To Carolyn and Cap
From Bening
Florida – with
admiration and
warmth,
Esther M.
Brones

S0-BCM-559

Her
Mothers

OTHER BOOKS BY E. M. BRONER

Summer Is a Foreign Land
Journal/Nocturnal and Seven Stories

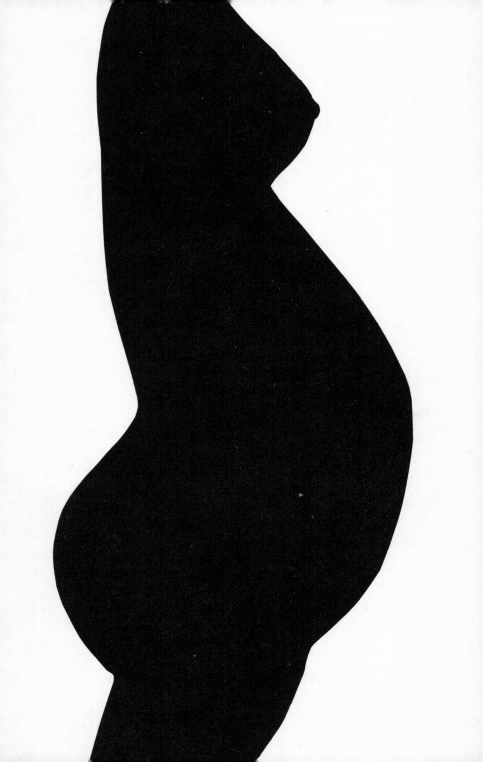

Her

E. M. BRONER

Mothers

HOLT, RINEHART AND WINSTON / NEW YORK

Copyright © 1975 by E. M. Broner

All rights reserved, including the right to reproduce this book or portions thereof in any form.

Published simultaneously in Canada by Holt, Rinehart and Winston of Canada, Limited.

Library of Congress Cataloging in Publication Data
Broner, E.M.
  Her mothers.

  I. Title.
PZ4.B86824He [PS3552.R64]   813'.5'4   75-938
ISBN 0-03-014721-2

First Edition

The section "The Sheller" was published in slightly altered form in *New Letters*, Winter 1974.

The sections "Looking for Mothers: Biological," "Primer: Ten Ways to Lose Daughters," "Peopleography," "Where Do Daughters Go When They Go Out?" were published in *Moving Out*, Volume 4, Number 2.

The section "Foremothers" was published in slightly altered form in *Elima*, Volume 2, Number 3, Spring 1975.

The sections "Remnants (1) and Remnants (2)" were published in *Shdemot, Digest of the Kibbutz Movement*, Volume 1, Number 3, Spring, 1975.

THANKS TO THE OSSABAW ISLAND PROJECT FOR
BOTH ATTENDING TO HER AND GRANTING HER PRIVACY.

Designer: Sandra Kandrac
Printed in the United States of America

Grateful acknowledgment is made for permission to reprint from Bertolt Brecht's *The Caucasian Chalk Circle*, translated by Eric and Maja Bentley in *Parables for the Theater*, University of Minnesota Press, Minneapolis © copyright 1948 by Eric Bentley.

Her Special Mothers

MARCIA FREEDMAN, MEMBER OF KNESSET, ISRAEL
JULIE JENSEN
VIRGINIA KELLEY
RUTH KROLL

"A woman writing thinks back through her mothers."
—Virginia Woolf
A Room of One's Own

Looking for Friends

1944

A Girl Should Have a Girl

A.
"I'm pregnant, mother."
"Have a girl."
"Why?"
"A girl should have a girl."

B.
"Mother, I'm pregnant with a girl."
"How old is she?"
"Seventeen years old."
"Then you're pregnant with me."

A 1944 maroon cardboard cover, not padded like the navy cloth cover of the year before. The war has come, and, with it, austerity in the yearbook.

"Wasn't it <u>fun</u>!" someone has written in her yearbook.

Another writes, "Your French class pal."

She does not remember the green ink of "Wasn't it <u>fun</u>!", the round, good-girl penmanship of her French-classmate, or "Michael Schwartz" in brown ink. She does remember her French teacher in purple ink who has written, "*A ma chère . . .*" The pencils have blurred, the ink faded with the people: "The swellest kid ever! Oh you gorgeous kid!" He was obviously not looking at her.

"One of my oldest friends," she has not seen since.

Whom does she know? She studies each page of twenty-five head shots per page, twenty pages of five hundred faces, another short page of an additional sixteen heads, braided, fluffed, cropped, in ROTC cap, plus eleven dark names without pictures, without study hall listing, majors, clubs, mottoes. It is a game book of 516 mounted heads, eleven faceless beings.

"Losers. I know all the losers."

Even the winners were losers.

There is the head of Shirley Panush. It is wide-eyed and intelligent. Now it hides those wide eyes and its 172 IQ in Rabbi Panush's attic room. Shirley was voted "The One to Make Hay With" by the Zionist Organization of America. There she lies on straw in the attic, her room too hot in the summer, drafty in winter. She had been kissed enduringly in high school and could endure it from no one else since.

There is a dark print of the head of Janice. Janice, however, was swarthy, though Jewish, and she did marry a Dark, a Black, and her parents sat *shivah*. But the Black left swarthy Janice, for she was a nag. But her parents will not renew acquaintanceship, for she has been tainted. And what has been mourned cannot be reborn.

There is the head of Pauline, some acne on the forehead, attributed to irregular menstruation. That was not all that was irregular in her life, parents, diet, place of abode. Once Pauline wanted to be an architect. She decorated the doors of her Murphy-bed closet with pictures of Frank Lloyd Wright.

Now Pauline lives with the owner of a liquor store in a flat above the store.

The eyes, forehead, hair, chin of Lois Goldman, lover of chemistry and daughter of a Romanian pharmacist. The Romanian pharmacist left his business to Lois's brother, for a girl cannot carry on the family trade or the family name. The brother has fulfilled his father's expectations. The business is a success, issuing few prescriptions but making money on a liquor license.

Lois Goldman married a doctor who cannot administer to her. She has lost forever her family name.

Beatrix searches that book of years. A girl with dark pitted skin and oversized teeth is listed as being on the Swimming Team. Beatrix remembers her. In Beatrix's constantly revised list of Best Friends, Swimming Team had a low number. Another low number is a girl with one undeveloped eye. Under her name is no list of accomplishments. She's a nonswimmer, even. Beatrix knew her well, had played dolls, Monopoly, Michigan Rummy for long hours on the girl's front porch. Beatrix left her for a girl friend with two eyes.

Roz's head fills the oval, Roz, Commercial, overweight, kinky-haired, who walked home from school each day with her. A blondie with big earrings and a big smile has inscribed on herself, "To my honey." She's Norma, everyone's honey. A fat-faced boy with the beginnings of a moustache is gazing at Beatrix. He had a crush on her. She was not flattered.

Her own face comes upon her: a fox from the woods, Jack from his box, a car swerving at her. She does not dimple like Shirley Panush. Her hair is not neat as Inez Muller's. She does not have lifted eyebrows and an amused smile like Marcia S. Liebowitz. She is not blonde, blue-eyed, frilly-bloused like Razel Schiller, who can only manage a General curriculum and belongs to Girl Reserves.

Beatrix has half her face in shadow. Her lipstick is 1940s purplish red. Her hair is newly washed and shapeless. To this day, her hair would be frowned on by neat Girl Reserves or Home Ec Club.

Her eyebrows are painfully plucked, not by her own hand,

5

but by the hand of the beauty parlor. She had not the courage to pull out those thick hairs from the heavy brows. The blouse she wears has a peter pan collar, is made of soft rayon material, white, with capped sleeves. She is not exactly frowning, but she is more than serious. Grim perhaps. Or grave. There is a vein visible in her forehead. The lines from nose to mouth are deeply shadowed. Her face is smooth, a little puffy, seventeen. What is she looking at? Her eyes bore into something. Her hair is ruffled as if by sudden wind. It is the most peculiar, self-conscious picture among all those 516, amidst all that mounted game. Maybe she deserved to walk home with overweight Roz.

Even the ugly girls look nice, a large flower in the hair, light eyes catching the cameraman's flashbulb. But only she among all of those intelligent faces, only she—*not* like IQ'ed Shirley, mechanically gifted Pauline, athletic Janice, scientific Lois— only she among the girls in College Prep glasses, with reflective faces, she, a nonsinger in the Spring Festival, a noneditor of the Yearbook, non-Spanish Club, non-Latin Club, never having spoken in the Speaker's Bureau, only she of the strange wild hair, throbbing vein in the forehead, intense, almost angry eyes, puffy eyebrows, jersey blouse stretched over breasts so flat the bra cups folded inward like craters on their cones, only she is still known.

It is for her, Beatrix Palmer, that BOB'S BICYCLE AND REPAIR SHOP can be proud they advertised in the Yearbook, next to LLOYD'S FURS, THE DAIRY BAR, BATES LUGGAGE, GROSSBERG'S GROCERY, THE ROMANIAN PHARMACY (of Lois Goldman's Romanian father), MEN'S HABERDASHERY (of Janice's dashing father), and Mr. Aishikin, who wrote: "V . . . —FOR TOTAL VICTORY."

C.
"I'm pregnant with a girl, mother."
"What is she doing?"
"She's going to a reunion."

Which she did do twenty-five years later. Beatrix was the only one with a date, her assistant book editor. Beatrix was also the only one at the reunion whose child was unaccounted for, whose husband had disappeared years before.

The assistant book editor held her arm like a sling, up the carpeted stairs of the nightclub. He yawned. He disturbed the three-master of a hanky riding on his jacket pocket to wipe his face, his hands against this press of people. He has accompanied her to the reunion for she is on the program to talk up her book.

Sarcastic Cynthia is ahead of Beatrix, her shorter husband two steps up, and Cynthia a step ahead. She has also moved ahead in other ways. Cynthia has moved East while Beatrix has stayed a rung down in the Midwest. She does not recognize Beatrix. Or she recognizes her and is annoyed. Bea's name is on the program. The program, moreover, is printed on thick stock to make up for wartime deprivation. Cynthia is holding the thick name of Beatrix Palmer.

Perhaps Cynthia is shy and has nothing to say. Perhaps Cynthia is ashamed. She is ashamed about her undergraduate major which began as English but, by Junior Year, became Beatrix's husband.

That year Beatrix lost her husband, her friend Cynthia, and, for irregular attendance, her semester's credit. Beatrix did gain, that same year; she gained about thirty pounds, a daughter, implanted while the husband was dreaming of Cynthia.

The husband is on the West Coast now, no one knows where. The daughter is traveling eastward, no one knows wherefor, whereto.

In Senior Year, Cynthia raised her goals, from classmate to graduate student to her instructor. There he is ahead of her, but still the same height. And, for all her villainies, Cynthia looks wonderful. She exercises every morning, doing The Elbow Touch, The Wrist Pushes, Small Arm Circles, Forward Arm Crosses, Arm Curl, Arm Pulls, Four-Count Toe Touch,

Tummies Aweigh. She does her facial exercises: the Buccinator, Caninus, Mentalis, angulare, orbitale. She dyes her hair carefully, strand testing it beforehand, making sure it is one shade lighter than her hair used to be, for her face, twenty-five years later, is also one shade paler. She can wear trim skirts, even though she menstruates, for Cynthia, unlike clumsy Beatrix, can insert Tampax. Cynthia is determined, an engineering sort, and the tampon rests in the vagina, held in place by constricting muscles. Cynthia is also a connoisseur. She tastes tea. She knows that it belongs to the camellia family, is grown on tropical and subtropical estates, and comes from India, Ceylon, and Indonesia.

Why, then, is Cynthia looking dour? Why does she seem bored? Perhaps she thought her name should have been listed in that class catalogue. The Program was full. One Most Likely to Succeed from twenty-five years ago was listed, as well as One Who Did Succeed. They were two different names, both of men. One Most Likely succeeded in being the first to die, of leukemia, the summer after graduation. One Who Did Succeed employs twelve oral surgeons in a dental complex managed by his sister, who has had banking experience.

About whom is Cynthia speaking so loudly? About the four best friends of Beatrix.

"Shirley is a hermit," says Cynthia, now recognizing Beatrix. "Is that right?"

Beatrix looks at her date. He is sensitive to the requirements of the escort and envelops her in soft-voweled, consonanted conversation.

Cynthia has dieted, culturally informed, and sun-lamp tanned herself for this reunion. She is not to be put off.

"Where's Janice?" she asks Beatrix. Explanatorily to her husband, "The only one of that group that did anything. . . ."

The husband frowns. He's not a bad sort.

Is Cynthia saying that Beatrix did nothing of interest?

"She married a Black man," Cynthia tells her Full Professor. "Her Hadassah mother must have died."

Actually, the mother did die, and the father and Janice's younger brother, too, all from diseases, but Janice's family blamed her for having weakened their defenses.

Lois Goldman arrives with doctor. She gives Beatrix a shy smile, for she has known her, and Cynthia a large one, for she has not known her very well.

"That's another," Cynthia checks. "What did you do, Lois? What ever did you do after graduation?"

"I've been a wife and mother," Lois begins. Cynthia has turned away.

"What's that all about?" Cynthia's husband asks softly.

They meet again in the Ladies. Overweight Roz is there, jolly, not kinky Jewish but wigged. Norma Honey is there, still small, still bosomy. She measures her four feet ten inches against Roz's five feet ten inches. Marcia S. Liebowitz is in Ladies, her amused graduation picture no longer so arch. She has suffered from Bell's Palsy and one side of her smile has slipped. Razel Schiller of blue eyes and frilled blouse has not attended and is not inquired after.

Cynthia and Lois are waiting, each first in line for the two toilets.

"Where's Pauline?" Cynthia asks Lois.

"She's not doing anything much," says Lois.

"Nor was she when I knew her," says Cynthia.

A strange thing is happening to Beatrix. Women ignore her. She has been in Book Review sections and on Morning Shows but the women do not see her. She, waiting for the booths, is a threat to each inside the booth. She is a reminder of high honor-point averages, of hands lifted eagerly in class, of mind gone to small matter.

Being ignored is, to Beatrix, worse than being dealt with rudely. Beatrix feels as if she will topple backward, like a cardboard Jackie Kennedy doll her daughter had Before Assassination, whose feet kept bending and who would stiffly, slowly fall. Beatrix Palmer feels the room is too close. Her face dissolves, nose sinking into its own cavity, eyes and mouth

stretching to meet each other, neck flesh melting into tendons.
" 'Fess up," says jolly Roz from her booth. "Who has The
Migraine? Who has The Change?"

Cynthia flaps her hands dry, not waiting for the warm air
flow.

The enemies are still enemies and the friends have drifted.

THE PROGRAM

    I. Introduction of Emcee
   II. Emcee introduces Faculty of 1944
      (1) Chemistry
         (Bald, even in 1944, an enemy of Romanian Lois's,
         and, in addition to being anti-Romanian and anti-
         woman, he has been consistently anti-Semitic in an
         all-Jewish school.)
      (2) Shorthand
         (An enemy of College Prep.)
      (3) French
         (A ma chère Beatrix.)
      (4) Math
         (Jewish Math, the only Jewish teacher in the high
         school and solemn with the responsibility of it. He
         also teaches Hebrew on Sunday.)
  III. Orchestra
      (1) Miller Medley
      (2) Ink Spots Spot
  IV. Our Authoress. . . .

Beatrix is introduced. The emcee gives her a generous, long
introduction. Her former classmates fidget. It is Auditorium
again. The emcee cuts his introduction. Beatrix comes forward
carrying note cards. The emcee groans. The classmates laugh.
The emcee is someone with the same last initial—P—who had
shared the same alphabetical study hall, someone Beatrix has
not seen since last marking. He grabs Beatrix by her 3 x 5's.

"Why should she speak when she's so beautiful?" P asks.

10

He rips her 3 x 5's. Band crescendoes, applause for fleeing Bea. People are still ascending the stairs as she and her date go against the current. People are registering at the desk of Judy and Johnny, high school sweethearts, winners of First Married. Up the stairs puffs the boy who once had a crush on Beatrix, the boy with a premature moustache in those hairless days. Now he has no moustache but has grown full sideburns.

He tells Judy and Johnny, high school sweethearts, "I sat up all night memorizing the names and faces, especially of the guys. I know all the guys' names. No use memorizing girls. They change their names."

Beatrix has changed her name back to her high school one.

D.
"Mother, I'm having a baby girl."
"May she be a doll, a living doll."

THE LIVING DOLL

She plays on the floor beside her grandfather. He wrinkles his nose at her. She brings him the doll. He kisses the doll's nose and lifts dolly to kiss mommy's nose.

"Sweet cheeks," he calls her.

The grandfather cries, real tears, when his little grand girl is broken like a dolly, when her nose is broken. He sighs and cries. He never again enjoys seeing her. There is a slight hump remaining, a fault in Lena's doll face.

E.
"Mother, I'm pregnant and I don't want her."
"Go to an abortionist or a psychiatrist."
"Which?"
"They're the same. They're different."
"How the same? How different?"

11

"They both look into your womb. The abortionist sees the
fetus there, the psychiatrist your mind."

F.
"Mother, I feel ill. What's happening?"
"You're being born."

The Physician's Book

We are all in that obstetrician's book. We are born into the
book with a case number, an admitted-into-hospital name. We
already have an address and a date of admission, a period of
gestation, the diseases from which we suffer, our father's full
name (his name precedes the mother's), our mother's name
secondarily. They are both living. But the grandmother, Lena
Gurnev, oh she is dead, although her husband David Gurnev
lives.

The child is recorded, July 5, stillborn, legitimate, male,
white, died on the same day. No cause of death is filled in. In
proper order the doctor signs his signature, the nurse hers, the
father his. No mother's signature.

How is the child disposed of on that same July 5? "Under-
taker" is written, in a slightly European pen stroke, instead of
the usual, "Home."

The male Palmer heir died, the eldest heir. Beatrix was
conceived into the obstetrician's book and taken "Home"
instead of to the "Undertakers" although only a female.

Mother Palmer does not err again. No more stillborns.
No more white females. She brings home two more male
Palmers.

G.
"Mother, I'm pregnant with a girl."
"What is she doing?"
"She's crying."

The daughter of Beatrix Palmer fell in love with a four-year-old when she, Lena, was three. Lena, named for her missing great-grandmother, had brown sausage curls and a print dress that said "I love you." She had a cloth doll whose matching print dress loved *her*. Everyone loved Lena, her mother, her grandmother, her grandfather, her dress, her doll, everyone but the four-year-old across the hall who loved his orange tractor shovel that was a model of his father's real tractor shovel.

Lena would await Howie's attention, holding her doll out to him. He, gruff as his construction-worker father, would knock the doll to the ground and run his orange tractor shovel over it.

Lena wept for hours whenever she left him. In her sleep, in the white lamb decal crib, she called his name. He, across the hall of the apartment building, slept soundlessly.

At the Study

Beatrix is at her study. Across a pitted old aluminum table are notes for her text on American women of the nineteenth century. She is reading *The Writings of Margaret Fuller, Love Letters of Margaret Fuller, The Roman Years of Margaret Fuller.*

She is at her study. She is reading *Louisa May Alcott, Miss Alcott of Concord, Louisa May Alcott: Her Life, Letters and Journals.* She is reading *The Journal of Charlotte L. Forten.* She is reading *Selected Poems and Letters of Emily Dickinson.*

She is reading. She is reading *Rosa Luxemburg Speaks*, in a crimson cover. She thinks of a title for a book, *Red Rosa*, but it sounds like a fairy tale to go with *Snow White*. She is reading J. P. Nettl's biography of Rosa.

Beatrix Palmer would know only heroic women. She would be a heroine.

She is at her study with documents scotch-taped onto the wall: the proclamation of the American Shakers, "Equality of the sexes, in all departments of life."

She is studying. Paper frames bend with their old photographs. Her mother, with then dark (though dyed) hair; the mother's cheek in her palm, the mother's face animated, her own responding, her hair dark then also (not dyed then also), her cheek in hand, both of them having cleared the table, the flashbulb shining on stacked glasses, saucers, the candles, the bit of photo of Einstein. (How her family would have loved its own Einstein, perhaps Baby Palmer stillborn that July 5.) There is another photo of long, rich, frizzy dark hair, the eyes averted, the face somber, the hair a curtain of night over that face.

Another photo. The dark-haired girl smiling, her hands on her belly. She is standing alone. No men are framed in the room, aside from a card in purplish ink signed: "Thos. Wentworth Higginson, Cambridge, Mass., March 21, 1884," aside from a postage stamp of Thoreau designed by Leonard Baskin, sent to her and canceled, hence canceled Thoreau. All other men have been canceled.

She is at her study. The globe turns lopsidedly, the globe is dusty, once that dark-haired girl's, seldom used since to see the world since the dark-haired girl saw the world. The globe lurches—it is the dark-haired girl's birthday. She is in a purple land between pink INDIA and yellow CHINA. Before that, cards arrived from blue SOUTH PACIFIC, from Auckland with the nipple mark for the seaport of North Island, from yellow JAVA on the INDIAN OCEAN. The mother never knew of such oceans or seas, Tasman, Coral, South China, Timor. She never knew of Micronesia and Melanesia. She never knew the map of her daughter's head, those bloodshot rivers in the eyes, the tongues her daughter spoke in anger, the ears where no sound intruded, where nothing vibrated, the chest where all sounds vibrated and drummed back messages of hatred.

There were blue shadows between the tight veins of Lena's forehead, greenish on her chin, the cheeks would flush pink,

and the hollows under her eyes would be yellowish green as if
healing bruises.

H.

"Mother, I'm pregnant with a girl."

"What's it doing?"

"It's menstruating."

A rare close moment between them. The daughter coming
down the stairs, her forehead bumpy, her chin picked.

"No breakfast. It'll make me sick."

The mother argues. She never learns. The mother will never
learn. She will always argue and drive opponent and proponent
from her.

But the girl is suddenly weary and weepy.

"It's something gross," says the little girl. "I can't tell you."

She tells her.

"Maybe it's the barbecue sauce with the chicken. It ran
through my stomach to my underwear."

The mother begins to feel air currents under her armpits, on
the soles of her feet; she feels tickles in the air, up the throat,
in the nostrils. She tries, she succeeds, in not laughing.

Lena, however, begins to weep.

"I have a dread disease," says Lena.

The daughter is right. She does have a dread disease and, by
the mother's calculations, made on the basis of her own mother
and grandmother, that little girl will have a dread disease for
forty years. No scientist will prevent the sting, the paleness,
the headache, listlessness, the kneading stomach, the burn in
the small of the back, the itchiness, nervousness, but each
scientist will practice the sin of incuriosity, and so her
daughter will flow, pale red, reddish brown, deep-staining
crimson, for forty years.

I.
"Mother, I have a surprise."
"What is it?"
"I'm pregnant with a baby girl."
"That's no surprise."

What will she, twentieth-century mother, say to her daughter?
She looks into history.
There are her mothers! Hello, Margaret Fuller, hello, my mother. She is one of Beatrix's historical mothers.
"MARGARET?"
Raucous male laughter at an American Studies Conference.
"A horse face," says a goat-bearded professor. "Do you know how she held her audience's attention at her Conversations? She froze them to their chairs in horror."
"Uglier than Emily?" asks a twittering, fringe-haired professor of Criticism.
"Emily?"
"The poetess."
"Uglier."
"Uglier than Elizabeth Peabody?" asks a young assistant professor, who *would be* a goat-bearded American Studies scholar or a fringe-haired critic.
"Taller, thinner, more solemn, but uglier," says the American Studies scholar, expert in Margaret Fuller.
Beatrix Palmer reads a paper: "The Easily Intimidated Ralph Waldo Emerson and His Intimidator, Margaret Fuller."
No one questions her substantially. They like to gossip.
"Was there any actual marriage certificate issued?"
They are speaking of Margaret Fuller and the Marchese Ossoli.
No one asks about Margaret's "History of the Roman Revolution," written from primary sources, with Margaret as a participant.
"Did Thoreau find the bodies?"

Thoreau, not intimidated like Emerson, rushed to Fire Island upon hearing that the boat Margaret Fuller had sailed on from Italy had capsized. He found neither Margaret nor the Marchese nor the "History of the Roman Revolution," but he found her Roman son, a baby, still warm but drowned.

They bypass Beatrix Palmer at the podium.

"Was she embraced by the Roman sun?" asks the twitterer, "and given a Roman son?"

His hand to his mouth, his cough of self-appreciation/deprecation.

But what if Beatrix Palmer were the mother of Margaret Fuller? Margaret and her decade-younger lover Angelo and little Angelino are sailing home. Margaret writes to Mrs. Fuller:

"When I think of you, beloved mother, of brothers and sister and many friends, I wish to come." (Joseph Jay Deiss, *The Roman Years of Margaret Fuller*, Thomas Y. Crowell, 1969, p. 302.)

(In Beatrix's family there are two brothers and no sister. Could Lena return to them? There was once that stillborn brother of Beatrix's, Lena's stillborn uncle.)

If Beatrix were Mrs. Fuller in that small New England town, awaiting her scandalous daughter, would she hope that they be shipwrecked off Fire Island and washed away?

Mrs. Fuller is not ashamed. She does not dread the ship's arrival. She stays at the Manchester, New Hampshire, home of her son and writes to that troublesome daughter:

"If we could know when you would arrive, we would be at the Depot to conduct you to our house, but all the drivers know where my son lives—at the corner of Chestnut and Central Streets. May the great God preserve you and conduct you in safety to your home." (Deiss, p. 313.)

The great God did neither.

Would Beatrix address Lena thus?

J.

"Mother, I'm going to have a baby girl."

"When?"

"When I become pregnant."

"Who will make you pregnant?"

"My lovers."

"Who are they?"

"A chick and a dude."

"WHO ARE THEY?"

"I haven't met them yet."

The night after the Reunion her assistant editor takes her to a blue film. It is in the way of business. Her company is letting go of trade editors and fiction writers to expand the text division. They are thinking of expanding *The Pioneers* further into text. The young assistant editor is currently editing a history of the skin flick.

"The porno film is an historical reality," he explains humorlessly, "and, must, therefore, be studied."

He is working from Brigitte Bardot and her towel, through *I Am Curious (Yellow)*, Warhol's *The Couch*, quickie nudies, the transvestite Cockettes. It will be academic—all but the book jacket.

The party is academic. When the flick begins, in living color, a heated argument develops on the couch between a Labor Zionist and a New Left universalist. Pillows and boos are hurled until the professors retire into the dining room and farther yet, to the punch bowl, for argumentation.

Beatrix Palmer is sitting on the rug, her back against the love seat. Her assistant editor is helping to set up equipment, to get the focus sharp, the sound clear before he returns to Beatrix, tripping over cords and legs on the way. He slips down against the love seat, his finger sliding under her arm and down her ribs. He would mount her but so would the host's German shepherd. Perhaps it is the porno affecting the

18

shepherd, or all those reclining figures. He even mounts a standing pants leg or two.

Two women in black fright wigs appear, one considerably older than the other. Both women seem to be Cleopatra types. They wear Pharaoh headdresses and snake bracelets. CU on one writhing woman, camera dollies in, woman is fondling her own breasts, shaking them, catching them, concentric circles, counterclockwise. Her hair is stiff wig black, her eyes are closed, camera dolly on down, black patch of hair covered by more black, the back of the head of the older Cleopatra, Our Lady of the Dike. ECU, this time, extreme close-up, of public pubic hair, labia, clitoris. Hand-held camera stops dolly action. CU on licked lady, mouth opened, eyes rolling, much as her breasts had rolled before. Enter the Hero, in furs—that is, a fur robe, not a fur coat, and a Viking hat—Hollywood Viking, a fur yarmulke with two horns attached. The ladies in the audience laugh and feel tender. He is a boychik, maybe sixteen, seventeen.

Up bolt both Cleopatras, down goes Hero. CU on erection. The camera becomes confused tracing the paths of each raven-haired seductress. There is Technicolor red, red tongues that look as if they have been eating candy hearts or cinnamon balls. The two red tongues meet on the erected tower. Hold. Slow motion following upwards the flicking tongues.

It is a brief film. Black hair, red tongues, brown Viking fur, grayish skin.

Beatrix is upset by the film. She can do nothing about the excitement. With her assistant editor it would be like Sweet Sixteen Viking. She is nervous and bad tempered. The editor takes her home. He cannot argue with her or be impatient. She is one of the better moneymakers of his publishing house.

K.
"Mother, I'm going to have a baby."
"Who will the baby be?"

"A Rani looking at Herself in a Mirror, a Rani with the Newborn Parasvanatha."

"How will I recognize her?"

"Her eyes will be edged in black. The iris will be blue. Her skin will be brown."

"Is that all?"

"Her earrings will be red stones in silver hoops, and she will be giving birth to a Hindu deity."

The mother is Western; in fact, Midwestern. Beatrix's mother is European. Beatrix's mother's mother, Lena Gurnev, is Sephardic. Lena is Eastern.

Lena says: "Steadfast a lamp burns sheltered from the wind; such is the likeness of the Yogi's mind."

This is the Bhagavad Gita.

Or Lena might say: "Betwixt me and Thee there lingers an 'it is' that torments me. Ah . . . take this 'I' from between us."

Lena has learned this from Hallāj.

Or Lena writes:

" 'Who is Me?'

" 'The Buddha who lives at my name and address.'

" 'Have you found him in the midst of the Ten Fetters, innumerable Defilements, Three Fires, and the Illusion of Self?'

" 'Not yet, but I am looking.'

" 'Who is looking?'

" 'The Buddha.' "

When the mother tries to speak to Lena, Lena's hands cover her ears.

Her mouth says: "The most important thing is Silence. In the Silence, wisdom speaks, and they whose hearts are open understand her."

Who are those people Lena is seeing, those Eastern people?

The mother is an archivist, a keeper of journals of Western women. Beatrix, for her first book, taped the voices of pioneers, women who went from Kiev to Cleveland, Sevastopol to Staten Island.

Beatrix had received a small anthropology grant to work on the oral history of the dying-off immigrants who came to the New World before and after the First World War. She and a photographer girl friend went into apartments, flats, private dwellings, old folks' homes, and hospitals with tape recorder and camera.

At first they interviewed the old men and the old women. It was difficult not to interview each of a pair. Sometimes an old sister or brother would chime in. Gradually, out of the trappings of a patriarchal society, Beatrix and her friend discovered that it was a matriarchy that put the costume of dark suit, skullcap, and beard on their men. They prayed for sons, but it was the women who held the families together when they were separated by the war—the women and children in Russia, Poland, Germany, Latvia, the men in New York, Chicago, Detroit, Canada. It was the women who invented ways to feed the family once they were reunited. Their book became one of pioneering women.

At first the old people were nervous at the sight of the "machine" and of the uncovered camera with its case dangling. Beatrix would not turn on the machine until the women were at ease, until they themselves said, "Put that into your machine. Why talk for nothing?"

They spoke and the photographer worked with high-speed film, with shots of old eyes lit in memory; pursed, animated mouths; gesturing, stiff hands.

Beatrix learned of their entrance into The Island, of the statue that greeted them with a poem by a Jewess. She learned that the Statue of Liberty was a Jewish landlady.

The book of transcribed and edited tapes with its accompanying photographs was called *The Pioneers*. It outsold the Museum of Modern Art's *The Family of Man* in Jewish circles.

Beatrix was invited to give readings from it to Jewish Senior Citizens Clubs; the members pursued her afterward with their autobiographies. Dances were choreographed from the lives of the book by everyone, from the American Ballet Company to Habonim Youth Groups. Her friend received royalties from the photographs, which were printed on rich paper and sold separately.

They had been under contract for some years to complete *The Remnants*, a book about the survivors of the Holocaust who came to the New World before or after the Second World War. The stories seemed more repetitiously tragic, and Beatrix and her friend were desultory in their work habits. The book dragged and was yet unedited and the photographs were not of the same quality as those in *The Pioneers*.

L.
"Mother, I'm pregnant. Who am I?"
"Your own mother."

M.
"Mother, I'm pregnant with a girl."
"Where is she?"
"At a restaurant."
"What is she doing there?"
"Misbehaving."
"What are you doing?"
"Slapping her hand."

Looking for Friends (1): Romanian Lois

Three years ago Beatrix Palmer was dined at Topinka's by her visiting executive editor. He wanted to expand *The Pioneers* into a sociological text for ethnic studies classes and he was concerned with the slow progress of *The Remnants*. Beatrix and her friend had already used up the advance.

Romanian Lois and her daughters were at Topinka's. They were lunching. They were waiting to have dessert with Lois's husband, whose office was in the Medical Building across the street.

Lois did not recognize Beatrix, for Beatrix had spent part of her advance on appearance. Not only were her eyebrows different but her hairline was reshaped by electrolysis, her hair recolored a reddish brown (the black tints had turned reddish in the sun anyway). Beatrix bought clothing in the expensive shopping mall in the Medical Building.

The puffiness of high school had left her face. Her face had not become haggard but that which made her face babyish and vulnerable and, perhaps, petulant, had left her.

Her eyes concentrate on Lois's table. She is distracted from her editor's discussion of paperback rights. The vein in Beatrix's forehead throbs at Lois. The lines from her nose to her mouth, though shaded with white underbase, are there, though faint. Her expression is not quite grim, more grave.

For Lois is slapping her youngest's hand, lifting the hand which dangles between her fingers and slap, slap, slapping the back of it. There is now visible a tomato juice stain on the tablecloth. Beatrix, at first, mistakes it for blood.

It is an earlier scene. At Lois's house. Her Romanian mother is slapping Lois's hand at the table, in front of dinner guest Beatrix Palmer, in front of the silently chewing older brother and the frowning father. Had Lois grabbed for food at the table? Had she spoken out of turn? Those claps, those thunderous slaps obliterated the cause.

The father rises, agitated with the disturbance at the table. The mother's hand is on her forehead. The brother's spoon is moving to and from his mouth, carrying, resupplying his dessert. Lois sits quite still. Beatrix asks to be excused.

Beatrix goes to the bathroom but cannot vomit. She returns to find the brother's napkin across his plate, Lois and her mother clearing the table, and the father feeding bits of chicken to the canary.

"Here, cannibal," he jokes, feeding bird to bird.

Beatrix's dessert, a torte, has been refrigerated for her. She is not asked to help with the dishes, for she is a guest, although the mother is not fond of her and is reluctant to have her at their table.

The brother has a date. His mother smooths his hair, touches his collar, kisses him. He tweaks her. The father nods proudly from his armchair in the living room.

"Good night, sir," calls Lois's brother.

(Beatrix is thrilled. A Jewish boy talking like that!)

Upstairs both girls rummage through the older brother's dresser. They find a variety of heroes, Trojans, Ramses among them, as well as Dr. Long's *Sane Sex Life and Sex Living.* The girls sleep together in Lois's single bed, their backs together, each masturbating herself. Bea dreams of the older brother. He is feeding her chicken. She becomes his cannibal, chewing his meat. She is happy the next morning that older brother is sleeping late.

"He came home in the wee hours," tiptoes in and whispers Lois's mother.

Sometimes Beatrix loves this family. More often she is terrified by it.

Lois wishes to speak to her father. She wishes to get into the high school Chemistry Club, whose faculty adviser is bald Mr. Haddock. Lois told Mr. Haddock that she had read all of her father's volumes on Luther Burbank and all of the chemistry books at home and at the pharmacy. But the adviser will not let her into Chemistry Club. It is traditionally all boys, he explains to her, as is Chess, as are the Hi Y's. Mr. Haddock tells Lois to join the Home Ec Club and learn her kitchen chemistry there. Lois weeps before her father. He turns his tie inside out and wipes her eyes with the lining. Lois's father bends Lois into his lap. The mother comes in to see, drying her hands.

"Sarah Heartburn," says the mother.

She takes the heavy 78 rpms of *Romanian Rhapsody* out of the cabinet and stacks the records on the spindle. The machine is noisy, the records old and scratchy. Lois's father asks the

buried head on his shoulder to dance. The mother is watching.
Lois is persuaded to dance with her courtly father.

"I rather thought I was your partner," says the mother.

N.

"Mother, I'm pregnant with a baby girl."

"What does she want to know?"

"Will her mother be her friend?"

"No, her enemy."

"And her father?"

"He will court her but he will destroy her."

"She wants to know how."

"He will dance with her and hold her close in order not to see
her. He will sing to her in order not to hear her."

O.

"Mother, I'm pregnant with a daughter."

"What's she doing?"

"She's dating her best friend's lover."

Looking for Friends (2): Shirley and the Ritual Slaughterer

P.

"Mother, I'm pregnant with a baby girl, and she wants to kill
someone."

"A best friend or a casual acquaintance?"

"A best friend."

"That's easier. You see each other more often and can take
better aim."

"Genja," said her father.

"Let me!" The aunt pushed into Shirley's room with the food
tray.

So how did it go from Genja to Shirley in one person? The same way it went, in one family, from Muny to Charley, Paltiel to Benny, Nuny to Anna, Marcus to Max, as they became name-changers and tried to become natives in the New World. Beatrix was native-born and Shirley foreign. In high school Shirley became the native and Beatrix the foreigner.

What changed Beatrix's citizenship from New World to Old? What changed her grading, in that judgmental time, from Jumbo Egg to Small?

Beatrix erred in choice of friends; for instance, Beryl Blumberg, a German boy. Beryl was a mime, but the class shifted uncomfortably when he simpered across the stage. He painted his face clown white, his lips red, but the class saw only the lipstick. His wrists were mobile—fish flops, dying butterflies, a sustained parting gesture. The class saw no athletic throw of the arm and, also, that he was no club man. He was, though, club-footed. And he was a grade lower than Beatrix, thus precipitating her downgrading.

Beatrix erred in mannerisms. Although American, she was a peasant, a *mouzhik*. She ate soup noisily, her soup spoon shoveling toward her, instead of lifting away from her. In a restaurant nothing on the menu looked familiar. She had no idea what to do with the multiplicity of spoons and forks, like weapons laid down in a truce. Her voice was loud when it should have been hesitant, shy when it should have lifted.

Beatrix's ways were unbecoming; that is, it was apparent to those of higher aims that she was becoming nothing to which they aspired. Their aspirations were to be the nonprofessional wives of professional men, the dependent wives of independent businessmen.

What was unbecoming about Beatrix? Her hair, makeup, dress, gestures.

Her hair was uncontrollable. Her eyebrows grew together. A sense of the hirsute prevailed—from legs, armpits (where sweat collected and which no amount of Arrid could dry), upper lip, that wild hair. She began to shave here and there, the way she polished shoes, streaking her legs, cutting painfully under her arms. She plucked her eyebrows until the tender skin puffed red and they became like an epicanthus fold. She bleached her upper lip. But everything was to distract from, to counteract what was there. And what was there was Mediterranean, although Bea's ancestors were once from the steppes of Russia (Lena Gurnev had, far back, been from the steps of the Inquisition).

Beatrix's lipstick was dark purple although her skin and eyes were pale. It was a threatening mouth whether or not she used it to threaten.

Her skirts hung; her small waist and fleshy hips were unfittable in teen-age clothing. Her blouses were girlish; her sweaters extra large. Her blouses were tight across the broad shoulders and under her arms; she floated inside the extra-large sweaters like a fetus. Her shoes were sloppy saddle. If she used Esquire White over the white section, it smeared onto the blue. If she brightened the blue with Shoe Blue, it ran into the damp white.

Her voice was unmodulated. Her hands either fluttered or jerked in excitement, narrowly missing the eyes of people with whom she was intensely conversing.

In contrast, Shirley Panush was Nordic blonde, her hair controlled, her makeup slight, dress fitted, gestures royal.

"Cheer up your room a little," Shirley's father said. "Use color."

Shirley wanted no color, fought off the painter while he was doing the rest of the house.

"Be reasonable, Genja," said her father. "We can't have him back again just for your room."

Shirley chose red. Her father said that was too dark. Why not a sunny yellow, a sky blue?

"White," said Shirley, in those days of dark green.

"That's all?" asked the father.

That was all. But her aunt *would* bring in pretty pillows, a quilted spread. Shirley threw them out of her attic room window.

"You can't have a bare bed," said her aunt.

"Bring me black sailcloth," said Shirley.

They did, hurriedly. She made a spread on her aunt's old treadle machine, which the aunt and the father had dragged up to the attic for Shirley.

"Why lie in black?" asked Shirley's father. "It's like mourning."

"So it is," said Shirley.

Soon she would begin to scream. They would have to wipe her with cold water and hold ice cubes in washcloths against her face. They didn't argue.

Once she brought them pleasure, pure pleasure. She made up for the loss of her mother and of their country, she was so agreeable, so pleasant.

It was a time of fire and color. These high school children held hands through newsreels of burning vessels, oil slick on the ocean from sunken submarines, the conflagration of London, flaming ships in Pearl Harbor. It was a confusion of flares, bombs, explosions, an amusement park of war for those waiting children who necked and petted and let Kate Smith love America for them.

Shirley Panush's father left Germany, the large synagogue where he officiated, and his wife's remains.

Bolts of material had arrived in their community, containing the stamped, identical Stars of David. The rabbi asked the women of his congregation to be proud, to embroider yet more stars for the altar, for the holiday tablecloths. But his wife did not care for that regular, repetitive pattern. She would pin it on sometimes, sometimes not, even though it was to be sewn on all clothing. Her nature was more brilliant than regular, as was her appearance.

Where her family was cool and deliberate in speech, her German sounded Italianate. They were cool in coloring, but she was all the primary shades with her blue-black hair, naturally red lips and cheeks, tawny yellow eyes. Her daughter, Genja, had green eyes, apricot skin, pinkish-purple veins when she flushed. She was of secondary colors.

The mother was a linguist and pianist but the mechanics of living were not always clear to her.

"Mother, my baby girl is a linguist and a pianist."
"Tell her that is not important."
"What is?"
"Whom she marries."
"That's all?"
"No, also if she can find her way back home."

Frau Panush called everything a machine.
"Turn off the machine," could be the radio, iron, phonograph, the light switch.

If she went to pay a visit, she would wander in the wrong direction and have to phone home "on a machine" to ask her husband, the rabbi, where she was and where he was.

One day on the streets Frau Panush told an SS man, "Officer, I am lost."

"Where are you going, Frau?" he asked gallantly.

She told him the locale of their house and that it was near their synagogue.

She did not return, charged with failure to wear the armband, intent to disguise her identity, and accosting an official of the state.

"Mother, I'm pregnant with a baby girl and she's a *rebbetzin*."
"Then she's nobody."
"But she's in danger."
"Then she'll die."
"She's married to a rabbi."
"He will live."

Rabbis survived if no one else. Religious organizations paid handsomely for them. Out came Genja, her father, her father's sister. But the rabbi was less than he had been. American synagogues want American rabbis, but they do not care if the one who officiates over the slaughtering of their meat has an accent. Rabbi Panush became a ritual slaughterer and also a *melamed*, tutoring slow Bar Mitzvah pupils in Hebrew.

"Mother, I'm pregnant with a baby girl."
"What is she?"
"The daughter of a *melamed*, a teacher."
"Then she will learn nothing."
"The daughter of a ritual slaughterer."
"Then she will be ritually slaughtered."

Rabbi Panush was strict, even with his slow pupils, teaching the *aleph beth* with the edge of the ruler. But Shirley was gay. She sang with the melodic voice of her mother, giggled like a Viennese, flirted like a Hungarian, was as ambitious as an American.

"Mother, my baby girl has a girl friend."
"Tell her it's impossible."

Shirley had her mother's artistic nature. She took the few art courses taught in high school, all by Miss Rose Cogley, B.S., M.E., and she won the Sunkist Oranges Poster Contest. The prize was a trip to Florida for Shirley, her father, and Miss Rose Cogley, B.S., M.E. The old aunt sulked at home and refused to put on lights while the family was out of town. She fretted in dusk and went to bed as soon as darkness fell. She cleaned in light. Shirley returned from Florida with her hair blonder and her skin tanner.

"Mother, I'm pregnant with a baby girl."
"What's her problem?"

"She has a blonde girl friend."

"Tell her never to stand next to her."

Children crowded the rabbi's front porch until Beatrix, Lois, Janice, and shy Pauline were crowded off onto the stairs. They sat there watching, coveting.

The old aunt never invited the children inside but watched from behind the living-room drapes.

"Mother, my baby girl has good taste."

"What does she want to do?"

"Select the drapes."

"Tell her the one who selects the drapes darkens or lightens the house."

The drapes were selected by the aunt—climbing, waving, stretching rubber-plant leaves. All of the furniture in the *rebbe*'s house was selected by the aunt for practicality, frugality, and sentimentality.

When a boy on the porch smoked, the aunt would knock against the window, her mouth pressed against the pane, a fish mouth, not clearly heard, but calling, "You'll set the porch on fire."

Everything else was on fire. There were fire wardens in London, saboteurs in France. There was the RAF being shot down in flames. There was Jimmy Cagney parachuting behind enemy lines in *16 Rue Madeleine*. There was Gregory Peck, leading his fellow patriotic Russians in the forest, a tiny band against the Nazis.

"Mother, I am pregnant with a baby girl and she is worried."

"Why?"

"The boys are fighting."

"But what are the women doing?"

"They're dancing."

The girls were in a chorus line, like Rita Hayworth waiting for Gene Kelly to discover her.

It was too much excitement, that combination of war and death. Love had to come along, had to be a little like war, like death, like being blitzed together in London—yet distant, for these children were but spectators. So they bombed into each other, exploding, leaving shrapnel of themselves.

"Mother, I'm pregnant with a baby girl and she's speaking."
"I'm listening with my stethoscope."
"She says her girl friend's brother has *not* been drafted."
"Then he must give an explanation."
"But her girl friend has also *not* been drafted."
"She need never explain."

The brother had a bum knee.

All the men at home had to give explanations, even movie stars on and off screen.

"Why are you out of the army, buddy?" a screen comrade asks Gene Kelly early in the film.

"Enlisted and wounded right off," says Gene Kelly.

He is then free to entertain the troops and to discover Rita Hayworth in the chorus line.

One late afternoon, Romanian Lois's brother arrived—the one with the bum knee—but he could still drive his father's car. He was sent to bring home bad girl Lois. Lois had not cleaned her bedroom before going to school and she was going to clean it now before the day was over.

"Mother, my baby girl has gone to school."
"Did she make her bed?"
"My baby girl has gone to work."
"Did she make her bed?"
"My baby girl has gone out into the world."
"Not if she neglected to make her bed."

"Hello, kid," said Lois's brother to Beatrix Palmer.

Bea blushed. *Sane Sex Life and Sex Living* before her.

"Hello, kid," says Lois's brother to Shirley Panush.

He then sat on the porch and smoked nonchalantly. When the aunt knocked at him, forming her soundless words from the other side of the window, Lois's brother went to his car, took a lap robe from the back seat, fastened it against the window, leaned the porch chair there, and continued to smoke. When he left to drive Lois home, Shirley was invited to accompany.

"Mother, I'm pregnant with a baby girl and she's dreaming."

"Don't let her tell anyone."

"Her dreams are betrayed!"

"She told someone."

The children still gathered on the porch but Shirley was not among them. Rabbi Panush would ask Lois where her brother was. The crazy aunt would shake her finger at Lois from behind the glass.

"I used to know where he was," Lois said to Beatrix.

"Where was he?" asked Beatrix.

"Sleeping with my mother," said Lois.

"You don't mean it!"

"I don't mean it."

Beatrix didn't ask her again.

They all went to a ZOA hayride. Some of them had dates. Beatrix did not. The girls watched Shirley disappear into the straw while kissing Lois's brother. She stayed under until Beatrix began to scream, afraid Shirley was choking to death. The couple sat up. Beatrix thought they looked terrible with glazed eyes and smeared faces.

Like dog paws in their laps, like a bus window opened on a windy day, so the abruptness and shock of Senior Prom.

"Mother, I'm pregnant with a baby girl."
"Does she have a date for New Year's Eve?"
"No."
"Does she have a date for the Senior Prom?"
"No."
"Then tell her not to be born."

Distraction. Shirley Panush passed out in American Lit. At first she laid her head down on the desk. She tried to raise her hand to be excused. Excusing her was complicated. A request had to be submitted to the office, but Shirley felt too ill to go alone. A message was returned from the office that someone would have to accompany Shirley. Miss Richardman, the American Lit teacher with the bobbed hair who taught "Thanatopsis" as a contemporary American poem, refused to jeopardize the health of her students. Shirley could be contagious. Miss Richardman herself could not take time out to deliver Shirley to the office, for American Lit had so much material to cover in so little time. Shirley fell from her seat.

The nurse told Miss Richardman that when she phoned Shirley's house the next day the old aunt hung up on her. The nurse tried again, alarmed at Miss Richardman's suggestion of contagion.

The father's tired voice had said, "No, not contagious, certainly not contagious. More like a hemorrhaging."

"A hemorrhaging?" asked the nurse.

"More like appendix," said the father.

"Mother, I'm pregnant with a baby girl and she is crying."
"Why?"
"Because she is pregnant and her lover is not."
"How does she know?"
"Only she is hemorrhaging."

The girls *had* to speak to each other. About the Prom.
"Is Sarcastic Cynthia going?" Beatrix asks.

34

"Yes, she's going."

Beatrix doesn't want to know with whom.

"Is Roz going?" Lois asks.

"Yes, she's going."

Lois wants to know with whom.

"Her cousin in the Eleventh Grade."

"She has no pride."

"She had to go. Her mother bought her a dress."

"Did you see it?"

"No."

"Didn't she want to show it to you?"

"Yes."

"Is Shirley Glazer going? Razel Schiller in General? Marcia S. Liebowitz? She's not going?"

"She's going."

"Norma Honey's going."

"Norma's always going."

"Who's she going with?"

"The son of Lloyd's Furs."

"Who's Marcia going with?"

"A Bob's Bicycle boy."

Lois's brother enters the kitchen.

"Hello, kid," he says to Beatrix. "Hello, sport."

Beatrix has Noxema on her pimple.

"I have the tickets already," he tells her. "Want to go?"

Lois is mad at her but Beatrix wants to go.

Cynthia comes over to say hello to Beatrix. She is also very pleasant to Lois's brother.

Beatrix is not a good dancer. The brother holds her close so she won't fall. He bends her into the HiLi position, pressing his lips to her forehead, his stomach against hers. When they straighten up, Beatrix's back is sore.

He puts his hand on the bare back of her borrowed formal.

("A borrowed formal and my borrowed brother," said Lois. "It's disgusting.")

"Does it hurt?" he asks.

His voice is very deep. Maybe he has a slight Romanian accent. He is sympathetically rubbing Beatrix's back.

"Better?"

"A little," whispers Beatrix.

They dance and he blows into her ear.

"Like that?" he asks.

"No," whispers Beatrix.

"Why not?" blowing into the other.

"It tickles."

"Then you like it," he says, "a little."

After the dance he buys hamburgers. The pickle and tomato slip out of the bun onto Beatrix's lap, for she is squeezing the bun too hard. He takes her for a drive and parks under the street light.

"We'll be in shadow that way," says Lois's brother.

He also says that the hamburgers didn't satisfy him; he's still hungry. Could he nibble—on her cupcakes? See the cherry on each top? He knows everything. He's been reading Dr. Long also.

Beatrix looks down at her bra. He has pulled it away from her cupcakes. His nails are carefully filed. He has a golden watchband. He has a white shirt and cuff links. But he is Lois's brother. He is Shirley's love. His hands cup around the cupcakes. Beatrix sees her chest heaving. His hands rise and fall. She begins to sob.

"Take it easy, kid," he tells her.

She begins to perspire, onto his white cuffs, dripping from his cuff links, wetting his wrist under the watchband.

He tries to kiss her but her lips are trembling. She closes her eyes and feels her face dampening with tears, her nose running.

"What a mess!" he says.

He moves the car. She is driving down Main with her bra hanging under her breasts. The bra flaps like an empty egg carton.

"Jesus Christ!" he says.

He reaches into the back seat at the next traffic light for his lap robe.

"Do something with yourself," he says, throwing the robe at her.

By the time she does something with herself they are in front of her house. He walks her to the steps and lets her climb alone. The living-room lights are on. Her parents are waiting up for their Prom girl.

The door opens.

"Miss America!" says her mother.

He drives off.

Lois calls the next day.

"He didn't come home in the wee hours," she says.

In careful detail Beatrix tells Lois about the HiLi, the back rub, blowing into the ear, nibbling at her cupcakes. Beatrix is giggly and breathless. Lois is attentive and quiet. Beatrix knows what she is doing. She is neither giggly nor breathless when she hangs up, and Lois is not quiet. Lois is not quiet to Shirley whom she visits that afternoon in the hospital. Shirley begins to scream. Shirley's father is phoned. Shirley's father forbids Lois's brother or Lois or any of the girls to see Shirley because they overly excite her.

Shirley's aunt will keep them away. When they come to the hospital, she is crocheting outside of the door. She calls, "Nurse! Nurse!" down the corridor. When Shirley is released from the hospital, Lois's brother visits her at home. He comes up the porch stairs, and the old aunt, behind the window, pulls the shade down on him.

Shirley waits for him to visit. One night she runs out of the house. Her aunt had dozed off, but the father hears the front door opening and rushes after her.

He is chasing her, he, the *melamed*, and she, the poor learner. He must teach her the holy way, the holy tongue, and he must beat her with the ruler on her shoulder, on her head, on her heart until she learns.

"You're killing your mama all over again," says the rabbi. He is the ruler. There is a double welt on Shirley's cheek.

"Thank God she isn't alive," says the rabbi.

"She was right," says Genja. Her voice is cool. "She was right to choose to go out in the daytime."

The rabbi pauses. What is her logic?

"To choose to leave off her armband."

The ritual slaughterer waits.

"To choose to see an SS man."

The rabbi begins to raise his arm, as he would the knife against the throat of beef, of chicken.

"To speak with him, to choose to leave you, to choose rather to die than to live with you."

His face is ashen.

"I make the same choice," says his daughter.

The ruler has fallen. Left on the ground. The rabbi takes Genja home.

"Mama, I'm pregnant with a baby girl."

"How is she?"

"She's dying in the womb."

"Why?"

"Her lover has left her."

"She's so young. Tell her to live."

"No, there's nothing else to live for."

Looking for Friends (3): Black Janice

Q.

"Mother, I'm pregnant with a baby girl."

"What color?"

"She doesn't know."

"Mother, I'm pregnant with a baby girl."

"How is she spending her time?"

38

"Visiting with girl friends."
"What are they doing?"
"Loving each other."
"How?"
"They talk, they console, they caress, they kiss."
"Is your baby rich or poor?"
"Poor."
"Only the rich can afford such a friendship."

"Mother, I'm pregnant with a baby girl."
"What is she doing?"
"Enjoying herself."
"With what?"
"With the war. With race riots."
"Tell her she'll never have so much fun again."

My Spanish teacher joined the Navy and was torpedoed and killed. In 1942 we had the race riots.

On Janice's porch there is a new glider. There are also hooks above us for a porch swing. This was taken down, to my regret, and replaced by the tame glider. I told my parents about Janice's swing, rusting in the garage. They warned me never to ask for it. We have old kitchen chairs on our porch which my parents take in every night so the paint won't peel.

The action in a glider is like floating on a rubber tube in Walled Lake. There are no surprises. But, as Janice and I talk and glide and slide from side to side, we soon enter the house and go into her bedroom. We masturbate ourselves or each other, depending on how late it is in the day. Broad daylight, we do ourselves. Dusk, each other. One day we forgot to lock the bedroom door. Janice's mother entered. It was dim in the room but she could see our bodies squirming under the cover. I was Dirty Bea, not allowed back in the house again. Janice's mother threatened to tell my parents while I sobbed and put my panties on. It was more humiliating than when I was caught stealing *Peggy Goes to London* from S. S. Kresge's.

And yet, yet I had the impression that Janice's mother could not understand *why* I wanted to *touch* Janice.

"One thing makes a riot," Janice's father said to his wife, his daughter, and his son (not in order of favor but of chronology). "Strangers."

In her house Janice was the stranger, the daughter of a dainty mother but built like her muscular father. From a family of light skin and hazel eyes, she had a wide nose, full lips, skin that tanned blackish brown in the summer, fading slightly in the winter. Her mother never accepted Janice's size. She would return from shopping with sample-size dresses for Janice, too short, too high waisted, with tiny calico prints that emboldened Janice's already broad face.

Janice's father laughed. Her younger brother, much like Janice in appearance, also laughed.

"She looks like Baby Snooks," said her father.

"Why, daddy?" mocked the younger brother, a big-mouthed, ugly Fanny Brice with her baby radio voice.

Janice would stretch her mouth between her fingers at her brother.

"Look at her! Now she looks like Joe E. Brown," said her brother.

Janice's body was like her flat, wide face. Her nipples were wide and flat, her breasts and stomach flat. A poor appendectomy left lobes of flesh like an ear listening at her side. Her thighs rubbed when she walked. If she wore corduroy pants, they squeaked.

Her mother, looking past Janice, always saw Cinderella's foot for the sample slipper, a wisp of a waist for that Deanna Durbin dirndl, slender white hands to give the manicurist each week.

To the brother, honors accrued: captain of the Jewish Center Swimming Team, captain of the Junior High Basketball and Track. If he were in High, he'd be several lettermen, just as his sister before him had captained Girls' Soft Ball, Girls' Stick Hockey, and was Lead of Synchronized Swimming.

Janice, at Synchronized Swimming demonstrations, was weightless on water, executing the most beautiful butterfly stroke, back stroke, breast stroke. She was the Center in the Center of the Flower routine, while the other swimmers were merely petals. She was the Sea Horse in the Dance of the Sea Horse and Swan Princess in a nautical version of Swan Lake. She would arch, dive, flip, leap while her parents attended the meets at the damp, bluish-green chlorinated pool. Her mother sighed at Janice's dripping short black hair, at her shape in the tank suit, and, after the meet, at Janice's slumbrous, sullen walk.

At the time of the riots Janice was making up Biology in summer school.

One morning the class watched while the National Guard encamped on the high school grounds. The class was having Biology class break and Janice had been batting balls over the fence into the encampment. The young guardsmen gathered along the fence.

"Yeah, Blackie!" they called. "Sock it, nigger."

"Blackie" to Janice who still attended the Sholem Aleichem Yiddishkeit Institute.

"Mama, I'm pregnant with a baby girl and she wants to be other people."

"Who does she want to be?"

"Razel Schiller and Norma Honey."

"Why?"

"They unfurl Razel Schiller's frilly blouse. They call after Norma Honey, 'Look at those big earrings shake!' "

"But those are insults!"

"She envies their being insulted."

A guardsman, one of the older members of the company, threw a hard ball over the fence straight at Janice's head. She saw it coming, could have ducked but caught it bare-handed and made off with it.

"Whoo-ee!" yelled the guardsmen. "She got one of your balls! Good thing you didn't throw the other!"

Janice took the ball to a corner of the field. In the soft dirt around the roots of a black ash she buried it and sat there nursing her hand. A young guardsman, leaning against the tree on the other side, watched Janice paw the earth with one hand, bury the ball, tap down the ground.

Janice looked up and saw him watching her. He went back to writing to his little sisters, messages on the back of Ford Assembly Line postcards. Janice returned to Biology.

The next morning, during Biology break, the class crowded at the Good Humor truck or threw a softball around. Janice walked to the black ash and had her Creamsicle there. Her hand was in her book.

"How is it?" the young guardsman asked.

Janice took her hand out of the book and showed him. The index finger was in a light metal splint, the bone chipped.

"How long?"

"A month," she said. "No sports."

"Not even swimming?"

"Yes, I can swim."

"That's good. It's hot."

The others were wandering into the building. Norma waved good-bye. Razel Schiller stayed there. She wasn't even registered for summer school.

The guardsmen called, "Come back for night school!"

"I'm off tonight," the young guardsman told Janice.

Janice said nothing. She felt like the bark of the tree, stiff, encased.

"You want to come by?"

"I'll see if I can."

"Ask them."

Which she did not, could not, even though the boy was all her mother would have had her be: slender, delicate-featured, soft-spoken, blond, shy, even a homebody writing to those sisters.

She walked by the field after dinner, nervously, not knowing where to look for him. The guardsmen lined up against the fence—but he was waving to her from the corner so she could avoid the encampment. Her walk became exaggeratedly casual and athletic, while he glided next to her, stepping softly, looking down at the sidewalk. At the next corner she, watching him, stumbled. He took her hand.

Then her walk became less lumbrous and his more affirmative. They walked past the Eagle Dairy and he asked her what she wanted. She was afraid to eat. He had a double-dip orange pineapple and gave her licks. They walked to the movie house and looked at the stills, but she couldn't be gone that late, movie-late, in the middle of the week.

"Study hard in the school year and you can stay up longer in the summer," said her dad when she told him she was going to a friend's.

"Which one?"

"Beatrix Palmer."

"Your mother said she's a bad influence on you."

"Maybe Shirley's—just two blocks away!"

"That girl's doing something with all those guys on the porch, even if her father's a rabbi."

"Pauline in the apartment around the corner."

"Nobody's ever home at Pauline's. She's always alone."

"I'll ring the bell and tell her through the intercom to come out."

"What'll you do? Stand on that main street in front of the door? You're asking for trouble."

"We'll go to the Viennese bakery for éclairs."

"You don't need the extra weight."

"I'll just walk. It's a nice night to walk."

"It's a rotten night to walk, hot and humid."

She went down the stairs and out, lying no more.

Janice and the guardsman walked home, a short walk but a long time. He told her about Ironwood, mostly farms and farmers drinking, and the boring little high school he went to. He had no plans. Maybe he'd go into regular service. Did he think about the war? He laughed. We think about the crops, he said. He liked to swim, to ride his old horse. He liked, best of all, his pigs.

"Smartest animals in the world," he said, "smarter than any dumb old dog. They can be watchdogs, I mean it. They'll squeal and warn you about strangers coming."

"You mean watch *pigs*."

They squealed. They laughed. They were a barnyard of noise. And, not thinking, she told him how to get to her house, and there they were. On the glider, not reading his newspaper, staring at Janice holding hands with, shame of shames, not even a regular soldier, that farmer National Guardsman, in that wrinkled uniform—was Janice's father.

The father rose and shook the newspaper at the boy. Jan and the boy thought the father was squawking, that it was part of the farm game. They laughed until the farmer came down the porch steps, rolled the newspaper, and slammed the guardsman with it. The boy walked off, not looking back.

"Mama, I'm pregnant with a baby girl and she's grieving."
"Why?"
"Her love is leaving."
"He'll come back."
"No. They never come back. They never look back."

I was not allowed to see Janice at her home. In school she became irritable, sarcastic, and did small violent acts. What began as playful slaps on the back, became cuffings of the ear, a slugging match with Norma Honey, a tripping of Marcia S. Liebowitz on the way home from school, goosing and hooting at fat Roz, spitting at Razel Schiller and calling her "bitch."

Janice phoned at eleven that night to apologize, but Razel's parents would not disturb Razel, gone to bed, and Janice did not apologize in person or by phone again.

"Mama, I'm pregnant with a baby girl and she hates."
"Whom?"
"Every girl she knows."
"That's because she's not allowed to hate boys."

College. Janice hitches into town without phoning her parents, staying at one girl's house or another's. She complains about the food at State, creamed *drek* on toast. Lois and I, enrolled at City, eat at home.

Janice's parents begin calling around. Janice has not returned to State, and Student Affairs has sent an inquiry. Janice's father phones shy Pauline, who stutters when he accuses her of withholding information. He calls Romanian Lois, but Lois's mother intercepts and will not allow him to speak to Lois. He phones Rabbi Panush's house. The maiden aunt hangs up. Then he phones me.

Janice's father says to me, "You should know where Janice is. My wife tells me you were so—so *friendly* with Janice."

I tell him, "Janice should have left home a long time ago."

He is silent. Perhaps he will apologize.

"I wish," he says, "I wish you a miserable marriage and crippled offspring."

Which became somewhat prophetic.

"Mama, I'm p. with a baby g. and she's run away from home."
"You have two choices."
"What are they?"
"Hire a detective or don't hire a detective."

Which Janice's family did, and which I did not do years later. The detective agency, after a month, found Janice on the

South Side of Chicago, living with one soldier after another. She met them while helping out at the USO.

"Mama, I'm p. with a baby g."
"Who is she?"
"A niece and a daughter."
"Who are her uncles?"
"An optometrist and a dentist."
"Who is her father?"
"A haberdasher."
"Who is her mother?"
"Nobody."

Janice's father consulted with his brother, the optometrist, and his brother, the dentist.
"Drive her to work with you," they advised the haberdasher. "Let her do something there, keep books, keep busy."

"Mama, I'm pregnant with a b.g. and her father wants to keep her."
"What does he want to keep her?"
"Busy."

"In the meantime," said the uncles, "we'll look around—a nice predental from the University, an optometry student from Chicago. She was in Chicago. They'll have something to talk about."

"Mama, I'm p. with a b.g. and she can't solve her problems."
"She's not supposed to."

The uncles said, "We'll find somebody to solve her problems. It's a case of high spirits which, unless controlled, could blacken her name."

46

Janice did not phone us upon her return. A couple of years later she phoned me—from Los Angeles. Her mother had written Janice that I was getting married. She wanted to know what shower gifts I received. She, although married before me, had received no shower gifts, no wedding presents. I sent her my silver pitcher and creamer, still in their plastic wrapping.

I apologize for doing that, member of my family who gifted me. I apologize, Harold, my ex-, for not having told you. I received no thank-you note from Janice.

Janice worked simple ledgers for her father. She worked in hats, ties, shirts, handkerchiefs, underwear, socks, wallets, suspenders, belts, sweaters, pajamas, bathrobes, and cloth slippers. She worked in his shop which, three years before, was in the riot area.

She was paid generously and bought expensively for herself. The parents approved. Her younger brother invited her to track meets. She was pleasant to the customers, respectful to her parents, distant from her friends.

"Mother, I'm pregnant with a baby girl and you will be proud of her."

"Why?"

"She is pleasant to the customers, respectful to her parents, distant from her friends."

"An ideal daughter."

One Friday before three o'clock, Janice went out with the deposit and did not return. Stock was also missing, the father discovered when he did inventory. The same detective agency found Janice in Colorado with a Black man, a good customer of the haberdashery, whom Janice had outfitted in accessories. They were married. His family was willing for an annulment, as was hers. But Janice and her husband moved farther yet, to California. Janice's father wearied of the chase.

She sent letters home in a year or two. They were returned

unopened. She sent a package of photographs of her children. It was returned. She phoned and her parents hung up. Once the brother answered and said, "Haven't you done enough damage?"

She let her little sweet-voiced daughter phone. The parents, on the other end of the line, were shocked and silent, then softly hung up.

The brother was injured at a sports meet, suffered a concussion, hemorrhaged, and died. Janice's aunt phoned Janice. She called home.

"Mama?" she asked. "Daddy?"

"Come," they begged. "Leave that man. Leave his children."

She came, spent a week in mourning, thinking it over. Thinking over the comfortable house, her room still unoccupied, the polite but stiff greeting from her uncles, her father's chain of haberdasheries.

"Take my husband into the business," she said, "and I'll return."

"There is no husband," they said.

In the mornings Janice's mother brought her hot chocolate in bed. Her father shared the newspaper with her and listened to her political opinions. She had become a Communist and a Unitarian but he commented on neither.

The phone rang at the end of the week of mourning.

The father handled the receiver nervously.

"It's for you," he said.

"Mama?" asked her daughter.

She returned to the West Coast, wearing a new wardrobe and dissatisfied. Within five years both parents died. The uncles handled the estate, a few thousand for Janice, the rest divided up among the Midwestern family, a Jewish Old Folks Home, and a room donated to Bethel Hospital.

Janice's young daughter was accepted into Talented Children's Art Classes, Saturday morning at the museum. The son had perfect pitch for the piano and was a perfect pitcher, besides, said his daddy, in Little League. Janice coached the

Girls' Swimming, and her husband the Little League, but they found neither peace nor happiness, for Janice nagged while her husband dragged. He left her for no other woman, faithful indeed to both wife and children, but he left for a quiet room, some Sunday fishing, a little joy.

"Mama, I'm pregnant with a baby girl."
"What does she want to know?"
"Will she be happy in marriage?"
"Let her stay in the womb, for once she is out of it, she could marry a baby boy who would crouch in *her* womb and refuse ever to leave."

Looking for Friends (4): The House That Pauline Built

R.
"Mother, I am pregnant with a baby girl."
"Then tell her there are no alternatives."

That last year of high school, Beatrix could do nothing to please Pauline. Cause and effect were not connective. Why did Pauline stop talking to her for the month of November? Why did she suddenly wait for her in the cold after school to begin talking again? Why did Pauline not respond to her apartment bell? Beatrix was sure the intercom was on and that she heard Pauline breathing when she identified herself.

She would beg, "Press the buzzer, Pauline. Let's go to the Chinese restaurant." No sound. "We can go to the Viennese bakery for chocolate éclairs." A click and the static of communication would cease.

Before every school event Pauline became depressed: a football event, the French Brunch, Christmas vacation, the Prom, Senior Skip Day, Graduation.

Beatrix, the good girl, attended what she could, miserably. Pauline missed all, miserably. Beatrix went to the football game and pinned a large school badge to her plaid skirt. She cheered, leapt, smiled, and walked home alone, except for the peanut shells a sloe-eyed former New Yorker had tossed into her hair. She sat on the bleacher step, and he, above her, kept leaning over. When Beatrix returned home her mother laughed shrilly at the outsized football medallion and asked Beatrix what that growth was on her hip. She asked it several times in front of Beatrix's father and some aunts and uncles who were visiting. Bea went up to her room where she saw the peanut shells in her uncontrollable hair, realized why the sloe-eyed New Yorker was leaning so close to her, and loosed uncontrollable tears.

Ah, they were all a crowd of shrieky, teary girls who abused their parents! Except for silent Pauline who abused no one but sipped water from a cloudy glass, clicked it slightly against the ceramic plate, and tapped the white dish with her fork, staring ahead, tap tap blindly, in that Chinese-American restaurant.

Beatrix looked for her at the French Brunch, held at the French teacher's house. Tea and croissants had been prepared by the French teacher's old French mother.

There, too, the girls cliqued up. Sarcastic Cynthia went with Rose Anne Epstein, who was going to go to Smith. Marcia S. Liebowitz had a girl friend. The French teacher patted the seat next to her for Beatrix, "*ma chère*, my little partner." It was wallflower time again, but Beatrix, at least, had tried to climb the wall.

Pauline, although A in Grammar and Style, could not be graded on Oral, for she refused to speak when called upon. She refused to attend when notified of French Club meetings, although she had paid dues for the whole semester.

"Mama, I'm pregnant with a b. girl and I'm selecting her name."

"Name her after someone deceased."

"Then she will start out partially dead."

50

Pauline was named for her grandfather, Palti, a bad-tempered grocery store owner. Palti disliked his two sons for monopolizing his wife's attention. In spite, he died before Passover, leaving his small wife to fill all those Passover orders and his two young sons to deliver them.

The wife squinted when she read the Yiddish paper. The sons wore thick glasses when still young. Palti found offense in this and accused them of being scholars in order not to support him in his older years. Eventually, the older son stayed with the mother but left the grocery store. The younger stayed with the store but left the mother to marry.

"Mother, I'm p. with a b.g. and she's married."
"To whom?"
"To a man who visits his mother."
"The mother and son—what is it they do together?"
"They confide, kiss, caress, dine, settle accounts, and whisper."
"Whisper? Then the b.g. can sue for divorce on grounds of adultery."

S.

Pauline's father married a flit, a girl given to permanents which burned and frizzed her hair, to flutterings of the hands, and wrinkling of the nose. She would not help out at the grocery.

"Mama, I'm pregnant with a b.g. and she wants to grow up to sell."
"To sell what?"
"Housecoats, budget dresses, and lingerie."
"On or off her body?"

The husband worked at the grocery with his mother and his wife went to work for Daisy's, a chain of cheap clothing shops. She worked in a Polish neighborhood where Daisy rented its lower level to a beauty shop. The customers emerged from the salon with Polish braided hair in fantastic twists, glazed and decorated like Easter bread.

"Mama, I'm p. with a b.g. and she wants to work when she becomes pregnant."
"And then?"
"She wants to work afterward."
"And then?"
"She wants to work while the child is growing up."
"And then?"
"She doesn't want to come home after that."

After Pauline's birth, her mother frequently took the bus to Daisy's to show Pauline off to the other saleswomen, to her former customers, and the beauty shop operators. Soon Pauline was provided with a playpen in the back room, while her mother sold lingerie, dark prints, and pastel formals at Daisy's for thirty cents an hour.

"Mama, I'm p. with a b.g. and she put her baby into a playpen."
"And then?"
"And then into a Murphy bed."
"And then?"
"Into a restaurant."
"And then?"
"Into the closet."

Beatrix visited Pauline in her small, dark apartment. Pauline's apartment faced the alley. The front of the building was on a busy bus route. Next door to the apartment building was the Viennese bakery. Across the busy street was Chinese-American cuisine.

Pauline's father moved back home with his mother and brother.

Beatrix went down the corridor to Pauline's apartment. The

door would be blocked by the Murphy bed. Pauline would have to lift the bed to let Beatrix in. Her mother slept in the back bedroom. The doors of the closet that housed the Murphy were decorated with photographs: white cottages with shutters, antebellum houses, brick houses in rolling hills, and, last year in high school, Frank Lloyd Wright houses. With Chanukah money Pauline subscribed to *Architectural Forum.*

"Mama, I'm p. with a b.g. and she wants to be an architect."
"What does she want to do?"
"Design houses."
"Impossible. She has to be a housewife, not a designer of houses."

Pauline's mother moved. She moved in with the owner of the liquor store, a block down from Daisy's. She lived above the liquor store but she continued to rent the dark, little apartment for Pauline. Pauline stayed in the living room on the Murphy, although the bedroom was not being used. The mother did store some old clothes there which took up much of the dresser and closet space.

Pauline's mother would come by with her key, leave a few dollars in the kitchenette or leave a shopping bag with specials at A & P, apple butter, jars of lime-flavored pears, pickled beets, Ann Page breads.

Pauline ate, most often, in the Chinese-American cuisine near the bus stop. Beatrix, waiting for a bus, would see Pauline sitting at a starched white tablecloth, which she did not have to worry about staining, did not have to clear of dishes. Beatrix would see the red-jacketed boys nodding and smiling and whispering themselves back into the kitchen so that Pauline, unlike Beatrix, did not get stomach cramps from table dispute, from family accusations. There sat Pauline in the picture window, twirling her water glass thoughtfully, an elbow on the table, a fist at her chin, three other chairs around the table pushed in.

Pauline's mother left notes in the apartment for her daughter:

"Did you remember to wash your greasy hair this week?"

"Do your clothes have to go to the cleaners? Smell the armpits."

"Did you clean your hairbrush yet? I noticed that it was full of hair and looked as if it had fallen under the bed."

Sometimes Beatrix agreed with Pauline's mother. When Pauline slept over—not often—Beatrix would ask Pauline to shower. Pauline would think about it. Usually she would not shower.

She had strange motivations for her decisions. In Pauline's apartment there was no shower, only a tan tub standing on its legs, in a tan bathroom. It was a toy bulldog of a tub on bowlegs, staring while Pauline read on the toilet. The senior year in high school Pauline painted her bathroom lavender and the bulldog black. It was not much better. If anything, the black bulldog was more ominous than the tan had been, and Pauline became constipated.

Pauline's father visited Pauline once in a while. He was relieved not to see his wife there. When any of the girls were visiting—Lois, Janice, Shirley, or Beatrix—Pauline's father would lecture them on sex.

"Watch out for men," he told Beatrix. "They want only one thing from a girl. When they get it, they're through. They go on to the next girl for the same thing."

"Mother, I'm p. with a b.g., and she's being lectured."

"By whom?"

"The father of her girl friend."

"About what does he lecture her?"

"About her erogenous zones."

"What information is he giving her?"

"He touches her erogenous zones and says, 'These are your Maginot Lines, the weakness in your defense.' "

"Tell her not to worry. He's an old soldier who talks and doesn't shoot."

Graduation. Beatrix unhappily wearing, under her black robe, the graduation dress selected by her mother. Beatrix had gone with Pauline down to Daisy's and had purchased a turquoise rayon, skin-tight dress with a maroon parrot perched on one hip and nestling one breast. Pauline's mother had been generous with her time while Beatrix tried on dresses.

At first Mrs. Palmer laughed shrilly and asked Beatrix, "What have you there, a costume?"

Then Mrs. Palmer was incensed that Pauline's mother had sold that dress to Beatrix. She insisted on being driven to Daisy's for a refund. It was not the policy of the store to refund. You could get credit for another purchase, but Beatrix's mother told the manager of Daisy's that she would report this shop to the Better Business Bureau for selling unfitting and ill-fitting merchandise to a young girl.

Said Beatrix's mother to Pauline's mother, "Don't treat her as you do your own daughter."

The money was refunded. Beatrix's mother, who knew Beatrix's size better than anyone, bought a tasteful, long-sleeved blue frock with rounded collar and softly falling pleats. Beatrix wore it for years. It wore well but all of her life Beatrix remembered the parrot's beak under her breast. She had reason to remember this, for when Pauline came to graduation and removed her robe, it was Pauline who was the parrot. She parroted in that dress, her hair washed and rinsed and as golden as Shirley Panush's hair (Shirley was given a diploma *in absentia*). Senior boys reached for the bird of her, for her feathery-soft hair. Pauline smiled, her back to them, her head slowly turning, like Betty Grable in her picture to the fighting troops.

At the end of June Beatrix, pressing Pauline's buzzer for minutes, was interrupted by the super.

"Moved out," said the fat woman.

Beatrix looked then at the name plate, blank as an empty eye socket. She did find Pauline at Daisy's. Pauline was distant and affronted on the telephone.

The other girls, less close to Pauline, could now be closer. Beatrix was given reports. Janice, in from State on one of her secret weekends, told Beatrix that Pauline had become puffy and stuffy and was promoted to Head Sales and Bookkeeper of the Daisy branch. Her mother worked under her. Pauline was living with her mother and with the owner of the liquor store.

The girls were silent.

Janice phoned Beatrix on her next trip into the city.

"Pauline fired her mother!" said Janice. "Oh, if we could all do that!"

Pauline allowed Beatrix to lunch with her and Janice a month later at a delicatessen. It was a Chinese-modern delicatessen. Pauline, with her knowledge of Louis Sullivan and Frank Lloyd Wright, of Form Follows Function, looked around at the pagodas, with prices of corned-beef sandwiches lettered on them, with slanty-eyed girls shouldering tilted parasols—club-sandwich prices on the parasols. On another mural, Tea Drinking Ceremony, BEVERAGES was lettered in oriental-style script.

It was Sunday afternoon.

"Where are you going now?"

Janice was hitching back to State. Beatrix was sneaking home. It was forbidden for her to see Pauline, after the business with the dress. (It was also forbidden, by Janice's mother, for Janice to see Beatrix.)

"Where are *you* going now?"

"I'm dropping in on my mother," said Pauline.

"I thought you lived with her," Janice said.

"No. She's back at the old apartment."

"Where are you?" Janice asked.

"With the owner of the liquor store," said Pauline.

We lined up at the cashier's.

"First a Chinese restaurant," said Pauline, "then a Chinese delicatessen. That's my life, from crazy to crazier."

Looking for Beatrix

T.

"Mother, I'm pregnant with a girl. What will she be?"

"What she was."

"What if she doesn't want to be what she was?"

"Then she will change, slightly."

"Beatrix," asked her father, his head in her crib, "what will we do to free Sacco and Vanzetti?"

This was the first of unsolvable problems put to her.

"Beatrix," asked her father, interrupting her Ninth Grade Social Studies homework. "They're killing our people. What will we do?"

He was reading the Belsen Black Book.

Beatrix wrote a report for Ninth Grade Social Studies: "The Nazis and their Death Camps." The teacher pointed out Beatrix's misspellings and disbelieved her information. The class was informed that this was an example of historical bias and racial exaggeration. The teacher was a Southerner, Miss Sample, whose specialty was The War Between the States and The Failure of Reconstruction.

Beatrix, news editor of the McAfee Intermediate Bulletin, incorporated her information into her column, "Bea's Bonnet." The principal censored the paper and refused to let the issue come out. Beatrix stormed home. Her parents averted their eyes. They held each other's hands.

"The principal must have a reason," said her mother, said her father.

"Beatrix," asked her father when she was in high, "what will we do about your middle brother who has an acne'ed back?

57

What will happen to your youngest brother who is stunted in growth and stutters?"

The middle brother's back inexplicably healed, but the younger brother neither gained in growth nor in speaking facility. Beatrix investigated and discovered an elementary school, slightly farther from their neighborhood school, with students less competitive and faculty less oppressive.

"You are jealous of him," said her father. "You want to send him away so that he should not get better marks than you at your old school."

"You already count him a failure," said her mother, "so you send him with the other failures."

The youngest brother learned to control the stuttering by never speaking. Although normal height was eventually gained, he thought he was short for he humped in and out of places, shrank before others, slunk, shadowed in day, retreated at night.

"Beatrix," asked her father, "what will you do about the British?" Beatrix was doing Government homework for City. "They are preventing our people from escaping to Palestine. They are another extermination camp."

When Beatrix's father cried, Beatrix became his mother. His eyes wet her blouse collar, her heart. She had access to City's ditto machine, on which she had been sending out "City to the Service"—a newsletter to City students fighting the war.

Beatrix poured her wrath into purple ditto until her parents received visits from City Journalism Department and the Army Information Service about the anti-British propaganda Beatrix was disseminating. Her parents made Beatrix promise she would discontinue publication.

"Beatrix," asked her father, wringing his hands, "what will we do about anti-Semitism in the land?"

Beatrix was still living in her old room, without Gene Kelly, without Gregory Peck, without Harold Steiner, with Baby Lena.

"Where?" asked Beatrix.

"California," said her father, "in the congressional campaign."

Beatrix left Baby Lena with her grandparents and traveled out to Los Angeles to campaign against R. M. Nixon, Republican candidate for Congress. He was waging an anti-Semitic campaign against Helen Gahagan Douglas. Helen Gahagan Douglas was not a Semite but she *was* a congresswoman *married* to a Semite. She was accused in leaflets and pamphlets and speechlets of following the Communist and Yiddish party line. Her voting record paralleled the CP line, and her husband, Melvin Douglas, followed the Yiddish Theater line.

When Congressman Nixon was elected, Beatrix's parents worried that he would take vengeance on his opponent, Beatrix. When he became Vice-President, her parents urged Beatrix to unlist her phone. When he became President they waited for the pogrom. Not that it didn't come—but no one came to take Beatrix to jail, or the pale, or an internment camp.

The girls knew about Beatrix's mouth. They knew that fearful and trembling, she was yet a dragon slayer. It was Janice who urged Beatrix to plead for less supervision of Janice's life. It was Beatrix who lectured the haberdasher father. Hence the father's curse upon Beatrix.

Maybe a curse has a life of its own, a force that enters our lives. We fight that curse, always expecting to be defeated by it. Bea, the Dragon Slayer, knew that when her love asked for her hand in marriage, one day he would release that hand, that when Sarcastic Cynthia asked to be introduced to Harold, Harold would, in turn, introduce himself into Cynthia. For the Dragon Slayer, every adventure presumes a battleground, a dragon, the possibilities of being slain, of slaying, or of running from the field in defeat, garments sullied, eyes glaring, blood from superficial wounds speckling the tall grass.

U.

"Mother, I'm pregnant with a baby girl."

"What's happening?"

"She's being aborted."

"Tell her not to take it seriously. She'll get used to it."

V.

"Mother, I'm pregnant with an abortion."

"Tell her we are all abortions—and more."

"What more?"

"Intrusions, conditions . . ."

"She doesn't want to listen to you."

"That's why she's an abortion."

It was an abortive year for Beatrix. Her husband had left her, unsettling her. A publishing house that had an option on her proposed cookbook, *Cooking Without Fear*, let the option drop. When the firm became infirm and Beatrix was generally unhoused from home and publishing house, she determined that everything that could be developed, completed, concluded would be so.

She finished her degree in Anthropology. She began preparing Lena for adulthood. She completed the cookbook, using Lena's ominous drawings of vegetables: cabbages with growths inside, translucent leaves over humped shadows, tomatoes dripping juice like blood, spears of carrots, pregnant zucchini with puffy features.

"M., I'm p. with a b.g. and she wants to do everything."

"She'll need help."

"Her helper won't let her do everything by herself. He wants to do more and be more."

"Then he needs help."

"M., I'm p. with a b.g. and she wants to be a writer."

"That's penis envy."

"But she wants to write cookbooks."

"Then that's an acceptable degree of penis envy."

"But her doctor wants to write cookbooks with her."

"That's womb envy."

Beatrix was deep into treatment, substituting doctor for father-lover-editor. Her doctor, in turn, was pleased that Beatrix, although invading the male domain of publishing—indicating penis envy by her need to exhibit herself—was yet working on a womanly subject. He enjoyed the topic, how Beatrix conquered her fear of the kitchen. That fear, he explained in a Foreword to the book, was instilled by her own mother's reluctance to share the role of homemaker.

"M., I'm p. with a b.g. and she's afraid of the kitchen."

"It's your fault."

"Why is it my fault?"

"If life is mundane, the kitchen is woman's sole domain."

"M., I'm p. with a b.g., and she wants to learn to cook."

"Don't let her."

"She wants to prepare breakfast."

"Then she'll have to carry it upstairs on a tray."

"She wants to bake a birthday cake."

"Then she'll have to carry it into the dining room for the guests, with its candles blazing."

"She wants to roast the Thanksgiving turkey."

"Then she can carve her future on its carcass."

"She is not allowed to carve the turkey. The man must carve. She enjoys serving the meal."

"Good, then she's prepared to be a servant."

The doctor allowed himself a smoke of a Freudian cigar while devising topics for the revised cookbook: Your Mother-in-Law Is Coming for a Visit; Your Former Husband Comes for Brunch and a Visit with his Child: What to Serve? Your

Mother Is Coming to Console You. The last has subtopics: Mother Brings Something That Doesn't Go With the Meal and Insists on Filling the Company Up With What She Brings Before the Meal Is Served, or, You're into an Organic Bag and Your Mother Calls It *Milchiks*.

The doctor was a playful man who rode a bicycle in good weather during the ten-minute grace period between patients. He thought the book would be therapeutic for his other patients. He invited them, as well as therapist and analyst friends, to write comments, forewords, afterwords. He promised that this group book would be group authored. When he insisted upon being listed as chief editor, Beatrix quit therapy.

"M., I'm p. with a b.g. and she's in therapy."

"What does her therapist do?"

"He plays eagles."

"How is that game played?"

"He throws her the baseball bat; she catches it. He places his hand higher than hers on the bat. They hand-climb up the bat, alternating hands until his cupped hand grabs the curved handle of the bat. He perches there, the eagle."

"He's grabbing the end of his penis. He's masturbating. Throw away that bat. What does she need that dirty thing for?"

Beatrix dropped the idea for the book, dropped her doctor, kept her fear of cooking and her daughter, bore her relationships with mother and father, and began a new book.

She called it, tentatively, *Unafraid Women*, women who both cooked and lived without fear. She had to go back a long way to find them, about a hundred years for some of them.

W.

"M., I'm p. with a b.g. and she can't find her mother."

"When did she last have her mother's address?"

"A hundred years ago."

Beatrix finds Mothers Margaret, Louisa, Emily, Charlotte, and other mother superiors in this convent of her search.

"M., I'm p. with a b.g. and she is looking for her mothers."
"What is Mother Margaret Fuller doing?"
"Mother Margaret is there, her mouth opened in Conversations. She is planning the Roman revolution."
"What is Mother Louisa May Alcott doing?"
"Mother Louisa is piquing her father. He is opposed to corporal punishment but he must whip little Louisa for her disobedience. Mother Louisa is also writing herself to death to support her father."
"What is Mother Emily Dickinson doing?"
"Mother Emily Dickinson is falling in love through the mails. She is also writing seventeen hundred seventy-five poems and publishing seven."
"What is Mother Charlotte Forten doing?"
"Mulatto Mother Charlotte says, 'Unless it be about slavery, it has slight interest for me.' "

Beatrix is taking years with *Unafraid Women*. She is afraid of them.

X.
"Mother, I'm pregnant with a baby girl."
"What is she doing?"
"Remembering."

In such a state of being unloved, untreated or mistreated, unpublished, unheard, Beatrix discovers that her friends are all in town at the same time. Even Shirley Panush spoke to her on the phone about a reunion.

They take pictures. The girl friends stand clustered around an oak, their faces in shade. Shirley is seated on a park bench. The photo captures her crutches leaning against the bench, for Shirley cannot walk without help. Her legs have given way to varicose veins, swollen ankles, trick knees, and thrombosis. The blood clot travels and must constantly be dissolved and her blood thinned out before it reaches Shirley's heart, lungs, or brain.

In the photo, Janice, the athlete, has indistinct features. She has tanned herself dark in California and the photo is contrasty. Janice is darker than her brown husband. Although her features are unclear, one can discern a scowl, but perhaps Janice is squinting at the sunlight.

Lois is lovelier than she was in the Yearbook, that crimson book with its cheap cardboard, wartime cover. Romanian Lois is less Romanian, more slender, her shape controlled, her hair flowing. As is the hair of her daughter who wears white dresses and whose straightened hair is blowing in the slight breeze.

Y.
"M., I'm p. with a b.g. and she has kinky hair."
"Straighten it."
"And she has crooked teeth."
"Put braces on them."
"A projection on her nose."
"Smooth it."
"Acne'ed skin."
"Treat it."
"Fallen arches."
"Fit them."
"Turned-in toes."
"Correct them."
"Then what should I do with my b.g.?"
"Sell her."

Lois has a hand on each girl's shoulder.

Beatrix is somber and armored. She holds Lena like a lance, the sword hand of her mother. Lena's features are hidden

64

under Lena's brown hair. She has been crying because she wanted to play with Howie, her four-year-old neighbor. Instead, she had to come into the sunlight for the photo.

The photographer is Pauline who will not allow herself to be shot, she says. She has quickly taken over the reunion. She has ordered the girls around as if they were in her shop at Daisy's. She has told them what positions to assume, where to stand, when to smile, how to place the children. Pauline is The Boss.

"M., I'm p. with a b.g. and she wants to be the boss."
"Of what?"
"She doesn't care, just boss."
"That's because she has never been in charge of herself."

Z.
"Mother, I am pregnant with a baby girl and she has stopped growing."
"Why?"
"She is finished."

Beatrix is alone in the room at Hillel House. The phonograph is playing and Beatrix practices dance steps. She is a self-conscious dancer still, from those Prom days, but she is now a woman with fleshy hips, small waist, full calves. Her shoulders are wider than Joan Crawford's. Her breasts are large-nippled, pointy, and small.

She dances, puts the tone arm on automatic, and repeats the dance on the 78 rpm. From a couch turned away from her rises a young man.

"Not again," he says and turns off the record.

Beatrix is about to give combat. The young man changes his mind, replays the record, and offers to dance with Beatrix. She refuses. He will not accept refusal. He holds her close. She stumbles as she did at the Senior Prom. His thighs guide her. He dances slowly, both hands on her waist, swaying her, preparing her, lifting her slightly. She is gradually subdued. Her eyes close. When lifted she soars and is surprised to be returned to Hillel carpeting. She opens her eyes. He, eye level, is smiling. Laughing at her? She becomes defensive and stops dancing. His hair is curly. So are his lashes. His eyes are laughing hazel.

Beatrix will not date. It is against her Socialist principles. Nor will she wear dresses or skirts anymore. She has explained it to her professors. She must wear slacks until the day when men's legs are also remarked upon. She must wear flannel shirts until the day when men, in addressing her, look at her eyes and not the eyes of her breasts. Her professors are startled at this outpouring and agree that she be given permission to wear slacks. It is practical in this cold climate. Madame Bosse disagrees. She will not allow slacks into French. Beatrix drops French.

Beatrix wears no makeup. She pickets fraternities, barber-shops, the campus restaurant and bar because they discriminate racially. Beatrix is an EVD Socialist—Eugene V. Debs Socialist Study Group, although her father calls it BVD. The EVD'ers have formed a campus cooperative and several couples have moved in, as well as four singles—Beatrix and three male EVD'ers. Sometimes guests visit and Bea finds her room occupied. She is annoyed. Are *they* Socialists? On those nights she sleeps home.

Her room now, in fact, is occupied by a capitalistic couple. Beatrix is wandering through Hillel House, looking for a place to study.

If Beatrix returns to the home of her parents, she will, for no reason, begin screaming at her mother. She will, for that reason, be excused from the dinner table by her father. She will cause her stuttering brother more speech difficulty, and her acne'ed brother will become self-conscious. Yet Beatrix's parents want Bea to stay home, are suspicious of the co-op, sure it will be her downfall, the shame of the name. The only way for Beatrix not to shame the name is to marry and change it.

This Hillel boy is different because he is in English studies, and that is a non-Jewish, nonreformist field, as well as nonpreprofessional. He is *not* prelaw, predental, premed, pre-ed. He *is* lighthearted, dresses with style, and is very pretty, which confuses Beatrix, with her emphasis on mental prowess rather than bourgeois appearance.

Who are Beatrix's friends besides Pauline at Daisy's, Shirley in her attic, Lois studying Chemistry for Early El—where there is no need for Chemistry—and Janice eloped to California? Besides—in later life—Mothers Margaret, Louisa, Emily, Charlotte, Rosa Luxemburg, Eleanor Roosevelt, Anaïs Nin, Kate Chopin, Mary Ann Evans, Frances Perkins? Who are her friends—in later life—besides the psychiatrist who will attend her and offend her, besides Lena and Lena's four-year-old love Howie and all those they will meet? Who are, who will be, her friends?

She is best friends with Bert. He disappeared soon after she met him. Perhaps he starved. When she knew him at EVD's, he had no money for food, no place to bathe. (There was only cold water at EVD.) Beatrix's mother fed him occasionally but would not let him use a towel.

"M., I'm p. with a b.g. and she wants to bring home a friend."
"Who's her friend?"
"He's a deeply pitted, emaciated Irishman."
"He can't come here."
"He's IWW, he's bitter, he's humorous."
"He can't come here."
"He's her guardian."
"That's all right but he can't come here."
"Who is allowed here?"

"Those who already have a home, who have eaten and bathed beforehand."

Bert is the guardian of Beatrix in that co-op. And Beatrix and Bert are also friends with Norman and Norman's duck walk and the large pimple on Norman's nose, because Norman will be a worker's lawyer. Bert, Beatrix, and Norman also love Charles, the Black elevator operator.

"M., I'm pregnant with a b.g. and she has a friend who is Black."
"What does he do?"
"He is the elevator operator on campus."
"That's all right."
"He is working for his tuition."
"Then that's not all right."

Black Charles is majoring in drama. He takes Beatrix to the People's Theater where he performs in *Stevedore* and in William Saroyan's *Hello Out There!*

Beatrix talks for hours in her room at the co-op with IWW Bert, pre–worker's lawyer Norman, actor Charles. They tuck her in at night, each kissing her forehead (Norman), cheek (Charles), hand (Bert).

And yet, in this her life, her parents cannot accept her and Beatrix cannot accept herself. It is Harold who accepts her, Harold with his rich speaking voice, slight body, spiral hair. He accepts the fact that she stumbles when she dances yet dances, that she screams at her parents, teases her brothers, and yet returns home, that she would make the land more civilized but lives in the hovel of the co-op. He accepts the fact that she is a virgin yet three men kiss her good night every night.

He accepts her slacks, her face pale without makeup (for she would attract no one by artifice), and that she weeps when he kisses her at the end of an evening. She closes her door on him, yet opens it to others for she knows that he would kiss the forehead, the cheek, the hand—he says, until she is damp between her thighs and that he will then kiss his way up or down them.

And so Beatrix and Harold marry. It is a proper marriage with a hall, two rabbis from her and his parents' respective synagogues, and with a catered dinner. After the dinner there is a sweet table. To the sweet table she is allowed to invite her EVDs, Bert, Norman, and Charles, as well as any of her old high school friends. She sends invitations to Shirley, Janice, Pauline, and Lois. Janice's invitation is returned with the hand on the envelope pointing to: Whereabouts Unknown. The other three girls do not respond in the special, stamped enclosed envelope for responding.

Harold will not move into the Debs co-op. He says that he has nothing against it but its lack of privacy, filth, bedbugs, and nosy people.

Harold and Beatrix, without income, become children again in her parents' house, using a bedroom and forcing the acne'ed and stuttering brothers to combine into one room so that the young couple can have a bed- and study room. Harold moves in with the pictures of Gene Kelly, Gregory Peck, and Eugene V. Debs.

It is not long before Harold and Beatrix are looking for more privacy from the family and from each other. They even visit the co-op but Bert has left the city to organize in the field, Norman has been busily studying for the bar, and Charles, the Black in drama, has dropped out of City because the Drama Department theater has been turned into a library for the returning World War II vets. There is no place for Charles to act on campus.

Cynthia, from Advanced French, begins to invite Beatrix and Harold to her house. She is an only child and it is quiet there. They talk, take classes together, and attend films, this troika of friends. Cynthia switches out of French to major in English. Beatrix and Cynthia love each other.

One afternoon Beatrix cannot find Harold. He is not under

the Big Clock in Main, where he had promised to meet her. He is not at the drugstore across from City, at the library in the theater. He isn't at Hillel. She walks to the co-op. It is cold, a draggy winter. Spring is late. Beatrix's shoes become wet and her hands stiff. She knocks on Norman's door. The room is quiet, the door locked. Charles's room is empty. She tries the door of her old single. The shades are down. The bed is full. She cannot make out the figures clearly but she knows them. Harold's curls are growing out of Cynthia's groin.

Historical Mothers

Looking for Mothers

"Mother, I'm pregnant with a book."
"Hard or soft cover?"

Beatrix sits at her desk. A book falls from her nineteenth-century shelf, the spine bouncing on her little toe. She is in pain. So are her authors: Margaret, Louisa, Emily, Miss Forten of Philadelphia and Sea Island. There are other mothers hovering on other shelves: Red Rosa Luxemburg, Mother Doris Lessing, Mother Anaïs Nin.

Beatrix is notating and recording, for they are each other's mothers and daughters. Why didn't Turgenev write *Mothers and Daughters* rather than *Fathers and Sons*? Why didn't D. H. Lawrence write *Daughters and Lovers* instead of *Sons and Lovers*?

Looking for Mothers (1): Mother Emily

What did Beatrix learn from her mother Emily? She learned valuable mathematical data. In fifty-six years of life Emily wrote 1,775 poems. During her lifetime, she published seven. That means Emily had 1,768 unpublished poems. That also means that if Emily wrote poetry every year of her life from birth on, she would have written thirty-one and some poems each year. Since that premise is illogical, Emily probably started writing at eighteen or nineteen, and then she would have written about forty-eight poems a year. That means she would have written a poem every week in the year but four, or a little less than one-seventh of a poem a day.

"Mother, I'm giving birth to a poetess."
"Tell her there's no such thing."

From her Mother Emily, Beatrix learns to work and to sustain. But from fluttery, stuttery Emily, Beatrix has to learn not to flutter and to let her youngest brother do the stuttering. Emily fluttered to her correspondents. She made her diminutive self more diminutive, her own meaning demeaning.

Two of Mother Emily's loves were Reverends, who maintained their reverential distance. Each she probably met once. Reverend Charles Wadsworth she addressed, in her correspondence, as "Master," and she was his "Daisy." Reverend Thomas Wentworth Higginson she called "Preceptor," and she was "Your Scholar," "Your Gnome."

LOOKING FOR MOTHERS (1A): MOTHER EMILY IS ASKED QUESTIONS. SHE ANSWERS ELUSIVELY

Mother Emily's voice, through the scrawly handwriting, is either throaty or babyish. Perhaps she lisps. Consciously.

Thomas Wentworth Higginson is puzzling over a letter with handwriting like fossil bird tracks, with little punctuation, mostly dashes. The letter is unsigned, but, on a separate card, within a smaller envelope, signed in pencil, is the signature— "Emily Dickinson from Amherst."

Mr. Higginson finds therein four poems and a letter.

Mother Emily's voice is throaty, unsure—carefully unsure— with this correct gentleman:

Mother Emily: "Mr. Higginson—Are you too deeply occupied to say if my verse is alive?" (Emily Dickinson, *Selected Poems and Letters of Emily Dickinson*, ed. Robert N. Linscott, Doubleday, 1959, p. 5.)

Mrs. Higginson is sitting in a wheelchair where she sat herself some years ago in order not to have to move anywhere. Reverend Higginson tells Mary Higginson of the letter, this curious letter with the fossil bird tracks, little punctuation but dashes, unsigned with the enclosed, penciled card.

"Well, well," says Mary Higginson.

Mother Emily: "The mind is so near itself it cannot see distinctly, . . ." (*Poems and Letters*, p. 5.)

Reverend Higginson thinks that is very sensible.

"Humph!" says Mary Higginson.

Mother Emily (plaintively): "And I have none to ask." (*Poems and Letters*, p. 5.)

Reverend Higginson thinks that is touching.

"Mother, I'm pregnant with a baby girl and she's writing a letter."

"What is she writing?"

"She is begging for advice but she is being modest, maidenly, and retreating."

"Then she is manipulating her correspondent."

Mother Emily: "I inclose my name, asking you, if you please, sir, to tell me what is true." (*Poems and Letters*, p. 5.)

Mr. Higginson is flattered to be called upon for the truth. He immediately replies with the truth. He receives another letter. Mary Higginson, adjusting her lap robe, is incurious.

Reverend Higginson informs Mary (he informs her of everything always and asks her advice on every occasion, and he immediately marries someone else named Mary when she dies) that he really knows nothing about Miss Dickinson, but he knows everything about Miss Dickinson.

"Nonsense!" says Mary Higginson.

Reverend Higginson tells Mary that he does not know why Emily refuses to leave her house in Amherst, why she refuses even to try to publish, why she will not visit him.

"Perhaps she is wise," says Mary.

But, says Reverend Higginson, he has questioned Miss Dickinson and knows every aspect of her life.

Reverend Higginson: "I asked her what she looked like."

Mother Emily: "I had no portrait now, but am small, like the wren; and my hair is bold, like the chestnut bur; and my eyes, like sherry in the glass, that the guest leaves. Would this do just as well?" (*Poems and Letters*, p. 9.)

"Mother, I'm pregnant with a b.g. and she is asked for her portrait."

"What does she send?"

"A poetical, verbal description."

"Then she is indescribably homely."

Mother Emily: "You asked how old I was." As old as my verse.

"Mother, I'm pregnant with a baby girl and she's asked how old she is."

"What does she reply?"

"She's a poet, as old as her verse."

"Then she's not young."

Emily is thirty-two.

Reverend Higginson: "What did she read?"

Mother Emily: "You inquire my books . . . I went to school,

but in your manner of the phrase had no education." (*Poems and Letters*, p. 7.)

"Mother, I'm pregnant with a baby girl and she's been asked about her education."
"What does she reply?"
"That she had none."
"Then she is educated."

Emily went to Amherst Academy for two years and spent an additional year at Mount Holyoke Female Seminary.
Reverend Higginson: "Who were her companions?"
Mother Emily: "You ask of my companions. Hills, sir, and the sundown, and a dog, large as myself, that my father bought me. They are better than beings because they know, but do not tell." (*Poems and Letters*, p. 7.)

"Mother, I'm p. with a b.g. and she's asked about her companions."
"What does she reply?"
"Nature and animals are her companions."
"Then she has many male friends and goes to parties."

The house was full of young men, music, and small celebrations.
Reverend Higginson: "I asked about her family."
Mother Emily: "I have a brother and sister; my mother does not care for thought, and father, too busy with his briefs to notice what we do." (*Poems and Letters*, p. 7.)

"Mother, I'm p. with a b.g. and she's asked about her family."
"What does she reply?"
"That they are all distant from her and her father does not notice her."
"Then she is close to her family, attended by her sister and her brother and dominated by her father."

Reverend Higginson: "I gently probed her sense of worth."
Mother Emily: "I could not weigh myself, myself. My size felt small to me." (*Poems and Letters*, p. 8.)

"Mother, I'm p. with a b.g. and she's asked her worth."
"What does she reply?"
"That she's of little worth."
"That's because her correspondent is afraid of worthy women."
"No, mother, he loves worthy women. He has many friends amongst them."
"Then they must not attain greater worth than he."

Reverend Higginson: "I asked what made her write her poetry."
Mother Emily: "Because I am afraid. . . . Will you be my preceptor, Mr. Higginson?" (*Poems and Letters*, pp. 7, 9.)

"Mother, I'm p. with a b.g. and she's asked why she writes poetry."
"What does she reply?"
"She says that she writes because she's afraid, and will her correspondent teach her?"
"That means she's written many poems and needs no instruction."

When Mother Emily had written this letter to her preceptor, she had penned more than one poem. In 1858 she wrote fifty-two poems, copied them over in ink, and sewed them into booklets. By the year of her letter to Reverend Higginson, 1862, she had written another 356 poems.

Mary Higginson is wheeling angrily, round and round in her chair. Her husband is dozing, sitting upright.

"Why do the insane always cling to you?" she, a dervish, asks. "Why are you the rock moss adheres to? Why are you the wall climbers entwine? Why are you the last stop, end of the line?"

78

She peers into the reverend's face. He is smiling faintly. "Is he dreaming of her?" she brakes her chair. "What's happened to reality? What's happened to his sense of duty, my God, his Christian duty?"

A woman, a wild, uncorrectable, unmet woman is the danger to Christianity and to duty, while Mary, Virgin Mary, tart-tongued and contrary, is confined and refined and no threat at all.

Beatrix, choose carefully, for we can pick and choose not only our mothers but among their qualities!

Beatrix will forget this after Harold leaves. She will speak to men in her high, nervous Mother Emily voice. She has been trained to speak in this fashion. Her normally rich, low voice will be used for friends from the Eugene V. Debs Socialist Study Group, for Bert of the pockmarks, Norm of the duck waddle, Charles in the elevator. She will ask all other men, helplessly, to help her with math or to help her hang something on the wall or to help her fix her plumbing. Poor Beatrix, even a woman's plumbing isn't so hard to fix.

Mother Emily, what else have you to teach Beatrix? Oblique-ness and crispness. Parallel pain.

Mother Emily: "I never lost as much but twice, / And that was in the sod." (Thomas H. Johnson, ed., *The Poems of Emily Dickinson*, Harvard University Press, 1955, I:38.)

Beatrix too has a double loss, Harold and Lena, burying the memory of the former, keeping alive that of the latter.

Mother Emily: "To fight aloud is very brave– / But *gallanter*, I know / Who charge within the bosom / The Cavalry of Wo–" (*Poems of Emily Dickinson*, I:90.)

Beatrix can transcend this with the best of the Transcendentalists. Her own hardships become her book, *The Pioneers*. She will handle disappointment and bravely throw the ingredients of *Cooking Without Fear* into the garbage can, into the wastebasket of wasted effort. She will be brave enough to deal with *Unafraid Women*.

Beatrix will have to learn, beyond Emily's tutelage, how not to please. She will have to try to prop herself up on her elbows and not sag. She will have to learn how not to greet or to retreat. But not yet. She may never learn all that.

With Mother Emily, Beatrix learns physical passion. Not from Harold when she was that child bride.

"Please *me*, honey," he would say. "Please me." Groaning. "Please. Oooh. Please."

Little Beatrix Bride was not content but did not know enough to be displeased or to ask Harold for pleasure.

How did Mother Emily know pleasure?

Mother Emily: "Come slowly–Eden!" (How did she know the pleasure of slow entrance?) "Lips unused to Thee– / Bashful- sip thy Jessamines– / As the fainting Bee– / Reaching late his flower, / Round her chamber hums– / Counts his nectars– Enters– / And is lost in Balms." (*Poems of Emily Dickinson*, I:148.)

Only one way Mother Emily could have known all that.

"Mother, I'm pregnant with a baby girl and she's masturbat- ing."

"Good. It's the only pleasure she'll know."

What exactly did Beatrix miss the most? Meeting Harold after class under the Big Clock? Whispering with him between the rooms of her parents and that of her younger brothers? Or did she miss the stopper in her cork, the stopping of the draft in the chimney? It is as if all orifices remained open. Certainly her eyes took years to close, years to sleep, for she was vigilant against villainy long after the villain had departed.

Looking for Mothers (2): Mother Margaret

"Mother, I am pregnant with a baby girl."
"Have only a pretty girl. Don't have an ugly daughter."

Beatrix, undress. Look into the mirror. It is not obscene to be privately seen.

What do you like? Can't you say even to yourself? Then, what do you hate about your appearance?

Hair. All that hair, I hate. Hair on upper lip—faintly there—long stiff hairs on chin, wild hair on my head, even when shaped, quickly becomes shapeless, waves, curls, no hairline, just intruding tendrils. Mediterranean hair. Hate my pube hair, bushy, curly forest—primeval forest. People look at the top of my head and know what's down below. They don't know that I have a white hair in the patch.

My accordion-pleated navel I hate, my navel accordion pleated because of Lena. Stretch marks on the sides of my hips—one on each hip—like white stripes down uniforms—I hate those—those are from Lena.

Do you hate Lena?

Oh, no. That's not allowed!

Turn around.

I hate the back, my hairy anus, even that! My big hips. My stomach muscles have sagged. There is that protrusion under the accordion navel, over the black pube.

My breasts I hate—too small, nipples too large. The nipple on the r.s. larger than the nipple on the l.s. Beauty marks on the breasts, especially on the r.s., not so beautiful. Blue veins around the brown nipples; one stiff black hair on the nipple of the r.s.

Thighs, hate thighs. Loose. I'll be my mother again. Never will I be able to wear a bikini or a topless, or sun in Nice. Never can I wear hip huggers, for my hips cannot easily be hugged. Rubbing thighs. Black-and-blue mark on the back of my r. leg.

Legs too full, shoulders too wide, neck too long. Eyes are becoming smaller, elbows wrinkled.

Well, now, is there anything you *don't* hate?

I *don't* hate my shoulders, my full mouth, my winged brows, my dimpled knees, my rather aristocratic, narrow feet, my graduated toes.

My shoulders are Joan Crawford-wide. My curly hair is Jane Russell's *Outlaw*-ish hair. My mouth is good. My arms are long and no longer skinny. My eyebrows are clean. They never grew back after that frantic high school plucking.

Ah, I see something else I hate. My womb, my womb. I hate my womb.

You mean, you can actually *see* it?

Yes, when I sit down, between the walls of my vagina, like a nestling, like the ugly naked red head of a turkey buzzard, this featherless, blood-red womb protrudes.

Then it's all bad?

No, no. The effect is not bad. My back is not white and soft like Pauline's Betty Grable back. My hair is not gentile-straight like Lois's Romanian hair, my skin is not creamy like Shirley's used to be before she went up into her attic. I am not graceful like Janice in the water. I have freckles on my shoulders. But the effect is of a tall, slender woman.

So, you like it?

No, I hate it.

LOOKING FOR MOTHERS (2A): MOTHER MARGARET DRESSES

She spends an hour each morning dressing, brushing her long, light hair, putting a single, large, fresh flower into it. She is the eldest child, medium sized, with a proud walk. One thinks that she is tall.

"Mother, I'm pregnant."
"Have an eldest daughter."
"Why?"
"Then you don't need a father, then you don't need a mother."

Margaret's breasts developed early and they press against the bones of corsets and convention, against the soft silk across her bosom.

They are plain women, my Mothers Emily, Margaret, and Louisa May: Emily with her long face and staring eyes; bald Louisa May who lost her rich auburn hair in illness, who lost her teeth, at least in my copy of the encyclopedia; plainest of them, Mother Margaret, whom Ralph Waldo Emerson described: "Her appearance had nothing prepossessing. Her extreme plainness—a trick of incessantly opening and shutting her eyelids, the nasal tone of her voice—all repelled." (Ralph Waldo Emerson, William Henry Channing, James Freeman Clarke, eds., *Memoirs of Margaret Fuller Ossoli*, Phillips, Sampson and Company, 1852, I:202.)

Ugly Emerson, hypochondriac, effeminate Higginson, short, egocentric Mr. James Nathan (known only because he corresponded with Margaret Fuller), undersized, long-nosed Thoreau! A mother can have a homely boy, and he can still be a joy. A mother can have an eccentric son, and he is the center of her heart.

But, says Mother Margaret: "When all things are blossoming, it seems so strange not to blossom too. I hate not to be beautiful, when all around is so." (Mason Wade, *Margaret Fuller, Whetstone of Genius*, Viking Press, 1940, p. 80.)

"Mother, I'm pregnant with a baby girl and she wants information."

"What does she want to know?"

"What does it mean when men say, 'Up against the wall, MF?' "

"It means, Margaret Fuller."

"But why?"

"They're afraid of her."

"Mother, I'm pregnant with a baby girl and she's not beautiful."

"Then let her be the eldest and the support of her family."

"Mother, I'm pregnant with a baby girl and she wants some information."

"What does she want to know?"

"How can she learn to be independent and strong?"

"Let her always be short of money and the head of her family."

Mothers Louisa May and Margaret were always short of money and heads of their families.

All these Big Mothers write letters. Mother Emily and Mother Margaret do, and they write foolish letters.

The quill slides in the finger. The pen is smooth. The fingertips touch the paper. The pen is put to the mouth, to Emily's flat chest, to Margaret's full chest. Margaret touches her breastbone. She wishes on it. Mother Emily is thirty-two. Mother Margaret is thirty-five. Each writes to a gentleman, and each calls him her guardian, although that gentleman is the same age or a year younger than Little Ms. Emily and Ms. MF.

They bring themselves to their gentlemen. Little Ms. Emily has all those packets and baskets and tiskets and taskets of poems, but she asks for advice on the writing of poems. Ms. Margaret has brought a whole curriculum vitae with her, but implores Mr. Nathan to protect her.

Why didn't you hear about MF? You were too busy learning about Emerson and Thoreau.

MF has brought work experience with her, hard to come by for a little lady in the 1840s. She has edited *The Dial*. She has been literary editor for Horace Greeley's *Tribune*. She held Conversations for intelligent women in Boston, charging twenty dollars for ten lectures. She traveled westward by

84

covered wagon to Oregon and back and wrote a travel book on her adventures. Needing to research it, she was the first woman allowed into the Harvard Library. She wrote the feminist tract, *Woman in the Nineteenth Century.*

But when little Mr. James Nathan visits her, she forgets her vital curriculum, for her blood stirs with something elemental.

What has Beatrix to learn from Mother MF? That women make double entries, afraid of their heads and too full of heart.

Little Mr. James Nathan is thirty-four. He has gone from Germany to New York. He is a businessman. That is his experience. He is slight and blue-eyed and that is also his experience. He is Jewish, which is quite an experience, both for Mr. Nathan and for Margaret's biographers.

Biographer Mason Wade is impressed that Margaret knew a member of the Jewish species: "One of the many presentiments of Margaret's mystical period was that some day she would know intimately a member of the Jewish race." (Wade, p. 162.) "Intimate." Oh, come off it, masonic Wade.

Mr. Jewish Nathan was "A personification of all the romance of the East." (Wade, p. 163.) He was also, like his fellow Jews, "clever."

Beatrix is jolted into reality. She also "intimately" knew a Jew but he was not the personification of "all the romance of the East." Harold was more the personification of the Jewish northwest section of her city.

Everyone is surprised by Mr. Nathan. Mr. Joseph Jay Deiss (*The Roman Years of Margaret Fuller*, Thomas Y. Crowell, 1969, p. 21) writes: "To her surprise he revealed himself as a Jew."

Mr. Deiss, was it a quick peak? Was he smooth as a doorknob? Top of a mushroom? Did Jewish Nathan unzip before there were zippers, or pull out of his drawers?

Poor Mother MF, this attraction to a Jew was the first step in her downfall, leading to enslavement by Mediterranean types, to pregnancy with or without marriage, and certainly to death by drowning with a certain young Italian and their certain young offspring.

Looking for Mothers (2b): Mother Margaret Writes Letters

My Mother, what are you writing? Why are you doing this to me?

Mother Margaret writes to Jewish Nathan: "You must protect me. Are you equal to this?" (Margaret Fuller, *Love Letters of Margaret Fuller, 1845–1846*, D. Appleton, 1903, Letter X.)

"Mother, I'm giving birth to a baby girl and she must be protected."
"From herself?"
"Yes."
"From him?"
"Yes."
"From them?"
"Yes."
"There is no total protection. There is only submission, conception, contraception."

MF: "I know little about the mystery of life, and far less in myself than in others." (*Love Letters*, XI.)

"Mother, I'm pregnant with a baby girl."
"What does she know?"
"Little about the mysteries of life and far less in herself than in others."
"Then she chooses not to know what other baby girls have chosen not to know."
"What should she do?"
"Choose to know."

86

Beatrix is crying. She has mottoes from Mother Margaret on her boards: bulletin, sleeping, ironing.

"AS MEN BECOME AWARE THAT FEW MEN HAVE HAD A FAIR CHANCE, THEY ARE INCLINED TO SAY THAT NO WOMEN HAVE HAD A FAIR CHANCE." (Perry Miller, ed., *Margaret Fuller, American Romantic*, Doubleday Anchor, 1963, p. 143.)

"THE FRENCH REVOLUTION AT LEAST CALLED HER 'CITOYENNE' RATHER THAN SUBJECT, SO THAT ALTHOUGH SHE MAY HAVE BEEN GUILLOTINED, AT LEAST IT WAS AS A CITIZEN AND NOT SUBJECT." (Miller, pp. 143–44.)

Writes breast-heaving Mother Margaret: "Lead me not into temptation and deliver me from Evil." (*Love Letters*, VII.)

"Mother, I'm giving birth to a baby girl and she is praying."
"For what is she praying?"
"She is praying not to be led into temptation and to be delivered from evil and presumptuous sin."
"She is praying to be tempted, to be evil and to sin."

Mother Margaret is kissing the scented envelope before she sends it off: "Are you my guardian to domesticate me in the body and attach it more firmly to the earth? . . . Choose for me a good soil and a sunny place, that I may be a green shelter to the weary and bear fruit." (*Love Letters*, IX.)

"Mother, I'm giving birth to a baby girl."
"What does she want from life?"
"To be as the good soil, a shelter, and to bear fruit."
"Then she wants nothing from life."

Only the year before, my Mother Margaret wrote that, instead of frailty, thy name is woman, "FRAILTY, THY NAME IS MAN." (Miller, p. 138.)

Only the year before, my Mother Margaret wrote: "KNOW

87

THAT THERE EXISTS IN THE MINDS OF MEN A TONE OF FEELING TOWARD WOMAN AS TOWARD SLAVES." (Miller, p. 147.)

Beatrix ponders on what to do when one's mother fails her daughter, returns her favorite dress to the shop, laughs at the peanut shells in her daughter's wild hair? Still, that daughter has slept on her mother's breast on long rides.

My Mother Margaret writes to Mr. Nathan (né James Gotendorf): "I cannot do other than love and most deeply trust you, and will drink the bitter part of the cup with patience." (*Love Letters*, X.)

"Mama, I'm giving birth to a baby girl."
"What is she?"
"Patient."
"Then leave her in the hospital."

My Mother Margaret, as all women, would forget her accomplishments and her past. She must be nothing before a lover. She has forgotten her pleas for the Indians, for prisoners, for the rights of women. Standing eye level to Mr. Nathan, she has no rights. Therefore, she must bow. "I feel today as if we might bury this ugly dwarf-changeling of the past, and hide its grave with flowers." (*Love Letters*, X.)

"Mama, I'm pregnant with a baby girl."
"What does she want to do?"
"Hide her past."
"And then?"
"Bury the future."

My Mother Margaret is religious.

"Mother, I'm pregnant with a baby girl and she's religious."
"Has she been a minister, a priest, a monk, a rabbi?"
"No."

"Is she at the pulpit? Does she open the Holy Ark? Does she marry and bury others? Does she minister final unction? Absolution? Does she wear a tallith and make a minion? Does she carry the Torah around the synagogue? Does she hold the chalice of holy wine for the congregation? Does she sit on the listening side of confession?"

"No."

"Then she's not religious. She's stupid."

And yet my Mother Margaret has written: "Women are . . . the easy victims both of priestcraft and self-delusion; but this would not be, if the intellect was developed in proportion to other powers." (Miller, p. 169.)

One day my poor vain Mother Margaret received a poem from "S." She copies this poem out in a fair hand to make Mr. Nathan jealous and to show him how others have addressed her. No poet, Mr. Nathan instead gifted her with a puppy.

Friend "S" wrote to my Mother Margaret in 1844: "Thou are the Wind, the Wanderer of the Air, / The Searcher of the Earth." (*Love Letters*, XII.)

"Mother, I'm pregnant with a baby girl."

"What do they call her?"

"Wind, the Wanderer of the Air, / The Searcher of the Earth."

"Then she has no name and they will forget her."

As Beatrix reads these letters she is afraid. She thinks of her affairs, humiliations she submitted to, forgiveness she always requested, the effort to give him pleasure, his withdrawing, Bea left quivering.

Mother Margaret writes to the puppy-giver, "I shall expect you to-morrow, but I wish it were to-day. Twenty-four hours are a great many." (*Love Letters*, XIII.)

"Mama, I'm pregnant with a baby girl and she's waiting."

"For what?"

"For him to come."

"Then tell her not to be born."

"She's waiting for them to come."

"Then tell her not to be born."

"She's waiting to come."

"How many times?"

"Mother, I'm pregnant with a baby girl and she's coming."

"Ah, the little beauty. How many times?"

"Many times. She wants to know who else is coming."

"Tell her Mother Margaret is coming, Mother Louisa is coming, Mother Emily is coming, Mother Rosa is coming, Mother Doris is coming, Mother Charlotte . . ."

"Then she has many friends."

Mother Margaret: "My feeling with you was so delightful. It was a feeling of childhood." (*Love Letters*, XV.)

"Mama, I'm pregnant with a baby girl."

"How does she feel?"

"Childish."

"Tell her not to, for there are those who would have her act as an adult until she becomes one, and then make her regress."

Beatrix never tacked up photographs of men after Harold had ripped down Gene Kelly and Gregory Peck from her closet door. (Eugene V. Debs fell off unaided.) Now Beatrix is tacking up Emily. Emily's hair is parted in the middle, covering conches of ears so that they hear no stirring of tendrils, no waves of wavy hair.

Beatrix has Olivetti'ed two portraits of Margaret Fuller. Portrait One: A book opened in her lap, perhaps her own book of western travels. Her large eyes abstracted, hair more decorative than Emily's. Her dress has a dark ribbon and white collar under her full neck. White cuffs balloon from her wrists. Portrait Two: Similar pose to Portrait One, but Margaret is in Rome and the journey has tired her. Her hands are held in maidenly fashion in her lap, except that she is no maiden. A shawl warms her in the chill Roman winter. Her breasts are fuller, her neckline lower. What has her face given up from Portrait One?—innocence, romanticism. With experience in Portrait Two comes a compressing of the lips, a thinning of that full face, eyes less dreamy, waist expanded. She has traveled to where she would go in Portrait One. She will never be able to return from experience.

Why does Bea treasure these unattractive portraits of unattractive women? Why is Mary Ann Evans there or Rosa Luxemburg, Rosa wearing a great bird in her hat at a Socialist rally? She has a photograph of Doris Lessing, with Mother Doris's gray hairs unplucked, thicker than the black, all tucked into a bun. She has a portrait of Mother Anaïs Nin talking animatedly to women students. Why does Bea frame these photographs, these engravings, copies from paintings? Because the women are not looking at or thinking about men.

Beatrix is tempted to cheat. There are many heroes: soldiers, governors, statesmen, sportsmen, movie men, stablemen. Their portraits are lovelier than Margaret's. Even the heroes and the lover of Margaret are lovelier than Margaret. Bea would tack up Margaret's two Giuseppes and one Giovanni, but she must resist. Once she surrounds herself with photographs of men, she will begin looking at the shiny surface. She will run her finger over the face. She will bend to kiss it. Then she will have to run out of her house looking for a hero.

Giuseppe Mazzini, founder of the Roman Republic, is looking at Beatrix. He has a wide-browed face, a straight nose, large dark eyes. Romantic Giuseppe Garibaldi, commander in chief of the Roman forces, is standing in red cape and plumed hat. And Giovanni, a decade younger than Margaret, this Marchese Giovanni Ossoli, is sitting worriedly. He has short dark hair, a moustache, a worried brow. He is worried about being disinherited while he is creating a new heir. He is Margaret's lover.

Resist handsome images. Resist creating heroes. Resist doing their TV makeup, hand tinting their photographs, blackening their hair, whitening their reputations. This is no task for women. Let men seat themselves at the mirrors of their dressing tables. Let them switch on the thousand watts around the mirror to see Before and create After.

Mother Margaret, you have helped Beatrix. On Bea's refrigerator, next to the wheat germ recipe are MF's words that women will attain "REAL HEALTH AND VIGOR, WHICH NEED NO AID FROM ROUGE OR CANDLELIGHT TO BRAVE THE LIGHT OF THE WORLD." (Wade, p. 70.) Natural women will appear among unnatural men.

But who is Mother Margaret? She is truth to women. She is lies to men. What has she said to Beatrix? "I believe that at present women are the best helpers of one another." (Miller, p. 186.) And she knows sadly that: "Now there is no woman, only an overgrown child." (Miller, p. 188.)

And Bea meets the overgrown child, Childe Margaret, when she reads her love letters. We must learn how to read the love letters that women write. We must learn that they are lies.

Mother Margaret: "I like to be quite still and have you the actor and the voice. . . . You have life enough for both . . . I wish . . . to see you now and borrow courage from your eyes." (*Love Letters*, XVII.)

"Mother, I'm giving birth to a baby girl."
"Ah, soon she will have the gift of life."
"Oh no. He will have life enough for both of them."
"Soon she will have speech."
"Oh no. He will speak for the both of them."
"Soon she will be independent."
"Oh no. She wants to borrow."

"Borrow what?"
"Borrow courage."

ACH! thinks Beatrix. What is happening to Margaret's vision?

"Mother, I'm pregnant with a baby girl and she is sighted."
"What can she see?"
"The boy playing in the corner vacant lot, the grocer boy, the newspaper boy, the delivery boy, the class president—a boy, the head of the debating team—a boy, the head of the speaker's bureau—a boy . . ."
"Then she's a blind girl."

Beatrix is holding a man in her arms. He is weeping. He has given a sermon and the audience was inattentive. He spoke to his class and they shuffled their feet. He called to a passing bus and the driver drove on. Bea is stroking his head. His teeth are uneven, perhaps there is more than one set of them in his mouth. She asks him to open his mouth. The teeth are crooked and brown. There is only one set. They are, although tall, crooked and brown, his baby teeth. She feels motherly toward her love.

So does Mother Margaret: "I thought of you with that foolish tenderness women must have towards men that really confide in them. It makes us feel like mothers." (*Love Letters*, XIX.)

"Mother, I'm giving birth to a baby girl."
"What does she want to do with her life?"
"Be a mother."
"And then what?"
"A grandmother."
"No more?"
"A great-grandmother."

"And what else?"
"Nothing else."

How many cradles did Beatrix rock? Lena's, of course. But larger ones.

"I can't sleep!" cried the Pimpled Poet.

They were in a motel. She put a quarter into the vibrator and rocked the Pimpled Poet.

"My poems were rejected!" he sobbed.

The more he cried, the tighter she held him. He drank all of her liquids. Her lips became parched, her nipples sore, her womb juiceless. Still he drank, the drunkard.

Mother Margaret has a request: "Your heart, your precious heart (I am determined to be absolutely frank), that I did long for." (*Love Letters*, XIX.)

"Mother, I'm pregnant with a baby girl."
"What does she long for?"
"His heart."
"What will she do with it?"
"She will tear it apart and swallow it in slippery chunks the size of oysters."

Beatrix is walking by streetlight. There is a long shadow ahead of her. She was walking on the head of the shadow. Once it walked beside her but she had hurt it, and now she carefully paces behind. Why doesn't she hop on a bus and go home? The buses have stopped running. Why doesn't she call a cab? She never carries extra cash. The boy must carry the money. The girl must be spent on. How long does she walk? About two hours. Ah, then they are walking in the direction of her home? No, away from it. What will she do? She will walk until she collapses. What will the shadow do? Shadows never tire. They only shorten and lengthen.

94

Perhaps Mr. Nathan cannot take such passionate letters. She writes but her elbow is at his windpipe.

"Touch," says her cleavage. "Touch," say the parted lips. "Touch," say her restless hands in her lap.

Mr. Nathan touches.

"Don't touch!" says Mother Margaret.

She is mortified. Mr. Nathan, né Gotendorf, thinks she is "a dame."

"Mother, I'm pregnant with a baby girl."
"Whom does she love?"
"A Jew."
"Tell it to change its name."

Beatrix has loved Jews and non-Jews, capped and decapped. They both cause pain and discomfort.

Mother Margaret: "My Beloved Friend . . . Saturday, 19th April, 1845 . . . Pain is very keen with me. I cannot help fearing it. . . . Yet . . . I submit and say: when and how much Thou wilt." (*Love Letters*, XX.)

"Mother, I'm pregnant with a baby girl."
"What is she feeling?"
"Pain."
"That's good preparation."

Once Beatrix loved a musician. He entreated her to attend all of his performances. He questioned her about them afterward. He begged her to attend while he practiced. He asked her preferences as to his techniques, the passage played this way or another. He asked her to listen to the performances of rival musicians and to compare them to his. It took up all of her time. Beatrix was very flattered.

Mother Margaret: "I keep your guitar by this window; if only I could play upon it." (*Love Letters*, XXI.)

"Mother, I'm pregnant with a baby girl."
"What does she want to play?"
"She wants to play upon his guitar."
"As he will play upon her organ."

Once Beatrix loved a psychiatrist. He took his temperature every day: "Now I am feeling a trifle sad. Now I am feeling rather glad. I am elated. I have slipped to plateau. I am at rejection." It took all of Bea's time. She was very flattered.

"Mama, I'm giving birth to a baby girl."
"Is she happy?"
"As happy as he."
"Then she feels nothing."

Once Beatrix loved a doctor. He told her all about herself: when her eyes were dilated and menstruation was coming, when her cheeks were flushed and a cold was coming, when her breath quickened and she was coming. He talked constantly. It took up all of Bea's time. She was very flattered.

"Mother, I'm giving birth to a baby girl, and I've chosen the obstetrician."
"Who is he?"
"Mother, the obstetrician has told me of a good pediatrician."
"What's his name?"
"The pediatrician has chosen a good gynecologist for my vaginal infection."
"I'm glad to hear of him."
"For my postpartum blues they've picked a good psychiatrist."
"His name?"
"In case anything goes wrong, they've chosen a mortician."
"Whose firm?"

"The Kaufman Brothers. And the rabbi came to see me, and the president of the synagogue."

"Who are those men?"

"They are all insurance salesmen."

Once Beatrix entered a literary contest. It was while she was nursing Lena and doing graduate work. She needed the money. She had many uses for it: a fan for her airless bedroom, dishes to replace her cracked ones, driving lessons, baby-sitting money. Her story was very good. Her friend, the Pimpled Poet, was also entering the contest. He had many uses for the money: skin treatment, insurance for his car, a necessary trip to inspire more poetry. Which would he choose? Beatrix asked him. He looked at her. "Skin treatment?" he questioned. He had chosen correctly. Beatrix did not enter the writing contest. They both lost.

One day Beatrix was weary. She had to rest her head on someone's shoulder. She had no telephone then because she was afraid of telephone curses. She went to a phone booth outside of a supermarket. All the shoppers parking saw her. All the shoppers pushing their carts through the doors saw her. She phoned the Pimpled Poet, the Shadow, the Musician, the Doctor, the Psychiatrist, the Preacher and told them she was weary and had to rest her head on someone's shoulder. They were all otherwise occupied that evening.

Mother Margaret: "My head is heavy, let me lean it on your shoulder, and you divine these deep things." (*Love Letters*, XXII.)

"Mama, I'm pregnant with a baby girl and she's leaning on her lover's shoulder."

"Why?"

"Because only he can divine deep things."

"Then either she is shallow or he's a carp."

Mother Margaret: "Said Beethoven . . . 'there is the god-like in man!' There is also the angel-like in woman." (*Love Letters*, XXIV.)

"Mama, I'm pregnant with a baby angel."
"Good. That puts her one down from God."

Mother Margaret: "I wish much I were strong, that I might be a fit companion for you." (*Love Letters*, XXVI.)

"Mother, I'm pregnant with a baby girl."
"What does she want to be?"
"A companion."

Beatrix was audience to her musician friend, but she never applauded loudly enough. She was nurse to her doctor friend, but she did not seem to sense his needs. She was patient with her psychiatrist friend, but he had more adoring patients. She listened to readings by her poet friend, but someone else taped him. She was congregation to her minister friend, but he, by his calling, belonged to the world. She trailed her shadowy friend, but in total darkness he disappeared. She reflected each one.

Mother Margaret: "I open my thoughts to the loved soul who has brought me so much sunlight . . . I know you ask nothing of your moon except a pure reflection in a serene sky." (*Love Letters*, XXVII.)

"Mother, I'm giving birth to a baby girl."
"What does she want to be?"
"A moon, a reflecting moon."
"Not a sun?"
"No, that's for a baby son."

"Beatrix, you have a baby daughter."
Beatrix stuck out a black tongue and mourned. She had had

a daughter by twilight. Her doctor wanted no trouble from her.

At his desk, Beatrix had explained:

"I want to help out in this birth."

"Certainly."

"I don't want to be overmedicated. I want to be aware of what's happening. I want to participate."

"Certainly, certainly, certainly."

He, therefore, prescribed twilight so that she would be overmedicated, not aware of what was happening, not help out or participate. It was, after all, his delivery.

"But I asked for other medication!" cried Beatrix.

"Did you?" Surprised. "I thought you were someone else."

Put their feet in the stirrups, all the riders look alike.

In the bed with Beatrix lay another, a profane, screaming, nightmarish woman, a dybbuk who entered Beatrix, scratched her face, bit through her tongue until it blackened with dried blood.

Lena was born in twilight, her hair wet and matted, her head misshapen from the long hours of travail.

When Lena was born in twilight, Beatrix put away the following:

1. *Boxing gloves.* No blue rubber boxing gloves tied to carriage. Pink rattle tied to carriage. No fighting, no punching, rather taming. Soft leather fitted gloves later on, garden gloves in middle age. No feel of gymnasium. No ropes. No coming fighting from a corner. The idea is to corner.

2. *Balls.* No football, soccer, volley. Later, men will accuse Lena of trying to steal their balls, of shifting their goals, foul play, netting them—when all they wanted was to put balls over the goalposts, over the nets, into the basket, into the bleachers. All they wanted was her to cheer for their tennis in summer, football in fall, ice hockey in winter, baseball in spring.

3. *Trains, schooners, buses.* Lena would not be a railroad woman. She will not aspire to Lionel trains, to skipper a

schooner, unleash a Greyhound. By land, sea, or air, she will have to be taken there.

4. *Microphone.* Lena will never announce, denounce, pronounce, renounce. She will not announce news, denounce dictators, issue pronouncements, renounce a throne to marry a commoner.

5. *Plumber's snake, tool chest, handsaw, tire wrench, jack.* Lena can use the plunger, even the screwdriver sparingly. She can use the small silver soldering iron to make cuff links for her love. When she gets a flat tire, she can smile at passing cars on the interstate highway until one stops and a brawny, handsome stranger emerges, walking slowly toward Lena to fix her flat.

6. *Superman pajamas.* No quick changing for Lena, rather careful training to match cosmetics with garments, phosphorescence for evening, delicacy for morn. No bursts of energy, no walking through walls. Lena's greatest fear was to be stuck against a wall as wallflower. No bullet-proof chest. Lena's chest hurt constantly from one reproof or another.

7. *Maps.* Why should she find her way? Let her stay close to home.

When Beatrix bore Lena in twilight, Beatrix's parents came at visiting hours. Harold had gone and was not heard from. Husband? asked the registrar. Beatrix had hesitated. The nurses tittered. Girls know you can't give birth without a husband. Lena later found that out and went looking to complete the form.

When Lena was borne in twilight, Beatrix's parents bought Beatrix the housecoat and perfume from the Gift Shoppe downstairs. They bought the layette and sent her flowers with Best Wishes.

When Beatrix, herself, was borne at twilight, her mother cried that she was no male heir, that the heir, born July 5 in the Obstetrician's Book, had gone to the Undertakers. Beatrix was the replacement. She would undertake to replace the male heir.

Beatrix's grandfather mourned his wife, Lena Gurnev.

"Name her Lena," he told Beatrix's mother and father. "Let her replace her grandmother."

But Beatrix's father also had a replacement, his late father Benjamin. Beatrix replaced a grandfather and a dead baby brother. Beatrix became a replacement for the males in her family.

When Beatrix's baby was born in twilight, Beatrix's mother had put Harold's clothes and books into the garage to mold.

"Don't name her after a man," said Beatrix's mother.

Beatrix's baby became her own great-grandmother, aged at birth, gestures feeble, her cry tinny, a dribbler, needing nursing and old wives' tales. When Lena was older, her skin smooth, head shapen, hair flowing and not matted, a shapely woman, then she became a baby.

"Mother, I'm pregnant with a baby girl."
"Of what religion?"
"Bahai."
"What?"
"Mormon."
"What?"
"Protestant."
"What?"
"Buddhist."
"What?"
"Muslim."
"What?"
"Parsi or Hindu."
"What?"
"Catholic."
"What?"
"Jewish."
"At last!"

Among the things that Beatrix gave away when Lena was born at twilight was the circumcision board. She was to be held in no Elijah's Chair by no godfather. She would not be fed whiskey and the tip of her uncovered. She would not have to sob as she was admitted to the race. No one would sign her Circumcision Book as witness. When Lena was born her genitals went unsnipped, unadmitted, unwitnessed. No one cheered her and she sucked no cloth dipped in schnapps to pacify her.

Mother Margaret is not feeling well. She writes to Mr. Nathan dolefully: "I have been very ill; last night the pain in my neck became so violent, that I could not lie still. . . . I went crying into town this morning, and nerves all ajar and the pain worse . . . it was a sort of *tic douloureux.*" (*Love Letters,* XXVII.) Why couldn't Mr. Nathan still that *tic?* Warm it, hold it, silence it?

"Mother, I'm pregnant with a baby girl."
"How does she feel?"
"She has a migraine."
"So will she always."

Later Mother Margaret will chronicle the Roman revolution, though that chronicle be washed ashore at Fire Island as Mother Margaret is washed ashore, along with her marchese and her still warm sonny. Mother Margaret's most important book, from primary sources, is never found, although friend Thoreau searched the beaches. He only found the still-warm body of the son.

There is a stone at Fire Island commemorating Mother Margaret. There is a stone in Beatrix's heart. She is an orphan.

Never mind the other letters. Do not learn your alphabet, women. Do not pen your letters.

MF: "Monday evening, 19th May. . . . You have so much more energy and spirit for the fight! I must try not to throw down the poor little silk glove again in defiance of the steel gauntlet." (*Love Letters,* XXX.)

"Mother, I'm pregnant with a baby girl."
"Is she ready for the fight?"
"She accepts no challenges."

From Mother Margaret, Beatrix learns to accept challenge. Never mind that Mother Margaret writes, Friday evening, May 23, about her letters: "Perhaps you had better destroy them . . . as they are so intimately personal." (*Love Letters*, XXXII.)

"Mother, I'm pregnant with a baby girl."
"How does she occupy herself?"
"Writing intimate love letters."
"He will never destroy them but will ask her to buy them back."

Which is why one must not "know intimately a member of the Jewish race."

Or a Pimpled Poet. Beatrix wrote long letters to the poet. He wrote couplets and quatrains in reply. Later she found her letters incorporated into poems and stories. One of his stories bore her name as a character and described her lovemaking habits. She did not object. She was flattered.

Above Bea's typewriter, against the built-in bookcase, Bea has tacked, from her Mother Margaret: "LET ME USE, THEN, THE SLOW PEN." Mother Margaret, too, is a slow writer. Bea knows that it is all right to take care and pains with a book. It's her inheritance.

Looking for Mothers (3): Mother Louisa

"Mother, my baby girl's father is a writer."
"Then she must be a book so he will read her."
"My baby girl's father is a dreamer."
"Then he has stolen away with her dreams."

"My baby girl's father is a wanderer."
"Then she will stay close to home."
"My baby girl's father is a spendthrift."
"That's all right. She will pay the bills."

What has Beatrix to learn from Mother Louisa? She studies a title page. Nineteen books by Louisa. And Beatrix is struggling with her third.

Beatrix is critical, as one must be with one's mother. The title page is deceptive, full of gaiety and romance. That is the fiction of Louisa's life. There is little gaiety to writing nineteen novels, to writing one's self to death. Mother Louisa's books are bouquets, *Under the Lilacs, Flower Fables, Garlands for Girls, Rose in Bloom*, yet no one threw, bought, or brought flowers to her. She does not escape to the circus, as in *Under the Lilacs*. Mother Louisa's escape, at the age of thirty, occurs when she joins the circus of the Civil War as a hospital nurse. She then escapes from the hospital and returns home with typhoid pneumonia. She has been gone six weeks.

"Mother, I'm pregnant with a baby girl and she's going into the world."
"I'll give her six weeks. That'll show her the world."

They all make an escape, one way or other, in their thirties, all those Big Mothers. Mother Emily, out of her back door, inside of an envelope inside of another envelope. Mother Margaret abroad. Mother Louisa to Washington, D.C., Mother Charlotte to Sea Island in her late twenties, to marriage at forty.

"Mother, I'm pregnant with a baby girl and she wants to make her mark in the world."
"Tell her to be thirty and a spinstress."

104

When did Louisa start becoming happy? At twelve, for at twelve Louisa writes in the diary that she kept in Concord: "Life is pleasanter than it used to be, and I don't care about dying anymore. . . . I had a pleasant time with my mind, for it was happy." (Ednah D. Cheney, ed., *Louisa May Alcott: Her Life, Letters, and Journals*, The Abbotsford Publishing Company, 1966, p. 40.)

"Mother, I'm pregnant with a baby girl and she's happy."
"How do you know?"
"She doesn't think about dying anymore."

Also at twelve, Lena went to an Abraham Lincoln costume and birthday party. Lena went as Ann Rutledge. She had uncovered her mother's white wedding dress. She found a white plastic flower. The children said Lena lay on the floor through the whole party, not speaking, eyes closed, holding that stiff flower.

Like Mothers Emily and Margaret, Louisa May is not beautiful. It helps Beatrix to look into her full-length bathroom mirror. Mother Louisa is six feet tall and ungainly.

"Mother, I'm pregnant with a baby girl and she's six feet tall."
"Then let her grow four feet of chestnut hair."

Which Louisa did and which she later lost to fever—all four feet of it.

Despite all of those books for little women and old-fashioned girls, despite garlands for the girls and *Lulu's Library*, did Louisa May like girls? No. Girls could not run races, jump from roofs, or be six feet tall.
Mother Louisa: "I have a fellow feeling for lads and always

owed Fate a grudge because I wasn't a lord of creation instead of a lady." (Louisa May Alcott, *Hospital Sketches*, Sagamore Press, 1957, p. 15.)

"Mother, I'm pregnant with a baby girl and she has a fellow feeling for the lads."
"She can't. She's not a fellow."

Did Lena want to be a laddie instead of a lady? Beatrix could not know. She had, by bearing Lena in twilight, eliminated names. Lena could not be (unless appended to):
Aaronson, Adamson, or Airman
Bronson or Berman
Clarkson
Donaldson
Edelson or Earlman
Fegelson or Fineman
Gerson or Gittleman or Goodman
Harbison or Haldeman
Isaacson
Jacobson or Gherman
Lewisohn or Lehman
Morrison or Masserman
Nathanson or Nieman
Olson or Operman
Peterson or Packman
Robertson or Rackman
Swainson or Sachman
Tilson or Tallman
Ullman
Williamson or Wineman
Youngman or Ziegman
Lena became Lena Gurnev Palmer-Steiner.

To what does Mother Louisa owe her success? To whom, answers Earl Schenck Miers: "To know Louisa May Alcott . . .

one must know also the father whose compassionate, indestructible nature was the warm kiss shining in her eyes." (*Hospital Sketches*, p. 12.)

Forget you, Earl Schenck Miers. That is a greater fiction than the nineteen titles on the title page. Men become characters because women have built their character.

Who made Bronson Alcott? Who were his mothers?

Little Fat Elizabeth Peabody was his mother, applauding his teaching techniques in his Temple School. His head was the temple, his brains the fount. Earnest Miss Peabody published transcripts of his techniques in "Record of a School." Bronson also notated his admirable practices in "Observations on the Principles and Methods of Infant Instruction." Except that he had not provided for his family during that time, or paid the bills. The constables closed the school, took away the bust of Plato.

Little Louisa stamped her foot at them, "Go away, bad man, you are making my father unhappy." (*Hospital Sketches*, p. 13.)

An employer insulted Beatrix's father about his age.

Little Beatrix stamped her foot. "Go away, bad man, you are making my father unhappy."

A woman insulted Beatrix's father on his size.

Little Beatrix stamped her foot. "Go away, bad woman, you are making my father unhappy."

A neighbor insulted Beatrix's father on his income.

Little Beatrix stamped her foot. "Go away, bad man, you are making my father unhappy."

A close friend insulted Beatrix's father on his daughter.

Both Beatrix and her father remained silent.

In the beginning, created Bronson Alcott Fruitlands, and moved his family to that spare commune.

Little Louisa writes in her journal, at ten: "More people coming to live with us. I wish we could be together and no one else. I don't see who is to clothe and feed us all, when we are so poor now. I was very dismal." (Marjorie Worthington, *Miss Alcott of Concord*, Doubleday, 1958, p. 13.)

Fruitlands decays, and the creator, Bronson Alcott, takes to bed with nervous breakdown.

Marmee Alcott nurses him to health.

Marmee Alcott stamps her foot at disaster and says: "Go away, bad event. You are making my husband unhappy."

Then it came to pass that Louisa May's daddy wanted to travel. He wanted to take his carpetbag to England and his good and worthy friend, Ralph Waldo Emerson, paid for the voyage. His good and worthy family, however, was left to its own devices.

When the bills became too great, Marmee went to work in Boston. When Marmee's health broke down, Louisa wrote. She wrote until she wrote herself to death. All the bills were paid.

"Mother, I'm pregnant with a baby girl and she wants to please her father. What should she do?"

"Tell her to be born on his birthday and to die the day after he does. That way, he'll have been taken care of."

Louisa obliged, being born on Bronson's thirty-third birthday in 1832. In 1887, Louisa was fifty-five and ailing and her father was eighty-eight and ailing. She visited him, but it was storming and she had forgotten her warm fur cloak. She died of pneumonia but not until the day after her father's death. She was laid to rest across the foot of her father's grave.

Up yours, Earl Schenck Miers of Edison, New Jersey. Miss Peabody, Mrs. Alcott, and Miss Alcott made up the character Bronson by applauding, nursing, and supporting him.

He was the guest conductor to a well rehearsed orchestra. He was the rooster who crowed long after sunrise, when the chickens had already laid the eggs.

Looking for Mothers (4): What Did Fathers Do for Their Daughters?

What did Timothy Fuller do for his daughter Margaret? He let her help with her sick mother. He let her educate her four younger brothers and her sister. He allowed her to work five to eight hours a day helping him write a history of America. For his daughter he died, allowing her to become head of the household. He allowed her to support her sick mother and four younger brothers and her sister.

What did Bronson Alcott do for his daughter Louisa? He was an eccentric who made her concentric.

Mother Louisa: "I wish we could be just a *real* family, like everyone else." (Worthington, p. 15.)

Bronson let his daughter Louisa forgive him over and over. If someone errs, someone else forebears.

One winter day Bronson Alcott was given ten dollars in cash to purchase a warm shawl for his wife, who sorely needed one. He walked into town with the money tucked into his pocket. He passed a bookstore and forgot about the shawl. When he proudly returned with his books, the family was indignant. How contrite was Bronson! How ashamed! He was immediately forgiven.

Bronson Alcott went off to seek his fortune—westward or through New England. Sometimes he wore a white, pocketless tunic so that he would not be tempted to carry worldly goods. Louisa worked, earning two dollars a week doing washing. Marmee worked, sisters worked. Four months later Bronson returns, one dollar earned. How contrite was Bronson! How ashamed! He was immediately forgiven.

Louisa May defined a philosopher as "A man up in a balloon who required at least three women to hold the ropes that would keep him on the ground." (Worthington, p. 56.)

From Bronson, daughter Louisa also learns total despair. Here is Bronson Alcott's suicide note in his *Journals*, after the failure of Fruitlands: "Shall I say . . . that I was not made by this world, not for it—wherefore am I placed on it if I was found unfit? And the world . . . bruised him with an iron hammer, as the bricklayer breaks an old brick to fill up a crevice." (Worthington, p. 39.)

Bronson took to bed to starve himself to death. Marmee daily left him a cup of tea. He daily refused. One day, the cup was emptied. He reached out for Marmee's hand.

How old was Mother Louisa when she looked into the river and thought of drowning herself? She stared down at the mill dam, at the running water below. Louisa was twenty-six. Her hair was thick and brown, her breasts full. No one loosened her hair. No one cupped his hands over her breasts. But, for practical Louisa, death is the final unemployment.

"There is work for me," she says and scurries away. (Worthington, p. 97.)

What artifacts did Miss Beatrix leave, typed on an electric typewriter? What last message to parents, Lena, to faraway Harold?

She was using a borrowed electric portable and was unfamiliar with electric machines. Her final note was unreadable. Words were broken in the middle or scurried to catch onto other words. The machine quadruple spaced the lines or typed lines one atop the other.

After the pills, Bea's head dropped onto the keyboard. Her hands pressed the whole alphabet. The borrowed machine buzzed. The keys pressed into Bea's face. She awoke, downed coffee, tea, and stimulants all night.

"There is work for me," said Bea.

She had to be home in case a letter arrived from Lena. Perhaps Lena, like Louisa, had gone to nurse in a hospital and had contracted a dangerous disease. Bea did not know with what Lena could have been in contact or contracted, for Lena had not contacted Bea for six weeks, six months, eighteen months.

Bea had to remain at home in case her father contacted her by phone. She now had a phone to curse or to hear curses.

110

"What shall we do to save Lena?" he would cry.

Bea would make a fiction. It was good writing practice.

"Lena is learning about life," she comforted. "Lena will soon come home."

"And Harold, too?" her father would ask hopefully.

Bea would hang up. To comfort someone else is to discomfort one's self.

Which is what Beatrix was not willing to do. She was not willing to learn: to spend money carefully; to drive; to fix whatever was falling, slipping, leaking, creaking, drooping, dripping, or sparking; to control Lena; to play cards; to read maps or find her way.

Since Lena cannot find her way either, no wonder Beatrix and Lena have found different ways.

Mother Louisa *was* willing to discomfort herself. She was willing to shovel snow, carry water, blacken a clergyman's boots, split kindling, make fires (all for four dollars for seven weeks' employment with that dastardly, shiny-booted clergyman), do sewing, teach children, take in washing, or write a book.

Mother Louisa: "I love luxury but freedom and independence better." (Worthington, p. 85.)

And Mother Louisa learns that though not a boy, she can go to war like a laddie, though not a son, she can "come out right and prove that though an *Alcott* I *can* support myself." (Worthington, p. 83.)

Eventually, Louisa makes a good financial investment, *Little Women*. Women are of some use, after all, especially if they are "little."

Louisa has done research for *Little Women*, internal and external. In research, Louisa has had a two-week romance in Paris with a Pole twelve years her junior. In research, Mother Margaret has had a romance in Rome with an Italian a decade her junior. What should Bea learn? To research.

Bea had a young friend. She led him by the hand. Sometimes he would pull back, but Bea would say, "It won't hurt." She softened love for her young friend. He was the virgin and she the de-virginizer. He was of smooth skin; the flesh of her upper arms was already loosening from the bone. He was blond and seldom shaved. Her legs prickled when the hair grew back.

With each young man, Bea aged. Her hair stiffened. The accordion navel, when squeezed, became a toothless mouth, gums, a devouring stomach. It frightened her lovers who thought they might never extricate from that hag of her mouth. Her face loosened its grip like the stomach.

Bea went for advice to a WW, a Wise Woman, Anne Marie.

"Anne Marie," said Bea, "Is it true what Mother Louisa has written in her column 'Happy Women'?"

"What is it she has written?" asked Anne Marie.

"She wrote that for 'All the busy, useful, independent spinsters I know . . . liberty is a better husband than love to many of us.' " (Worthington, p. 191.)

Anne Marie listened. Her face was wizened. She has had a busy, useful, independent spinsterhood. She opens her mouth to speak. It is a navel mouth.

"Men are the spice of life," said Anne Marie, "so handsome to look upon, thrilling to hear, decorative in the home with their shaving and pomading."

Anne Marie's eyes turned tawny in memory.

"But," she asked, "can we afford to keep them, afford not to work so they can be industrious, afford to let our muscles sag so that they can be strong, afford to age so they can stay young, afford to let them go outdoors while we peer out through curtains and blink in unfamiliar sunlight?"

MUSICAL HISTORICAL

While Beatrix is researching for *Unafraid Women*, she discovers that a Mrs. Gildersleeve, in 1863, asks Louisa May Alcott for a literary contribution. Mrs. Gildersleeve is writing an anthology called *Heroic Women*.

Bea startles! A hundred years ago? And she, Beatrix Palmer, is struggling with such an anthology yet. She must do

112

something different. Perhaps her heroic women, her unafraid females will sing instead of talk. She'll write, Life Is a Musical, a Musical Historical.

Mother Margaret will stride on stage, singing in a rich voice of Transcendentalism or of the Roman revolution.

Little Ms. Emily will sing a throaty bluesy to Higgy. From her letters Bea will excerpt:

> The sailor cannot see the north,
> but knows the needle can.
> The hand you stretch me in the dark
> I put mine in.

And she will add the refrain:

> Will you be my preceptor, Mr. Higginson?
> Your friend, E. Dickinson.

Miss Quadroon Forten will be a natural—a Motown song, Black blues infinitely better than white blues. Miss Forten will quote from a letter of her grandfather's. Perhaps she'll have an operatic voice, like Shirley Verrett's:

> Did the God who made the white man and the black
> Cast away His work and turn His back?

Beatrix, who cannot carry a tune, sings everything to "Three Blind Mice."

She has an inspiration for the book: *Singing Mothers.*

Beatrix stops. She turns off the tape. She puts down her pen.

Beatrix once belonged to the PTA of Lena's elementary school. The mothers sang at each meeting, dressed in navy and white, and billed themselves in the PTA announcement as: "The Mother Singers." When the school turned Black, they were mother others and stopped using that title.

It is all wrong. Beatrix has wasted another year of her life. Her women must speak, must not choose to please with each note. Mother Mary Ann Evans did not sing. Mother Rosa

listened to music but she did not warble a tune. Let Lotte
Lenya sing in her whiskey voice for all of them.

Rest, mothers.

HAVE CHILD / WILL WRITE CHILDREN'S BOOK

Bea has another idea. She will send to Little Golden, to Red
or Green Fairy, to *Jack and Jill* or Simon and Schuster the
stories she wrote for Lena. In each story, Little Lena does
something remarkable.

"Do you like them, Lena?" asked Beatrix.

"I hate them," says Little Lena.

"Why?"

"You took my name from me."

Each publishing house kept them not two weeks.

"These are private family stories," wrote the children's
editors.

It is no comfort, no provisions in the cupboard, to have
unpublished children's books, cookbook, musical historical. But,
on some things, you can't count.

Once Bea's mother told Bea's father, "There will always be
anti-Semitism."

"Yes," said Bea's father, "but don't count on it."

On misfortune, also, one cannot count. When one has
adjusted to self-pity, a certain squint of the eye, a discouraged
limp, then fortune befalls one. It may seem as abrupt as acorns
falling from an oak, unless one has spent years watching the
growth of the oak.

Fortune befell Beatrix Palmer, who, nevertheless, had been
preparing for it, blowing birthday candles to it, wishing on
stars to it, stamping it into her palm when white horses
paraded by.

This was *The Pioneers*, a book quickly conceived, lightly
pursued. She spent no more than a few visits with each of the
interviewees. She always came away, if not with stories, then

with goodies: crocheted flowered shawls that they had given to her for listening to them, embroidered tablecloths, sachets, decorated towels. Whatever their hands were not too arthritic to do, they gave to her. From one woman she received bottlecaps covered in purple and white thread, crocheted into a hot plate. They gave her aprons made for Senior Citizens Bazaars, cosmetic bags for curlers, sewn over gallon plastic milk bottles. Whatever they could do, they did for her. Whatever they could say, they said for her. She was being rewarded while she was working on it. For that she received royalties for several years. She could live modestly. Who needed more than five thousand a year? And she earned extra giving lectures to Senior Citizens groups, reviewing interview-type books for book pages. She became a consultant on geriatrics, even a panelist. Once on a panel of geriatricians and psychiatrists, she found herself opposite her former psychiatrist. He was effusive to her. She listened impassively to his remarks and frequently, thoughtfully contradicted them. His cigar went out.

Success is a group. Once she had royalties, she received grants. Once she had grants, she was admitted to MacDowells, Wurlitzers, and other writers' colonies.

Her life changed. Her parents' phone calls were respectful. Her father asked literary advice on letters to his friends. Her mother whispered at the beginning of each phone conversation, "Am I disturbing you?"

Bea begins to lose fears. She can change a typewriter ribbon without rushing her portable down to the typewriter store each time it types palely. She can insert new blades into her razor.

Orifices are less threatening. Until now, Bea was afraid of all orifices except anal, as her former psychiatrist, fellow panelist would have informed her. Her nose would become solidified walls of mucus, dry and unbreathing. When she ripped at the mucus, the walls bled. The nasal passages were unusually genteel then, sensitive without their coating, afraid of odors. Bea would apply deodorant everywhere—to bathroom odors, cooking odors, underarm and vaginal odors. Bea's ears would become blocked with wax. She would then be hard of hearing and was afraid that people were talking about her behind closed doors, behind her closed ears. She went to her ENT man who vacuumed out the wax. Then every whisper pierced her. Her urethra stung when she urinated, until she applied medication. Her vaginal walls clung together. Harold had said he had to pry her open.

Only her anus was open, generous, a playground slide.

With fortune, Bea's heart, hand, ENT, vagina walls opened. She bestowed love, generosity, attention, and the clasp of her womb on those who needed one or all from her.

It is the final generosity to embrace one's mother.

Looking for Mothers (5): Biological

"I love you," Beatrix one day told her mother.

Her mother commenced a series of statements: "It's about time," "So it's finally paying off," "What took you so long?" but choked them back. Bea's mother, instead, burst into tears.

Bea almost ran from the room, especially when her father rushed in and accused, "Haven't you done enough to your mother?"

But her mother waved him off and he left, looking amazed at the cannibalistic scene behind him: the mother chewing Bea's hair, her ears (without their wax), nibbling her nose (no more sinus trouble), kissing the lips with Hungarian Mira's nonallergenic lipstick, her neck, with anti-crepey neck on it, her shoulders. Bea's mother did *"Miesele, Meisele,"* little mouse, little mice, to each finger, tickling up Bea's inner arm.

Bea was in her mother's oven—baked, basted, fluffed, stuffed. Bea's insides began to drip like a Thanksgiving turkey.

116

Her eyes glazed over as if newly basted. Her arms felt like well done drumsticks, separating at the joints. Bea lay on the plate at her mother's feet.

The teeth of Bea's mother: Widely spaced. Threads were broken off between them, the tongue poked pink behind the white bars. They chewed carefully. The teeth of Bea's mother were a picket fence, tombstones, outposts. It was more heartbreaking when the teeth of Bea's mother had silver fillings than when her hair turned from brown to silver.

The hands of Bea's mother: Slightly bent, slightly chapped, slightly burned, slightly cut. When Bea's mother could no longer move the wedding ring over the knuckle, Bea wept.

The eyes of Bea's mother: Nothing abrupt, gradual coloration. Not summer blue skies, not warm twinkly eyes. These were thoughtful gray, twilight or dawn. No climate changed them. If they looked upon Bea, she suddenly became Birthday Bea or Tidy Bea, starched, bathed Bea, patent-leather-shoes Bea, Bea with sausage curls. If the eyes of Bea's mother shifted away from Bea, she was Bad Girl Bea. She had stolen from S. S. Kresge's. She had shaken the dusting mop into her mother's clothes closet, rather than opening the door on the cold air of the back porch.

The mouth of Bea's mother: Kid gloves, soft underwear. It was less a moving of the lips and a speaking of words, but the brushing of the lips against her. The lips of Bea's mother were European-shy. They did not believe in kissing a child's mouth. They kissed the forehead, the top of the head, the fingers, arms, knees. They bit the *tuchas*, but it was incestuous, it was spreading germs, to kiss a child's mouth. Unless there was a drowning. The lips also did not kiss animals or kiss anyone who did kiss animals.

Bea's mother asked her granddaughter Lena, "Did you kiss the cat?"

"Yes," said Lena.

117

"Then you can't kiss me," said the lips of Bea's mother.

One day Lena said, "No. I didn't kiss the cat."

Her grandmother allowed Lena to kiss her.

"I fooled you!" cried Lena. "I did kiss the cat!"

Bea's mother turned pale and rushed to the bathroom to brush her teeth, scrub with a washcloth at her lips, her cheeks, her forehead.

The feet of Bea's mother: In slippers, heelless slippers, or lace-up shoes. They used to be in shoes with little heels and in shoes with buckles, but now the feet of Bea's mother like to be blanketed, swaddled, put into buntings, laced and attached firmly to the ankles.

The breasts of Bea's Mother: Great bulges of dough with chocolate-chip nipples, saddlebags, pouches.

"Mother, I am pregnant with a baby girl."

"Has she told you that she loves you?"

"She is ashamed to tell me."

"When she tells you, press the words between the leaves of your Unabridged, iron them between sheets of wax paper, trace them, let them be as the rubbings of stone, a rare historical marker."

Bea says farewell to her parents. She is going to an island, the island of one of her mothers—Charlotte Forten of Philadelphia. Miss Forten sailed to Sea Island, off the coast of South Carolina and Georgia, in 1862 and stayed until 1864. Bea wants to celebrate the Centennial of her mother's visit.

"Must you go?" ask the lips of Bea's mother, drop the eyes of Bea's mother, cross the laced feet of Bea's mother, fold the hands of Bea's mother, click the teeth of Bea's mother, heave the breasts of Bea's mother.

We cannot stare into the features of our mothers for too long. It makes it difficult for us to leave, and we must leave our biological, our biodegradable mothers.

118

Looking for Mothers (6): Charlotte Forten

Bea had written:

Dear Owner, Caretaker, Scion, Real Estate Agent of Sea Island:
I am researching Charlotte Forten's stay on your island. She lived there from 1862 to 1864. Could I come down and look at the butterflies, trees, flowers, and skies that she described?

Beatrix Palmer

The letter was hastily typed. The alphabet suffered from her nervous touch: H's became N's, P's were O's—all tails wagged away, L's, S's were urgently, darkly pressed. It was the letter of an erratic.

The reply began:

Dear Typist, Historian, Writer or Real Estate Buyer:
I have no information on Miss Charlotte Forten, but come right ahead, little lady.

Beatrix stiffened. How did he know she was a "little lady"? Had he peeked at the size of her bra cup? Her vaginal opening? She was normal otherwise.

If it is convenient with you, we will send our ferryman over to the Hilton to ferry you across.

Jack Ferguson (Col.)

Harold Steiner had been gone for seventeen and a half years. Lena had been gone for one year. Beatrix Palmer was afraid to inform her parents of her departure. They felt her job was to be right at home, waiting for Lena. They asked her daily, the past year, if she had heard from Lena. They were to ask another 730 times.

"The row was delightful. It was just at sunset—a grand Southern sunset; and the gorgeous clouds of crimson and gold were reflected in the waters below, which were smooth and

119

calm as a mirror." (Ray Allen Billington, ed., *The Journal of Charlotte L. Forten,* Dryden Press, 1953, p. 128.)

Charlotte Forten was correct, as she was, also, in her description of the ride to the house:

"As we drove homeward I notice that the trees are just beginning to turn; some beautiful scarlet berries were growing along the roadside; and everywhere the beautiful live oak with its moss drapery. The palmettos disappoint me much. Most of them have a very jagged appearance, and are yet stiff and ungraceful. The country is very level. . . . There are plenty of woods." (*Journal,* p. 129.)

Beatrix's ferryman was not what she had anticipated. Perhaps she expected a furtive, hunched, graybeard to row her across Styx. Perhaps she expected to forget her past as she was taken to Sea Island.

Her boatman had long, light hair, Southern-blue eyes, was tall and slender. He was silent on the ride over from the mainland and when he spoke, she had trouble understanding his South Carolina accent. As she approached the island, her past *did* recede.

"Never saw anything more beautiful than these trees. It is strange that we do not hear of them at the North. They are the first objects that attract one's attention here. They are large, noble trees with glossy green leaves. Their great beauty consists in the long bearded moss with which every branch is heavily draped. The moss is singularly beautiful, and gives a solemn almost funereal aspect to the trees." (*Journal,* p. 129.)

"Is Jack Ferguson, Colonel, here?" Beatrix Palmer asked.

"No'm, he ain't," said her ferryman.

"Is he on the island?"

"No'm, he ain't."

He lifted her luggage—her suitcase, typewriter, ream of cheap paper, carbon, paper clips, eraser, pencils, ball-points, all the costuming of the writer.

All the separate parts of her profession nestled against him. The paper did not fly from him like gulls at the dock, like the white egrets in the rookery they passed. The paper clips did not click against him, the carbon rub, the erasers erase. He carried her profession into the mansion.

"Who lives here?" she asked.

"You and me," he said.

There were sounds in the kitchen. An ornate wooden door swung open. Cooks and servants, black and white, came to greet her in silence.

"Do they live here?" she asked her ferryman.

"They don't live in Main House," he told her. "They live in Middle House."

"Do you know of Charlotte Forten?" she asked him.

He was carrying her luggage up the staircase to her bedroom.

"Is she coming, too?" he asked.

"Yes," said Beatrix Palmer.

He deposited her belongings and went on down to the hall to his own room.

She unpacked until the dinner cord was pulled. She unpacked and hung her dresses in the walk-in closet. She unpacked and folded her sweaters and underwear into the 1920 dressers with their hand-painted roses. She unpacked and spread lipsticks, matching rouges, eye shadows, musk perfume, nail clippers, photo of Lena across the dressing table.

She descends for dinner, casually dressed. Not her ferryman. He is wearing good slacks, a Mexican shirt, a soft leather jacket. His hair is freshly washed.

There are two places set for dinner at the massive oak table in the baronial dining hall. She is seated at one end, he at the other. He is seated at the head, she at the foot.

What does the head say to the feet?

"Did you have a nice day?"

"Yes, thank you."

"Did you get yourself settled?"

"Not quite."

"It takes some doing."

121

"Yes."

"Colonel Ferguson said you were a historian?"

"Sort of."

"You're doing a history of the island?"

"Part of."

"Seems funny to find a woman Yankee historian working on a Southern coastal island. I never saw one of those before."

"I've never seen a ferryman seated at the head of the table, wearing soft hair and a soft leather jacket."

He smiled. She smiled. The head and the feet would get along.

"What are you looking for down here?" he asked her.

"Ghosts," she said.

"You'll find those aplenty!" he laughed. "More ghosts than egrets, and there's an egret rookery up the road."

"What do the ghosts do?" she asked.

"Different things to different people."

After the meal he escorted Beatrix into the living room. They poured coffee into Wedgwood cups from the silver coffee urn. He made the fire, lighting pitch pine as kindling for the oak logs.

Beatrix reclined, persuaded by the soft couch.

"I have a little Scotch," he said. "Want to come to my room for it, or want me to bring down a glass?"

"Bring down the Scotch," said Lady Beatrix.

They drank. The logs crackled.

"What kind of ghosts?" Bea asked.

"The kind you deserve," he said.

As the fire died and the room cooled, they were less amicable.

He kicked ashes over the last of the sparks and placed the fire screen before the logs.

"Shall I escort you to your room?" he asked.

"No," she said. "I'll sit here a bit longer."

"I might not hear if you call," he said. "I can't always make out a Yankee voice."

He ascended, taking off his jacket as he climbed the long stairway to the upper balcony. From her position on the couch she could watch him down the corridor to his room. She had not wanted to be alone, but she did not want to be coerced into company. After all, she had just come from the mainland.

The fire died. She heard rattling at the patio door, upstairs footsteps, pots in the kitchen. She heard laughter from girls and deeper-voiced men. The laughter blew in like a radio turned up with the station drifting.

Next to her a pillow suddenly dented and the air chilled. She sat clutching the arm of the couch.

"Hallo!" she called. What was his name?

Doors opened, all of the doors of the house seemed to open to hear her. His door also opened and she saw his shadow down the stairs. The dent in the pillow next to her released and the pillow puffed again. The cold air dissolved.

"I'll take you," he said.

He gave her his arm up the stairs. He opened her bedroom door and led her into the room. He turned down her covers for her. He crawled under them, for her. She was too chilled to undress but lay next to him in her jeans and shirt.

"That won't do," he said.

His fingers were warm against the cold ash of her skin.

Politely, he gave her his arm, around her back. He gave her his leg, she on top, his legs around her. He was her fiddler crab; he was a pointed, drill shell. They moved like crustaceans all night under the quilt, until dawn. The tree shadows branched onto her typewriter, onto her desk. The chair in front of her desk began to move. They awoke.

"Thank you," he said politely and went down the hall to his room.

She saw him at breakfast and not again for the day. Beatrix took her first walk in the woods, carrying *The Journal of Charlotte L. Forten*.

"Was there ever a lovelier road than that through which part of my way to school lies? . . . It is lined with woods on both sides. On the one tall stately pines, on the other noble live oaks with their graceful moss drapery. And the road is carpeted with those brown odorous pine leaves . . . sauntering along, listening to the birds and breathing the soft delicious air. Of the last part of the walk, through sun and sand, the less said the better." (*Journal*, p. 133.)

Bea spent her days walking in the woods, on the white sandy beach, looking at the sky and the Southern coastal birds: the brown immature egrets, the white mature ones, the big blues—heron, ibis. She avoided the island grazers, the wild ponies, feral pigs, some donkeys. She listened for deer, the raindrop-soft sound of them. She did everything she never did in real life. Perhaps that is why the unreal life entered her bedroom through the walk-in closet, the rose-decorated bedsteads and dressers, the orange-tiled bathroom floor, the double windows looking out on the river. The spider-crab shell on her tall dresser wiggled its legs. The clam shell, still attached by a bit of membrane, although opened out, began to clap open and shut. An island tiger-eye shell righted its self and snail-paced its way across the glassed top.

Her collected thoughts are like her shells: red-veined slippers, Florida Ceriths, sand dollars, white and red-ribbed scallops, jingle shells, eared-arks, moon shells, pen shells. Her thoughts jingled, ribbed, rubbed. She will come, in time, in two years' time, to know these shells intimately. Now time antecedes and predicts.

Beatrix listens and hears what Mother Charlotte heard. It is November 30, 1862, and her students are shout-singing, led by Prince. They sing a mother song:

> Old mother, old mother, where hab you been
> When de gospel been flourishin . . .
>
> My mother's gone to glory, and I want to git dere too
> Till dis warfare's over . . .
>
> I wonder where my mudder gone,
> Sing oh graveyard!

124

Graveyard ought to know me
Sing Jerusalem!
Oh carry my mudder in de graveyard.
Sing etc.
Oh grass grow in de graveyard
Sing etc.
Lay my body in de graveyard
Graveyard ought to know me
Sing Jerusalem!

(*Journal*, pp. 141, 142.)

Charlotte is not a mother's daughter. She is a father's daughter, as are Mothers Margaret, Emily, Louisa May.

"Mother, I'm pregnant with a baby girl."
"You'll carry it nine months; he'll carry it the rest."
"Who?"
"Her father."

Charlotte's grandfather, James Forten, was her mother. Her uncle, Robert Purvis, was her mother. Her father, Robert Bridges Forten, was her mother.

Grandfather James Forten preceded the Abolitionist movement by a generation and shaped the views of William Lloyd Garrison. Her uncle Robert Purvis was called Father of the Underground Railroad. Her father, Robert Bridges Forten, was an antislavery lecturer, a fighter of the segregated school system of Philadelphia, and died in the Forty-Third United States Colored Regiment during the Civil War.

Charlotte was made pregnant by her grandfather, her uncle, and her father. She was the bearer of the dream. Margaret Fuller's father Timothy impregnated Mother Margaret with *his* dream of writing an historical text. Louisa May was impregnated by her handsome father Bronson, who dreamed that his books would have widespread publication.

According to Editor Ray Allen Billington, Charlotte was a "delicate young woman of sixteen" in 1854 when she left

Philadelphia for Salem, Massachusetts, and commenced her journal. She was also "a person of color." Oh, off it, Editor Billington!

And yet, they *were* all delicate young women, all of my mothers. Margaret Fuller had migraines. Louisa had terrible aches in her joints. Charlotte would begin teaching and would suffer relapses in Salem, with her white students, and on Sea Island, with her Black students. The cause was clear, the symptoms also: energy, ambition, dreams equal migraines, joint pains, bodily weakness. My mothers were not trained to run the race, and, when a few of them did, their chests ached, their legs stiffened, they panted long before the finish line.

Charlotte began her journal (they were all journalists—my daily mothers, Margaret, Louisa May, Charlotte): "A wish to record the passing events of my life, which, even if quite unimportant to others, naturally possess great interest to myself. . . . Besides this, it will doubtless enable me to judge correctly of the growth and improvement of my mind from year to year." (*Journal*, p. 33.)

It is Salem, May 1854. She is going on Sweet Sixteen.

She has been denied entrance to two ice cream saloons with her friends. She has watched, behind the curtains of her grandfather's house in Philadelphia, the capture and manacling of fugitive slaves. She has had to separate herself from others on the omnibus and train. Her friends are not admitted to concerts, though they have tickets. Her friends are turned away from museums. She is Sweet Sixteen.

They were once all Sweet Sixteen, all of my mothers. *The Mother of Bea at Sweet Sixteen*: She had taken off her Russian schoolgirl uniform. She engaged in smuggling to support her family, dressing as a Ukrainian peasant, suppressing her Russian and Yiddish. Her family smuggled itself across the border to Poland and, from there, sailed to the Promised Land. The promise was a job in a laundry. The oil goes from her skin. Her face is either flushed or dried. Her wavy, soft black hair is matted or frizzled in the heat. She falls in love with an

126

educated man. She smuggles herself into his life. She has no time to read a book. She is Sweet Sixteen.

Bea is Sweet Thirty-Eight.

When Bea was Sweet Sixteen her friends gave her a compact with a large mirror and leather case. The initial on it is F. Why F?

"We could not find B or P," said Shirley, Janice, Lois, and Pauline.

Her parents give her a Sweet Sixteen party. It is not a surprise party. She has been informed that the relatives are invited and her friends are not.

Her grandmother gives her a green leather jacket. Bea is ashamed to wear it. It is too boyish. She returns it to the department store and her grandmother cries. When Bea is thirty-eight she finds that same-style green leather jacket in the same department store. She buys it and never takes it off, but her grandmother never knew for she died soon after Bea's Sweet Sixteen.

An aunt and uncle gift Bea with *Twentieth Century American Writers*. The paper is thick. The smell is not moldy or like shelving paper or drawer-liner or notebook paper. The smell of the book is of rich wood. The photographs of the authors are unbearded or of youngish women. Bea enters the book and never leaves it. She decides at Sweet Sixteen to lie between its pages.

Charlotte Forten is Sweet Sixteen.

"I wonder that every colored person is not a misanthrope. Surely we have something to make us hate mankind. I have met girls in the schoolroom—they have been thoroughly kind and cordial to me—perhaps the next day met them on the street—they feared to recognize me . . . Oh! It is hard to go through life meeting contempt with contempt, hatred with hatred, fearing with too good reason to love and trust hardly anyone whose skin is white." (*Journal*, p. 4.)

It is May 25, 1854, when Charlotte is almost Sweet Sixteen.

"Another fugitive from bondage has been arrested, a poor

man, who for two short months had trod the soil and breathed the air of the 'Old Bay State,' was arrested like a criminal in the streets of her capital . . . all this to prevent a man, whom God has created in his own image, from regaining that freedom with which he, in common with every other human being, is involved." (*Journal*, p. 34.)

Mother Louisa is watching this scene. Mother Louisa is Sweet Twenty-Three.

Mother Margaret is not watching. She had been active in the Roman revolution of 1848. She had recorded its betrayal and defeat. She set sail to America, suffered shipwreck and death on July 19, 1850. Mother Margaret has not been watching for four years.

Mother Emily is Sweet Twenty-Four. She is afraid to watch. Perhaps she is afraid to watch because she has weak eyes; perhaps, because she has other weaknesses. Mother Emily has now pursued her studies and is safely home. She will leave her home in nine years, 1863, while Mother Charlotte is on Sea Island. She will leave her home either for her weak eyes or for her faltering courage.

Mother Emily: "I was ill since September and since April in Boston for a physician's care. He does not let me go, yet I work in my prison and make guests for myself." (*Poems and Letters*, p. 13.)

Lena is Sweet Sixteen. Beatrix Palmer bakes a cake. She ices a pink "16" on the frosting of the double-chocolate cake. Beatrix puts the cake carefully into the refrigerator to allow the frosting time to harden. Beatrix tiptoes upstairs with Birthday Breakfast—French toast, 100 percent pure maple syrup, wedges of pink grapefruit that she had cinnamoned and heated. Beatrix knocks. Her hands are occupied, but she pushes open the bedroom door of the Birthday Girl.

The room is a mess. It is usually thus. The bed sheet rises in waves. The covers are ruffled like sand at the beach. Drifts of clothing, picked up and discarded, are strewn about. The bathroom is empty. The closet has also been emptied—of clothing. Lena will not be a captive, a fugitive slave. She has made her escape to Canada through the underground railway of freaky friends. The cake hardens in the refrigerator.

Charlotte Forten's father is in town, for "the excitement in Boston is very great. The trial of the poor man takes place on Monday . . . there seems nothing too bad for these Northern tools of slavery to do." It is Saturday, May 27, 1854, in Charlotte's Journal (*Journal*, p. 35.)

Also in town is the Reverend Thomas Wentworth Higginson, who will later encounter Charlotte on Sea Island. Bronson Alcott, Louisa's daddy, is in town. They are plotting the rescue of the fugitive slave.

Charlotte, on Wednesday, May 31, walks "past the Court House, which is now lawlessly converted to a prison . . . I believe in 'resistance to tyrants' and would fight for liberty until death."

Charlotte's daddy has failed to rouse opinion. Louisa's daddy has failed to rescue the fugitive. Mary Higginson's husband has also been unsuccessful in carrying off the fugitive slave.

On Friday, June 2, Charlotte writes: "Our worst fears are realized; the decision was against . . . and he has been sent back to a bondage a thousand times worse than death . . . I can write no more. A cloud seems hanging over me, over all our persecuted race which nothing can dispel." (*Journal*, p. 37.)

Charlotte is Sweet Sixteen.

Janice is Sweet Sixteen. Her parents rent the back room of Lully's Restaurant. The invitations, table decorations, and Sweet Sixteen dress are color coordinated. The table favors are red lollipops and red carnations. The invitations are Valentine's red and white. The cake is white frosting with red maraschino cherries. Sweet Sixteen Janice has a red sequined formal with a white cloth peony between her breasts. Her breasts are smaller than the peony. Her hips are larger than the dress. The side seams have split at the waist. Beatrix is not invited. It is to be remembered that she did not conduct herself in a ladylike fashion.

Pauline is Sweet Sixteen. The girls fill her Murphy bed with presents. Her mother has gone out to buy day-old A & P Ann Page cake.

Romanian Lois is Sweet Sixteen. She is sent to the beauty parlor. Her nails are manicured. When she returns, her father gallantly kisses her hand, her shaped nails, her clipped cuticles. Lois's brother drives around picking up the girls. They are invited for dessert with the family, and they are all returned to their own homes within two hours.

Beatrix Palmer is sitting on a piece of driftwood. She has walked in the woods until she came upon this lake. Beatrix Palmer reads her Mother Charlotte's journal. Her hand is falling asleep, her elbow hurts from being crooked with the book.

Charlotte Forten is not interested in anything unless it be about slavery. She quotes the words of her grandfather: "Resolved, That we will never separate ourselves voluntarily from the slave population of this country; they are our brethren by the ties of consanguinity, suffering and wrong." (*Journal*, p. 9.)

Charlotte Forten, long before the event, is preparing herself with indignation. She will sail to Port Royal, South Carolina. She will be ferried across to St. Helena's, the first schoolteacher of runaway slaves.

Beatrix Palmer is also preparing herself with indignation. She has been studying the faded writing framed and hung in the living room of Main House.

"1812," Beatrix reads. "Four lots."

Each column adds up to about $12,200. The page adds to approximately $48,000. She reads that Old Rose, age seventy-five, is only $20; Peg, thirty-eight, is $500; but Nelly, seven, and Betty, five, are $200 and $175 respectively. She reads that Cato, fifteen, is $350; Sarah, nineteen, is $400. Under Sarah's name, Stephen, five months, is only $50. In these lots relationships are not noted or known. Is Stephen, five months, a relative of Sarah, nineteen? If separated, will they long for each other, that Stephen and Sarah? Jacob, seventeen, is $400. Betty, fifteen, is $300; Tabby, two, is $125. Are Betty, fifteen, and Tabby, two, related? Was Betty a thirteen-year-old mother? Mary, two, is $125; Grace, four, is $175; and little Bob, five, is also $175. Sambo, forty-five, is $425, Black Sambo is.

Beatrix glances around as she reads those names. Is someone watching her? The names are blurred as if someone's hand passes between her vision and the frame. She looks closely. The four lots, each containing forty names, blur, tilt in their frame. Beatrix leaves Main House.

Beatrix, sitting at the shore, is lonely. She walks back again toward Main House. She walks through the woods. Woodpeckers loosen twigs. She hears, in the palmettos, rooting feral pigs.

It is dusk. Sounds reverberate; the pigs shake the palmettos. Donkeys and ponies and wild cattle thrash through the underbrush. Birds rattle leaves. Beatrix pauses to look at a rusted water tank that has fallen over on its side. Snakes begin to glide out of the water tower. Beatrix runs along the cattle path. She trips on a root and sprawls. Her hands are muddied as is *The Journal of Charlotte L. Forten.*

Beatrix returns to Main House, through the Servants' Entrance. The kitchen workers greet her. She shows them her muddy shoes, muddy hands and knees of jeans. She shows them, also, the soiled pages of Charlotte Forten.

They wipe her hands, brush the caked mud from her jeans, give her an old kitchen knife with which to lift off the mud that is stuck into her heels. They dampen the pages of the *Journal* and blot them with a kitchen linen towel.

If Beatrix hastens, she can bathe before dinner. Beatrix carries her shoes up the stairway, not to muddy the carpeting. She hurries into her unlocked bedroom, through to her unlocked bathroom. Water is pouring into her tub. Soaking off the mud from his hands, knees, and body is her lover.

The next day, Beatrix Palmer reads of Mother Charlotte's first school day for her runaway slaves:

Nov. 5, 1862, Wednesday: "Had my first regular teaching expedition and to you and you only friend will I acknowledge that it was *not* a very pleasant one. Part of my scholars are very tiny—unusually restless." (*Journal*, p. 131.)

On Friday, November 7, Mother Charlotte wrote: "the mocking birds were singing . . . I think 'my babies' were rather more manageable to-day, but they were certainly troublesome enough." (*Journal*, p. 132.)

Charlotte's delicate body tires. Her spirit wearies. She constantly admonishes herself: "Let me not forget that I came not here for friendly sympathy or for anything else but to work." (*Journal*, p. 147.)

All of her mothers examine and reexamine their motives.

"Mother, I'm pregnant with a baby girl."
"What is she doing?"
"Reexamining herself."
"Oohh, what pleasure!"

On her Sweet Sixteenth, Mother Charlotte wrote, Thursday, August 17, 1854: "My birthday.—How much I feel to-day my own utter insignificance! It is true the years of my life are but few. But have I improved them as I should have done? No! I feel grieved and ashamed." (*Journal*, p. 47.)

Three years later, Thursday, June 15, 1857, my mother Charlotte wrote: "Have been undergoing a thorough self-examination. The result is a mingled feeling of sorrow, shame and self-contempt. . . . Not only am I without beauty and talent, without the accomplishment which nearly everyone of my age, whom I know, possess, but I am not even *intelligent* . . . entirely owning to my own want of energy, perseverance and application." (*Journal*, p. 106.)

That is Sweet Nineteen and still of little worth.

Looking for Mothers (7): Daughters and Birthdays

Louisa May writes to her father on her birthday. She is in her chilly little garret in Boston. It is November 29, 1856. Louisa May's birthday is also her father's birthday. She is his birthday present.

Mother Louisa: "Dearest Father—Your little parcel was very welcome to me as I sat alone in my room, with the snow falling . . . outside and a few tears in (for birthdays are dismal times to me); and the fine letter, the pretty gift and most of all, the loving thought so kindly taken for your old absent daughter, made the cold, dark day as warm and bright as summer to me."

(During this correspondence, Mother Charlotte is Sweet Twenty-Two.)

Mother Louisa: "I will tell you a little about my doings, stupid as they will seem after your own grand proceedings. . . . I love to see your name first among the lecturers, to hear it kindly spoken of in the papers and inquired about by good people . . . at last filling the place you are so fitted for, and which you have waited for so long and patiently." (Worthington, pp. 82–83.)

"Mother, I'm pregnant with a baby girl."

"What is she doing?"

"She is praising her father."

"How is she praising him?"

"She is longing to see him first among lecturers, kindly spoken of and inquired about."

"She is not praising him. She is writing his obituary."

"Why?"

"So she can live."

In this birthday letter, Ms. Louisa has told her father that though an Alcott, she will support herself. She also tells him, "I can't do much with my hands; so I will make a battering-ram of my head and make a way through this rough-and-tumble world." (Worthington, pp. 82–83.)

Ms. Forten also makes a battering ram of her head and goes to St. Helena's.

Mother Charlotte, October 28, 1862, Tuesday A.M.: "Our ship rode gently along over a smooth sea leaving a path of silver behind it . . . have passed Edisto and several other islands and can now see Hilton Head." (*Journal*, p. 125.)

"Mother, I'm pregnant with a baby girl."
"What's she doing?"
"She's making a battering ram of her head."
"That's better than what he's doing."
"What's he doing?"
"He's making a battering ram of his prick."

Beatrix is ashamed. It is this sensual life that leads her to exploit her own body, to exploit even her mothers. It is the trees, the clinging moss, the shush of pine needles underfoot, the soft air, those clean sheets, that boat ride in bed every night.

Beatrix is weeping. She is darkening in shadow, she is reddening by fire. In the living room she mourns Little Billy, twelve, $325; Little Lucky, twenty-two, Nanny, sixty, $250; Old Granny, seventy-five, with one leg, a bargain at $25.

What would Mother Charlotte think about Beatrix's being on Sea Island?

Mother Charlotte: "It's another white making time out of this crime."

Mother Charlotte: "It's another Jew writing history on our misery."

John Davis, thirty-four, is $500. Lolly, twenty-four, is $400. Big Tom, forty-five, is $420. Buck, forty, is $350.

Beatrix Palmer: "You cannot be your mother; you cannot be your heroine; you cannot be another's color."

Beatrix is largely alone. Not Charlotte.

Charlotte meets Harry, who learns quickly to hold a pen correctly and to write.

"I must inquire," says Charlotte of her first adult student, "if there are not more of the grown people who w'ld like to take lessons at night." (*Journal*, p. 133.)

Unlike Beatrix, who is idling, Charlotte is useful. She sews for old people on St. Helena's. She makes a warm, red jacket for an old woman. She hears an old man tell what a happy year this has been, "nobody to whip me nor dribe me and plenty to eat." (*Journal*, p. 132.)

My Mother Charlotte speaks to Old Harriet and to Bella.

Old Harriet tells Mother Charlotte: "Three of [her] children have been sold . . . [because] master's son killed somebody in a duel and was obliged to 'pay money.' "

Bella "is rather a querulous body . . . One by one her children at a tender age have been dragged from her to work in the cotton fields. . . . She has had to see her children cruelly beaten." (*Journal*, p. 143.)

Beatrix wanders in the forest, but Charlotte visited Harriet Tubman one Saturday, January 31, 1863: "She is a wonderful woman—a real heroine. Has helped off a large number of slaves, after taking her own freedom. She told us she used to hide them in the woods during the day and go around to get provisions for them. Once she had with her a man named Joe, for whom a reward of $1,500 was offered. Frequently in different places she found handbills exactly describing him, but at last they reached in safety the Suspension Bridge under the Falls and found themselves in Canada. . . . Joe had been very silent . . . moody. . . . But when she said, 'Now we are in Can[ada],' he sprang to his feet with a great shout and sang and clapped . . . in joy. How exciting it was to hear her tell the story. And to hear her sing the very scraps of jubilant hymns that he sang." (*Journal*, p. 161.)

Looking for Mothers (8): Come Home Where You Belong

"Mother, I'm p. with a b.g. and she is leaving home."
"Her father will ask her to return."
"But she is getting her schooling."
"Her father will ask her to return."
"But she has gone forth to do her life's work."
"Her father will ask her to return home where she belongs."

Beatrix receives mail. Her ferryman has been to the mainland and back. He carries her letter in his leather pouch. She is the only one on Sea Island to hear from the mainland. Her father wrote:

> The weather is not good. Your mother's health is as good as can be expected, although the weather keeps her house-bound. She slipped on the ice on the way to the supermarket and twisted her ankle. When that repaired, she fell from a chair while hanging the kitchen curtains and bruised her ribs. Have a restful vacation. . . .

Louisa May's daddy wanted her back, too. Margaret Fuller's daddy died and couldn't have her back. Emily's daddy lived until Emily was forty-four and he had his baby with him all of that time.

"His heart was pure and terrible," wrote Emily of Lover Father, "and I think no other like it exists." (*Poems and Letters*, p. v.)

Twice during Mother Charlotte Forten's schooling did Father Forten write to Salem demanding that she return home. He had sent her to Salem in order *not* to send her to the segregated schools of Philadelphia, but his baby has been gone from him too long. He wants her back. He wants her back, Wednesday, September 27, 1864. He wants her back Friday, March 16, 1865. Each time her teachers intercede for her.

There are other fathers. Thomas Wentworth Higginson is not a father, but he is so viewed by Ms. Emily and Ms. Charlotte.

136

On Tuesday, August 1, 1854, Ms. Charlotte sees Mr. Higginson for the very first time: "Mr. Garrison gave an interesting account of the rise and progress of the anti-slavery movement in Great Britain. I had not seen Mr. Higginson before. He is very fine looking, and has one of the deepest, richest voices that I have ever heard." (*Journal*, p. 46.)

She sees him again, New Year's Day, 1863 on Sea Island. "I found myself being presented to Col. Higginson, whereat I was so much overwhelmed, that I had no reply to make to the very kind and courteous speech with which he met me. I believe I mumbled something and grinned like a simpleton." (*Journal*, p. 154.)

Should Beatrix make something of this? Something of Hig's "deep, rich voice," something of his "kind and courteous speech"? Should she turn this into historical fiction? Should she turn this shy friendship into passionate romance? *The Colonel and the Mulatto.* Think of the cover illustration: she is dressed in white, although she is brown. He is bending her backward, as in the Old HiLi dance at Beatrix's Prom. A river sparkles behind them. He is dressed in his colonel's uniform. Her lips are parted; her eyes closed.

What is Charlotte thinking? "Col. H. is a perfectly delightful person in private—So genial, so witty, so kind. . . . My heart was full when I looked at him. I longed to say, 'I thank you, I thank you' . . . and yet I *c'ld not.* . . . Words always fail me when I want them most." (*Journal*, p. 156.)

Why not a little historical distortion, projection, projecting itself from paperback to Celluloid, projecting Beatrix from poverty to income?

Beatrix squirms. She is not the only night rider in her bedstead/bedsteed. Charlotte rides horseback with her colonels, long, sensual rides. She hears that she is "more than" liked by a certain soldier. "But I *know* it is not so. . . . Although he is very good and liberal he is still an *American* and w'ld of course never be so insane as to love one of the proscribed races." (*Journal*, p. 187.)

It is again dusk. Beatrix trots down the path, so does a boar after her. A kitchen woman's white dog was gored by him yesterday. Beatrix has been warned, also, to stay clear of the marshes. The house lost a large pig there last week, when, during a heavy rainstorm, the alligator of the marsh caught hold of the pig's leg and pulled it under.

"The screams haunted me for three or four days," said one of the kitchen people.

"What does the alligator do with the meat?" asked Beatrix.

"Hides it on shore till it ripens."

As Beatrix trots back and enters through the gates of the estate, over the metal grating that keeps cattle out, she sees a light on in a tabby hut—an old slave hut made of limestone and oyster shells and whitewashed. Through the window she sees her lover, wiping his hands on a paint rag, looking at a small canvas on an easel. She pauses, then decides not to interrupt.

That night she is alone at the fire. She goes alone to the patio to bring in more firewood. Her lover is not there. She has had to dine alone. She has moved from the foot of the long table to the head of the table. The women bring in her shrimp dish, made from shrimp caught off the island—then close the heavy wooden kitchen door behind them. She hears her own utensils on the table. She hears her teeth against the fork. She hears her spoon against her dessert dishes, lifting the figs that have been picked from the fig tree behind Main House. She moves to the living room.

She will not go hunting for him, not at head or foot, not studio or stairs or bed. There are footsteps again. Either it is he or it isn't. She won't hunt. She hears other sounds: pistol shots, whip cracks, moaning, sobbing, laughter. Beatrix decides that Charlotte's *Journal* is breathing out loud, that women are describing the slave owners beating the slave children, the separation from families. Beatrix does not cower before fiction or fact.

138

The fire has burned a hole through the middle of the logs. There is a wooden ring around the flame. The finger of flame is consuming the ring. The ring crashes inward. It thunders outdoors. There is laughter and weeping. There is the crash of silver and gold. Pieces of eight shoot into the flame. Lightning shoots through the living room. Beatrix looks up. On the balcony, stories above, stands her lover. He is slowly beckoning, his arm outstretched to her, his index finger crooked, his third finger tickling at her. The cushion next to Beatrix is not dented. Cold air does not appear. All is still.

"Ben!" someone screams.

Patio scrapings, horse's hooves, revelers, clattering dishes, clinking treasure.

"BEN!"

Only the shadow of the hand of Ben, over the balcony, reaching, reaching down to Beatrix. Beatrix does not scream. Or the shadow would enter her mouth. She closes all her orifices. She lets the mucus dry up inside her nasal passages, closes off scent. She lets her ears wax over. She lets her womb walls cling to each other in terror. The shadow rubs her back, chucks her chin, passes over her hair. Her hair resolutely clings to Beatrix's head. Her chin presses down to her neck. The storm is over. The night has passed in a second. It is dawn, and the kitchen workers are banging the screen door. The tree branches are scraping fingernails at the window. Beatrix goes into the kitchen, stiff-legged.

"Help me pack," she asks the women.

They ascend with her. Her clothes are strewn around her room. (It is Lena's Sweet Sixteen.) The bathtub water is flooding onto the orange-red tile floor, over the carpeting. The chair is sliding in the water to and from her desk. Only some of her notes are dry. The women put her clothes through the washing machine and dryer in the Laundry Room. Beatrix puts her damp notes into the sun to dry.

Everyone is tired of the Civil War. Higginson is ill and must go North. Emily Dickinson is writing worried letters to him. Mary Higginson is writing worried letters to him. Charlotte Forten is ill and must go up North. Beatrix is becoming ill and must go up North.

It had been so brave. They had all been brave. Louisa May had joined up and fought the war as a nurse in the Washington military hospital in 1862. She had tended the victims of the bloody battle of Fredericksburg. The women are their fathers' laddies. Louisa May was proud of her brave white soldiers. Charlotte Forten was proud of her brave Black soldiers in Col. Higginson's Black Army Regiment. But everyone is tired.

"Ghosts of my mothers!" cries Beatrix.

She is packed and ready to leave Sea Island. She pauses at the patio where the voices originated the night before.

"Ghosts of my mothers!"

They are laid to rest, those motherly ghosts. They are too tired to sew any more warm red jackets, to teach adults how to hold a pen, to tend the wounded, to sew packets of poems, to hold conversations, write observations. Their fingertips are callused—poor, toothless, hairless Louisa May; their full breasts have dried—poor Margaret; their migraines and joint pains have disappeared—poor Charlotte; their sore eyes and sore nerves are soothed—poor Emily.

Beatrix must leave them. She must go past them, to prehistorical mothers, to foremothers, to the opening of caves of herself.

"Enter me, ghosts of my mothers!" she whispers in this Southern land.

They are tired. A yellow butterfly drifts by. A black-and-white, zebra-striped butterfly loops by. Two Monarch butterflies mate. They couple with double sets of wings, on the patio stones. They hold tight, leaping together onto the glass top of the wrought-iron table. They leap again upward, the reverse of autumn leaves, attaching themselves to the oak tree. The oak has leaves of butterflies. The grass has ribbons of snakes. The palmettos have spots of hogs. The ghosts have folded themselves, like seldom used underwear, old gloves, button boxes, back into drawers.

A limping Black man appears for Beatrix's luggage. His name is Jimbo.

"Where is Ben?" asks Beatrix.

"Ain't no Ben," says Jimbo.

"The other one, the one who brought me here," says Beatrix.

"I'se the one brung you from the mainland," says Jimbo.

"The ferryman," says Beatrix.

Jimbo does not understand Yankee dialect.

"Do you often see Colonel Jack Ferguson?" she asks.

"Not often," says Jimbo.

The motorboat rocks. They are in the wake of another motorboat. Jimbo is sprayed.

"Since he's not been on this earth for these many years."

"He invited me down," says Beatrix.

Fishermen in a passing boat have caught a seagull in their net. It is a brown, immature gull.

"What you doin' with him?" calls Jimbo.

"Fish feed," says one of the fishermen.

The fisherman twists the gull's wing. The gull snaps at him with loud clacking beak. The wing is broken, hanging only from one tendon. The gull tries to fly, falls, swims, spinning in the water.

"Colonel Jack Benjamin Ferguson?" asked Jimbo.

"Yes," says Beatrix.

"He must've called you from his grave, then," cackles Jimbo. "Maybe he's mad that I didn't weed the mound this month."

"Nobody by that name comes down?"

"Nephews of the late Colonel, they come down. They got title to the island for their lifetime."

"Does one of them paint?"

"Sure they does," says Jimbo, "they paints the woods red, they paints the deer, the hogs, the birds a bright red."

Beatrix is confused.

"Sometimes they paints people red," says Jimbo. "Once there

141

was a duel on the island and two people painted each other red. One was Colonel Jack Benjamin Ferguson, a red hole through his ear."

Beatrix begins to cry hysterically. Jimbo has to pilot. He cannot pat her shoulders.

"Ma'am," he calls behind him. The words come broken through the wind. "Sometimes they comes back, all the folks of the island—Black Bart, the pirates, the parties, the duelers. The chairs are filled with them. I always sit on their laps or step on their toes. It's like dancing with the days past."

Beatrix has been waltzing with her mothers. She has been walking on the shoes of her fathers.

LOOKING FOR BEATRIX'S MOTHER

Beatrix rushed across the water, through the air, by air terminal bus, by taxi, to her mother.

"Forgive me, mother," she said, "for everything I have done to you."

"I know exactly what you did," said her mother, and listed: (1) You had your father sign your report cards; (2) When you told about your day, about your night, you looked at your father; (3) When you spoke of foreign affairs, money affairs, travel affairs you looked at your father. . . ."

The mother was still listing when Beatrix left the house.

Mother Emily Dickinson had written to Higginson, when the latter inquired after her family: "I never had a mother." The mother outlived the long-lived father.

Looking for Friends Again

"Hello, I'm phoning an old friend. This is Beatrix Palmer."
"Who is this?"
"Beatrix Palmer."
"Who do you want?"

"Lois Goldman—the doctor's wife—I knew her in school. . . ."

"The mizus not at home."

"Can I leave a message?"

"Don't seem to be no pencil around."

"Hello, I'm phoning an old friend. This is Beatrix, Beatrix Palmer."

"Who's the old friend?"

"Janice."

Long pause. "My niece? She's been out West for years. Afraid I can't help you."

"Hello, I'm phoning an old friend. This is Beatrix Palmer."

Pause. "Hello."

"Pauline?"

"Yes."

"What are you doing, Pauline?"

Pause.

"What are you doing these days, Pauline?"

"Same as in *those* days."

She does not speak again. Beatrix prattles, slows, stops. She has offended once more.

"Hello, I'm phoning an old friend. This is Beatrix Palmer."

It is an old woman who answers. "Who? Who?"

Beatrix repeats. No one is on the line. A moment later, a man's German-accented voice.

"What is it you wish, please?"

"This is Beatrix Palmer, an old friend."

"Yes. What is it you wish, please?"

"I wish to speak to Shirley."

There is whispering, a conference.

"Hold the phone a little, please."

The conference moves away from the phone.

The father is panting on his return.

"She is unable to come to the phone. She remembers you. Very well. We all remember you. Call again, please. Perhaps she will be able to come to the phone."

"Hello, I'm phoning an old friend. This is Beatrix Palmer."

"Which partner do you wish to speak to, please?"

"Norman. Labor Law."

Norman of the Eugene V. Debs co-op does not remember Beatrix Palmer at first, does not want to remember the co-op.

Suddenly Norman remembers.

"Bert is dead, you know. Frozen to death downtown on some park bench years ago."

"What happened to Charles?"

Black Charles, the drama major and elevator operator, had traveled up to the top floor.

"Head of Harlem Theater. See him, my wife and I, when we fly to New York to do theater."

"Yes," says Beatrix.

"My best to your husband," says Norman. "Did you call, Beatrix, for business? Did you need a solicitor, a counselor?" When Beatrix said she did not, he repeated best to Harold and rang off.

Best to that marriage that froze to death downtown years ago.

"Hello, I'm phoning a friend. This is Beatrix Palmer."

"Who is your friend?"

"The photographer."

"The photographeress?"

"The woman photographer of your firm."

"She's not here now. She's off taking pictures of Southern coastal trees."

"Why?"

"She's doing a book for Time-Life. She's doing a book for

Friends of the Earth. She's doing a book for *Reader's Digest*."

"But she's supposed to be doing a book with me. *Remnants*. What does she know about Southern coastal trees?"

"What does she know about remnants?"

"Hello, mother, I'm phoning to see how you are."

"Why the sudden concern?"

"Hello, Bob's Bicycle Shop, are you still in business?"

"Sure, we're still in business."

"I want to fix my bicycle."

"We don't fix. We just sell new."

"Hello, Lloyd's Furs. Are you still in business?"

"Sure we're still in business."

"I'm calling about storaging a fur."

"Not if you didn't buy it here. We only storage what we sell."

"Hello, Bates Luggage. Are you still in business?"

"We're expanded."

"I need some lightweight luggage."

"That's no problem."

"I need some low-priced, lightweight luggage."

"That's a problem."

Good-bye, Marcia S. Liebowitz, French Teacher, Jewish Math, Shorthand, Bald Chemistry, Shirley Panush, Romanian Lois, Black Janice, Pauline. Good-bye, Bob's Bicycle and Repair Shop, Lloyd's Furs, The Dairy Bar, Bates Luggage. Screw you, Sarcastic Cynthia, Fat Roz, One-Eyed Susan, Norma Honey, Razel Schiller. Good-bye Judy and Johnny, high school sweethearts.

"Mother, I'm pregnant with a baby girl and she's looking for a friend."

"Tell her when she phones, her friend will be on the West Coast, will be affronted at being found, will be hiding in the attic, will be at the beauty parlor. Tell her not to look for a friend."

Foremothers

Looking for Past Mothers, Way-Past Mothers

If there is one grant, there are two. If there are Wurlitzer and Ossabaw, then there are also MacDowell and Yaddo. If all the writing colonies are full, there is a travel grant overseas. She is to work on *Remnants*. She goes to Israel, the land of the immigrant and the pioneer.

Her father phones. "Keep an eye out for Lena on the way," he says.

Four Are the Matriarchs: The First Matriarch

"Mother, I'm pregnant with a baby girl."
"May she be the mother of heroes."

She journeyed to the South for there was a famine in the land. Avram watched the shepherds moving past. They turned to look into her dark eyes, at her black skin, her black hair. They stared at the folds of cloth around her belly and hips.

Avram shouted, "You are seeking to entice!"

She had been leading the goats, now a dwindling herd. She had put up the tent she brought to her marriage bed. She had also brought her dowry of two striped robes and her neck beads. She milked the goat. She cooked the last of the kid meat.

Avram suffered from thirst, from fear. She, like a camel, did not seem to have his hunger or his need for water.

"Tell them," he commanded, "that you're my sister, not my wife."

She was asked. The shepherds asked. The soldiers asked. Other than that she spoke seldom, laughed never—was to laugh, later, *once.*

She told the soldiers, "We are traveling into Egypt together, my brother and I. We have no water. We have cooked our last kid."

They took their pleasure with her while Avram sat outside of the tent, drinking their water, eating their provisions. Then the soldiers brought her to the Great House. They pulled aside her garments from her body. Despite famine, the flesh curved. Despite thirst, the shoulder and buttocks meat was juicy. She was given to Pharaoh, who had her while Avram sat outside of the Great House counting his newly gained sheep, oxen, asses, camels.

This time, for the first time, the King of the World plagued Egypt, plagued the shepherds with loss of sheep, the soldiers with loss of battle, the Great House with loss of riches, the Pharaoh with loss of pleasure.

Avram sat by the crossroads, counting his flock.

Pharaoh came out of the Great House: "What have you done to me here! Why did you not tell me that she is your wife? Why did you say, 'She is my sister'? and so I took her to me as wife. But now, here is your wife, take her and go." ("In the Beginning, An English Rendition of the Book of Genesis,"

Everett Fox, translated from the German of Martin Buber and Franz Rosenzweig, in *Response* 14, Summer 1973, p. 36.)

Once again she traveled with Avram up from Egypt, only the journey was in stages and slower for they were rich in cattle and precious metal.

The nomadic years passed. Maybe because of the great journey in the desert, or the early famine, or the time she was had by shepherds and soldiers, by princes and pharaoh, Sarai in no way thickened, never bore fruit. All life around her fattened—the camel, the oxen, the she-goat. Trees bore fruit—the date, the fig—but she remained bony. Her walk did not fill the striped cloth of her robe. Her neck beads and hand beads were the larger on the scrawny neck, the veined wrist.

Avram saw her stirring behind the veils in her section of the tent. Her hand would crack bowls of nuts for his callers, but the tent was silent of children.

"You are truly sister," he said to her, lifting the curtain between them, "not wife, for you have borne me no seed."

Sarai, Contentious One, frighted and gave unto Avram her she-servant, an Egyptress—much as Sarai herself had been given away in an earlier day. Sarai could not look upon Hagar, not when Hagar came behind the curtains to prepare the meals, not, afterward, when Hagar's belly stretched and smoothed over. The eye of the belly stared at Sarai, the evil eye of the belly, until Sarai beat the woman upon her face and neck. When Sarai lifted a stool to plunge into the eye of the belly, Hagar fled. Hagar returned from flight for there was no other tribe that would have her thus.

The son of Hagar became thirteen. The master of Hagar was ninety-nine, and, on a day, the foreskins of the son and the father were cut with a sharp stone. On a day, three men appeared before the tent of Avram. They were given the hospitality of the nomad—young oxen, meal cakes, cream, and milk.

The men would have none of provision until they had asked, "Where is your wife?"

Avram lifted the curtains of the women's section of his tent. His wife was grinding meal. She was grinding her gums. She smiled, a wrinkled smile, at the strangers.

They went in upon her, upon her old bones and desert-dry skin. She, courtesan again, as in those desert-bright days of the Pharaoh, laughed within herself.

The three men left. (Some claim it was one man.) The sun was too bright. Avram was ninety-nine, Sarai was ninety—and the three men in the hot sun melted into one imperious man who shouted across the desert, "This set time next year, your wife has a son."

Her name would no longer be Contentious, but Sara, Princess, the mother of tribes. She bled for a month after the visitors left. She bled on the sand, over the carpets, into her garments. When she ceased to bleed, Avram entered upon her in one terrible painful night. He came in, unwrapped his body, took in hand his old familiar rod as if it were his walking stick, and ground it into her.

She, who had little flesh left, neither teeth nor hair, bore with green seed, and it came to pass within that time of bearing, that Sara's face smoothed, her hair grew in fuller, her lips reddened.

When the child was born, Sara was satisfied. She gave suckle to the baby. She laughed behind the curtain of the women's section, and the curtain stirred with her laughter. When Yitzhak was weaned, her breasts shriveled again, her lips paled, and flesh withered. Then she noticed Hagar. Then she noticed the thirteen-year-old son of Hagar, the circumcised Yishmael—"Heard by Elohim."

Sara was, as truly she spoke, not merely the wife of Avram. She was wife and sister-daughter of his father, but of a different mother. She was doubly jealous of Hagar—an Egyptress acquired while Sara was with the Pharaoh. This stranger, neither sister nor wife, had filled her womb. The God of the World had—when Sara was with the Pharaoh—stricken every womb in Egypt. No head came through, no shoulders shouldered their way out. It was because the sister and the wife of Avram was in the bed of the Pharaoh. When Pharaoh returned Sara to her brother-husband, so the wombs of Egypt filled. But this Egyptian womb had been filled and had given birth to the favorite of Avram, to the son hearkened to by Elohim.

Hagar was merry. Yishmael was joyful. Yitzhak, the baby, stared at the blue sky, at the desert bugs upon his fist, stared at the stripes on his rug.

Sara did not speak to Hagar. She spoke unto Avram—with the voice of his long-ago sister, the daughter of his father, the daughter of his mother, the voice of his past and his present.

Sara said, "Your future is with me in my tent. With my son. Kill Hagar. Kill her child."

Avram ceased patting the dark head of Yishmael. He ceased attending to Hagar. Sara waited. She kept her son hidden from Avram until a servant came unto Hagar, unto Yishmael and said, "You have been in the desert before. Go again."

Yishmael turned to go into the tent of Avram, but a sharp spear stayed his way. With spears they were driven from the tents, from the oasis. At the edge of spears they were sent into the desert.

The desert was cruel, mountainous. There was shade only from small trees. No water, no provisions were provided them. Hagar told Yishmael to crouch in the shade of the one tree, while she wandered looking for any of her tribe, looking for water. She found a well. She filled the goatskin with water and hurried back to give Yishmael drink.

Yishmael and Hagar lived in the desert, became huntsmen and bowmen. He remained with his mother, taking unto himself a wife she brought him from Egypt, another Egyptress.

Sara remained in the city of tents. She rested upon her couch and appointed another as handmaiden.

She was the First Matriarch.

Looking for Lena

"I saw her," said a warty woman with one long dark braid, carrying her basket of leeks on the Jerusalem bus.

"Where?"

"Right here."

"When?"

"Just now."

The bus driver asked the passenger to remove her basket of vegetables from the aisle of the bus. The woman refused. The driver stopped suddenly in the middle of the road and would not drive farther. The woman pulled long leeks from her basket and whipped the driver across his head and neck with the leeks. He continued his route.

"I know her," said a *sheitl'ed* lady. "I will never forget her."

"Why?"

"She was right here, against the Kotel."

We were standing at the Western Wall.

"What did she do?"

"She banged her head against these warm stones. She wept until mucus flowed into her mouth."

"Are you sure it was she?"

"No one has ever wept like that before."

"That's the girl," said a student at Haifa University.

"How do you know?"

"Because of what she did."

"What did she do?"

"She took the bus from the foot of Mount Carmel to the very top, to the university. Then she climbed out of the bus. I followed her. She ascended the steps of the new buildings, until the highest point of the campus. She climbed the steps of an unfinished building, taller than any of the others."

"And then?"

"She shouted, 'Higher. I want to climb higher!' "

154

"Did she climb down?"

"No. When I left with the last bus down the mountain, she was still sitting on the top step of that incomplete building."

"I know her," said the florist in Tel Aviv. "She bought so many flowers from me."

"Did you ask her why?"

"She said they were to decorate a grave."

"Did you ask her whose?"

"She said the person was not yet deceased."

Bearers of the Dream (1)

"Everything is to learn about," said Naomi.

Beatrix is shivering. Tel Aviv is cooling in the evening. Naomi rises and closes the door to her porch. They had dined among Naomi's plants, listening to the Sea of the Median, and to caged birds on a neighbor's porch.

Beatrix had lectured on *The Pioneers* at Tel Aviv University. Naomi, a Senior Lecturer in Biology, took Beatrix home for Turkish coffee and for a biology lesson.

They lie on Naomi's stiff Arab rugs. Naomi was not the instigator, originator, vilifier, seductress. They had showered, taking turns. They had dressed in long towels and spread the towels under them, against the itchy rugs. They had wiped a water spot from each other's limbs, from a nipple, a lower lip. They had mopped a poorly dried forehead. Their fingers on each other were stiffer than the hidden straw in the rugs. Their fingers made knobs of nipple and clitoris. It was not tickling. It was a rubbing, a mortar-and-pestling. They each knew what to do.

Beatrix lay her head on one of Naomi's breasts and then on the other. It was a fount, a spring, like this city of their lovemaking. There was the *tel* of Naomi's bosom; there were the springs of Naomi's nipples, armpits, juices of the belly,

155

sweat from the back of the legs, sand of the oasis, salt of Naomi's sea.

Afterward they did not ask:

"Do you love me?"

"Did you have other lovers?"

"How did you lose your virginity?"

Virginity is neither valuable nor valueless between women.

"Do unto another as you would have her do unto you," and they lay back after the *mitzvah*, after following the Golden Rule.

"Tell me your story," said Beatrix to Biological Naomi.

"I am here," said Naomi, "because my father wanted to be here."

"Where is your father?"

"Not here. There."

There in the Diaspora in America, Naomi was trained to return to the Land. There, a descendant, she was taught to ascend the Judaean Hills.

"I was raised in the movement," said Naomi.

Naomi's eyes are hazel, her hair thick brown, her lips full and warm red, her cheeks high-colored. There are no men for Naomi in Israel. Men have been depleted by the wars. Yet Naomi stays.

"Why do you stay, Naomi?"

"It was my destination. There is nowhere else after one's destination."

Naomi's father is an official in the Labor-Zionist movement. Independence Day is not the fourth of July; it is Israeli Independence from British colonialist rule. Elections are watched closely, not to Congress but to Knesset. Naomi knew about gun-running when she was three years old. She knew about Israel Bonds, cash-running, shortly afterward.

When Naomi finished high school, she moved into a Labor-Zionist co-op. Her father came to speak to the group, the Bayit, the House, on their Tuesday night cafés. He spoke on Israeli-

Arab relations, on Israeli poetry, on the British and French change from neutralism to Arabism. After her father's seminars, the Bayit would serve felafels, humus, and other Israeli-Arabic dishes. The whole co-op went as a group to Israel. There they split. Some went into democratic-socialistic kibbutzim. Naomi came to the city, where she tried to start a city kibbutz, an *irbutz*, with a young Israeli. When he was killed in the War of '67, she enrolled at Tev Aviv University, became a biologist and a Lesbian Zionist.

We lie in the dark, Naomi and I. We are holding hands. She has a large ring on one finger. Her hands are big and the ring is not too obtrusive for those hands.

"Are your parents alive?"

"Oh yes."

"What are they doing?"

"My dad is dreaming."

"And your mother?"

"She sleeps without dreaming."

"Of what is your dad dreaming?"

"Of his return to the Land."

"Is he proud of you?"

"No. He disinherited me."

"Why?"

"For leaving him to come here."

Beatrix sleeps on her towel, on the striped Arab rug. The colors are not color-fast and the stripes have bled through, becoming another, paler rug on the bare floor.

Four Are the Matriarchs: The Second Matriarch

Avram called for the eldest servant of his household.

"Swear!" said Avram.

The servant put his hand on Avram's testicles and swore by them that he would help Avram to carry on his seed.

Avram did not search out a sister for Yitzhak. But, among the people of Avram, the servant found Avram's niece, first cousin to Yitzhak.

To the niece gave the elderly servant "a golden nose-ring a half-coin in weight, and two bracelets for her arms, ten goldpieces in weight." ("In the Beginning," p. 60.) He himself put the ring on her nose, slipped the bracelets up her dark arm.

"Take her and go," said her brother Lavan and her father Betuel, for they knew that within the camel bag of the old servant were gifts for them. And the servant also brought out jewels for the brother and mother of Rivka.

Yitzhak was forty years of age when he beheld Rivka. Her face was veiled but he brought her into the tent of Sara, his mother, where he unveiled her face and her body, and Rivka comforted him on the death of his mother.

Although the servant's hand had rested upon the testicles of the father-in-law that the seed of the house of Avram continue and the tents multiply, yet was Rivka "a hardened-root." ("In the Beginning," p. 66.)

Her cousin, Yitzhak, is forty, the pampered son of old parents ("thy son, thine only son, whom thou lovest, even Yitzhak"). His mother is gone and this hardened root lies within her tent, heeding not the admonition of her brother Lavan, "Our sister, be thou the mother of thousands of ten thousands."

Yitzhak prayed, not Rivka, Yitzhak who besought the Lord as his father had done in Sara's old age. Rivka conceived, but her time was not happy, no laughter as with her mother-in-law. The movement within her belly was painful. She cried out but Yitzhak heard her not. She would put her hand on her belly, hoping to warm and calm a dissatisfied limb, to hold a knee, elbow, foot, or head. All within her was knobs. The boys came out embattled, one with fine baby fuzz, kicking off the clinging hand of the second.

That which Yitzhak loved did Rivka despise. Yitzhak, once

under the knife himself, loved only danger and those who sought it. Rivka, alone in this land but for her nurse, never again to see her family from the Aramean Field, sought quiet and companionship.

Her quiet son, her favorite, carried within him cunning, while the one who roamed had within him trust. Thus did the twins exchange themselves in part.

Yitzhak was sixty, and, like his father Avram, a dissembler. When the famine came Yitzhak went to Gerar, as Avram had done before him. Yitzhak enticed the King of the Philistines with a view of Rivka, for Yitzhak was sixty and Rivka yet young. The King let Yitzhak sojourn in Gerar.

And Yitzhak said unto Rivka, "You will tell the people of the place that you are my sister."

Although aging, Yitzhak was ever fearful of being harmed. He had faced death once in a glinting knife and ever after he squinted at it. He did not now want to be killed for a fair wife.

And it came to pass that the King of the Philistines craved Rivka and went to her. He found there Yitzhak fondling Rivka's breasts, touching her thigh, kissing her body.

The King had been about to commit mortal sin, lying with the wife of a guest, thinking the wife his guest's sister.

Yitzhak fared well with "sheep-herds and oxen-herds and many working-cattle." ("In the Beginning," p. 68.) His cousin-wife, like his own mother, like his father's sister-wife, would love one son, would revenge herself upon spoiled Yitzhak. She had been taken from the Aramean Field, from her mother and father and brother Lavan; she had been scorned and called a hardened root; she had been called his sister before the king, to entice the king during a famine. She would make her son her lover. She would husband her son, train him in cunning, help him to steal the blessings, the land and the love of his father from her eldest born. She would create enmity between Yaakov and Esav. She would warn Yaakov to flee for "your brother comforts himself on your account, to kill you." ("In the

Beginning," p. 73.) She would send him, my only son, my son, to the land of Lavan my brother until "your brother's anger has turned away from you and he has forgotten what you did to him." But it was she, Rivka, who had kindled the anger, fed it, quenched it only when it threatened to destroy her child.

Rivka dissembled. As Sara had attacked the women in her household, so Rivka attacked her daughters-in-law, the wives of her eldest son, Esav.

Rivka approached the bedside of Yitzhak. She had made him broth. She spoon-fed him while he held shakily unto her feeding hand. He was not only blind and senile; he was obedient.

"I loathe my life because of the daughters of Het," said Rivka. ("In the Beginning," p. 74.)

A drop of broth spilled on Yitzhak and burned his chest.

"If Yaakov should take himself a wife from the daughters of Het, like these, from the daughter of the land, what then shall life be to me?" ("In the Beginning," p. 74.) She wiped his chin.

So it was Yitzhak who ordered Yaakov to travel forth into the land of his mother, to the household of her birth, to the incestuous bed. There, among blood-cousins, he must take a wife.

Esav, the elder, saw that his wives, the two women of Canaan, were hated by his mother and were evil unto his father. Esav saw that, like his uncle Yishmael, he was the stranger.

Yaakov, the younger, traveled from Beer-Sheva to the Aramean Field, to the tent of his uncle Lavan. Thereafter he became the husband of two sisters, both nieces of his mother. They were to be the Third and Fourth Matriarchs.

Esav, the bitter, Esav, the fool, tried once again to please. He wed no woman of Canaan, no Hittite, but a daughter of a son of Avram, his cousin. But *she* did not become a matriarch.

160

Remnants (1)

Bea is working on *Remnants*, without her photographer. She is interviewing and documenting survivors of the Holocaust. She finds them everywhere. They drive taxis, dangerously turning around from the front seat to tell her their stories. They lunch on the old train, built during the Turkish rule, offer her cucumbers, yogurt, fresh Israeli bread, and their stories. Their arms are blue-tattooed, this special breed, this stamp of people, these middle-aged, aged, bald, these men with thick, graying hair on their heads, Brillo-like hair springy on their chests, these women who push crazily on buses, charging seats, disturbing the conductor. These survivors are still elbowing their way to air on the cattle cars; they are still filling their starving stomachs.

She sees the women in the Turkish baths. They are eating cheese-filled pastry. They are lying voluptuously naked on the carpets or sunning on the roof. They are bare-armed, bare-legged, bare-thighed, bare-breasted, but they are tattooed. They are dressed in numbers.

Her German florist and his wife are tattooed. The fishman at Super Sol's is numbered. The Polish bakery lady is not only tattooed but her face is half burned off. Neighbors across the street from her rented Jerusalem apartment rest tattooed arms on the railings of their balconies and watch their children playing soccer in the street.

She sees them at all the memorial places, looking into mirrors, at Yad Vashem, the Memorial to the Holocaust, at Holocaustal museums, watching Holocaustal films. Their children come, their grandchildren, their cousins in the Diaspora.

"It can never be seen enough," they explain.

Not everyone tattooed is marked as Superior Product, Grade A Beef. Not everyone is Blue Ribbon, but they are remnants, streamers from other lands, banners of another time, these streaming ribbons of people crossing the Mediterranean. No one led them out. No one divided the sea for them. In fact, the world was unified in preventing their departure.

One red-haired fifty-year-old, the treasurer of his village, and his widowed sister tell Beatrix their tale. In their twenties, some twenty-five years ago, they sailed to Palestine on a coal boat. The British turned them back. They were fleeing the Nazis, who had already killed their parents and their younger sister. But the British turned them back. They tried for five months to land, for five months not to be returned to Poland. Black with coal dust, coughing, their eyes streaming, they finally landed.

The sister holds up a photograph of her family. She is in uniform. They are the Socialist Youth Group. There she is, under her heavy chins, her thinning hair, twenty-five years ago, soft, round face, light eyes. Her brother, wearing a worker's cap, is next to her. The youngest sister poses in Youth Group uniform, with her hair braided on top of her head, her hands braided in her lap.

"She was *lakachet*," taken, says the sister, and wipes her eyes. She fits her thumb on her sister's face and leaves her print on it.

She sees other numbers. An Air Force security agent and his young daughter sit next to her on the train from Haifa to Jerusalem. They are going for the Maccabee Games. Air Force security kisses and pets the young daughter who has his own face.

"If you want to keep your daughter," he advises Beatrix, "give her everything she wants and don't bind her wrists, and you will keep her forever."

But he is afraid he will not keep his fourteen-year-old forever. She has blood clots in her legs. After the soccer games, they will go to the Western Wall to pray for the success of her leg operation.

The child sleeps on his shoulder. He encircles her head with his tattooed arm.

162

They are circus people. The Tattooed People. The Experimented-On People. Still, they live.

Bearers of the Dream (2)

In Haifa Beatrix visits a singer. She is small and half of her height is her black hair. She walks on platform dude shoes. She struts. Her voice struts. Her voice is a platformed voice, thrown higher than she is.

The singer talks about her throat problems, her tight vocal cords, the chest that is too resonant. She talks about theater problems. Eighteen-year-olds are getting all the singing jobs. Tall girls are hired first; short girls last. She talks and eats. She is staying away from milk products, however. They clog the throat.

"Tell me your story, Rina," says Beatrix. "Are your parents alive?"

"My father is alive," says Rina.

"Your mother is dead?"

"My mother was always dead, but she is not dead."

"What are your parents doing?"

"My father is dreaming."

"Of what is he dreaming?"

"Of singing."

"Does he sing?"

"He always sang. He played guitar, banjo, mandolin. He sang on the radio, played the banjo in family bars. We sang, when I was a baby and he not yet middle-aged, at the openings of auto dealerships. We did Chevrolet openings together. We did the new gas stations. He sang on the Yiddish Hour. We tap-danced Saturday afternoons at a downtown movie house. We were a team, my father and I, like Shirley Temple and Jack Haley, Shirley Temple and Bojangles Robinson, Shirley Temple and George Murphy."

"What did your mother say?"

"She didn't notice."

"What did your father teach you?"

"To sing and to go home afterward, not to go on the road. A single girl always comes home."

"What did you do?"

"I came here, where I can go home every night. It's a small country and it chaperones me."

"Is your father proud that you are doing what he taught you to do?"

"No. He has disinherited me."

"Why?"

"Because I am doing what *he* wanted to do."

"That's all?"

"And because I, a single girl, did not return to his house at night."

Four Are the Matriarchs: The Third and Fourth Matriarchs

What do I learn from my mothers? Sister against sister, woman betrays woman. The man is the seed and the woman the gourd, filled with seed and rattling or dried and to be discarded.

Beatrix learns what is praiseworthy. Avram is praised for offering up his son, his only son, but he offered up both of his sons, both of his only sons, one to the desert and one to the slaughtering place on the mountaintop. How is it that later both boys, brothers despite their mothers, bury their father Avram together? "Yitzhak and Yishmael, his sons, buried him in the caves of Machpelah." ("In the Beginning," p. 64.)

Mother, you made a contest of the womb. You named your children as prizes. And when you tired, you sent your maidservants to bear for you. You dissemble, mother. You make fools of your men.

Lea, older mother with weak eyes, with squinting, suspicious face, with graying hair, unable to find her own love, found another's, her younger sister's.

There was a plenitude of wombs for Yaakov, two wives, two maidservants. First he came into Lea. All night he rent her. All night he reared and pawed the earth. He did not know his mare. In the morning on his rug slept the head of that old gray mare, her face relaxed, her mouth crookedly open, a faint snore issuing. Her eyes, not clearly open in daylight, peered white beneath the nonclosing lids, like moon still visible in the morning sky. It was as if Lea watched him while she slept.

Lavan did not overly punish his son-in-law. Only for a week, a bride week, did he have to saddle and bridle her. Within seven days he would have Rahel, the one he had first kissed at the well. It was for Rahel that he had lifted up his voice and wept. (The old servant, another time, at the same place, had met the maiden Rivka at the well and had wept his thanksgiving. They are all wells, our mothers, wells of our generations. It is for them that the Old Testament, the Old Testicle, is written.)

For seven nights did Yaakov come in upon Lea. Did he dream, all that time, he was with Rahel? Or did he see the pretty maid Zilpa crouching in the corner of the tent? Did he dream of her soft flesh, for we dream of someone when we make love, either the person we are loving or the person we would like to.

Lavan not only gave Rahel unto Yaakov, but also her maid Bilha. Yaakov loved Rahel that bridal week until the tent stakes shook. Lavan was shrewd. With four women, Yaakov would work those extra seven years and not notice. With one daughter, Rahel, Yaakov would have turned swiftly back to Yitzhak and Beer-Sheva, the land of Seven Wells.

The women are bearers or hardened roots. For weak eyes, God, the Majestic Plural, compensated with strong womb. For Rahel's pretty face and fair form, God compensated with spontaneous abortions.

Lea held each of her sons before Yaakov. Why did he continue to come in upon her tent if she displeased him? Perhaps he came on her in anger. He would go into that tent, slap her, stripe her face like the rugs under her, hurl her down. And she would be so grateful, for she had that blurry vision, those bad, squinty eyes, and he dangled every year another son. She called those sons: Son's Sight, Hearing, Joining, Giving Thanks, and said, "Indeed, now will my husband love me." ("In the Beginning," p. 79.)

It was an animal pen in that tent, crawling, squalling babies. In Rahel's tent it was cool and quiet; yet Rahel wept.

Like her husband's grandmother, Sara, Rahel gave up her serving maid, Bilha, to bear for her. The child would be raised as hers when Bilha would have borne across the knees of Rahel. Rahel thanked God for Bilha's son and called him Judge, for God had judged and had heard the voice of Rahel.

The women contested. Bilha bore again; Rahel named the child Contester. Lea gave her maid Zilpa unto Yaakov. Zilpa bore. Lea went into the tent of Rahel with the umbilical cord dangling from the unwashed infant and told Rahel, "I call him Fortune," for God had made her fortunate.

And the sisters quarreled and bore through their maids. Yet once again Lea went into the tent of Rahel and held up another son and said his name was Bliss for he was her bliss.

Yaakov walked between babies in all the tents and there was no thought of any other thing.

The eldest son of Lea finds a magic root to make Lea full-bellied again. Son's Sight brings the mandrake for his mother but Rahel pulls at Lea's hair, begging for the mandrake.

Lea screams, "Is it too little that you have taken away my husband, / must you also take away the mandrakes of my son?" ("In the Beginning," p. 80.)

She intercepts Yaakov, coming home tired from the field. He must lie that night with her. He does. He cares no longer whose womb he is filling, so long as it is warm and tight-fitting.

166

Lea bears "Hire," for she has hired Yaakov for the night. Yet another night Lea rocks with Yaakov and bears a sixth son. She rushes to the tent of Rahel and holds him up, Prized One.

She also bears a daughter, Dina.

Lea's tent is full.

"How many children have you, Lea?"

"Six."

"But I see seven here."

"Six are my sons. We do not count daughters as our children."

So it is to this day in the tents of all Bedouin.

What is happening to Rahel? She bleeds irregularly. She grows listless and has nothing to add to the prophecy that her children shall cover the earth as the stars in the sky, as the tents in the oasis. And her tent flaps open to admit another baby, other nephews. They all look like Yaakov.

Then it comes to pass that Rahel, too, bears a son.

"God has removed my disgrace!"

She calls him: "May He add to me another son." ("In the Beginning," p. 81.)

When they flee from her father Lavan, it is Rahel, the one who could not steal the mandrake roots, who steals the totems of her father. Perhaps Rahel thinks these totems will impregnate her, that this tribal god of Lavan will do for her what it took Him too long to do. Lavan comes looking for them, as Yaakov moves his tribe back to Beer-Sheva. Rahel hides the totems. Lavan looks into her tent. She tells her father that she is menstruating and cannot rise to bid him enter, for menstruating women are as camel dung, only not so useful. Her father would be cursed by his totems if he entered the tent of a bleeding woman.

Yaakov comes to Shekhem, which is on the west bank of the Jordan. He drives his household and cattle as far as Beth-Lecham, the House of Bread.

Rahel has been traveling on camel, and it is her time. She

has been bumped. The sun has been merciless upon her head. Her bearing goes hard for her.

She is bearing, dying, and cursing her son with the name Son-of-My-Woe, but Yaakov takes him from the tomb of Rahel's womb and calls him Son-of-the-Right-Hand. Rahel cries, or sighs. The womb shudders closed. She is buried on that spot.

Yaakov puts a standing marker there where she has died and goes to his tribe to count out his sons, twelve, and his years and his father's years. When Yaakov goes from that place of Rahel's Tomb, Lea stays at the marker yet a moment longer, a faint smile upon her face.

The sons of Yaakov, twelve in number, what happens to them? They are named: Despoiler, Warrior, Ruler, Sailor, Toiler, Viper, Goader, Farmer, Seeder, Soothsayer, Devourer, Divider. The daughter, Dina, what is to happen to her? She will not be Rich Man, Poor Man, Beggar Man, Thief, Doctor, Lawyer, Merchant, Chief. She will be raped and then not mentioned again.

Mothers, what have you taught me? When we sing at the Passover table "Who Knows One?" One is the Lord in Heaven and on Earth. We come to Four are the Matriarchs. We come to Nine are the Months of Childbearing. Mothers, you have taught me that a woman is as good as her womb. If she bears, her sons will place a standing marker where she has died. And if she is barren, she is not part of the Old Testicle.

Mothers! Sara! Rivka! Lea! Rahel! You have taught your daughters that women fight for the penis of a man. The winner will be honored with burial in the Cave of Machpelah or under a standing marker on the road to Bethlehem.

Who named *you* my mothers? Who named *this* a matriarchy?

Remnants (2)

Beatrix completes her research on *Remnants*, for, as Yossef told his brothers: "God sent me out before you / to prepare you as a remnant on earth, / to keep you alive for a great deliverance." ("In the Beginning," p. 126.)

Their great deliverance is to be alive, is to be working extra time on *Shabbat* to supplement the income, is to send sons into the army to be killed.

But they are alive. Beatrix sees them in the green hills of Judaea, walking among the twisted, ancient olive trees. They are alive in development towns, working under the hot sun. They are alive on the boulevards of Tel Aviv. They climb Mount Carmel in Haifa. They are alive inland and in port cities, on mountains, in deserts.

Bearers of the Dream (3)

In the artist's village of Ein Hod she meets Ilana, a Russian potter. Ilana has a rounded belly, a rounded bottom, handles of arms.

"Tell me your story, Ilana," says Beatrix.

They have returned from a concert in the stone amphitheater of Ein Hod. Wild dogs had rushed across the stage while the chamber group bowed. A donkey with a scarred nose had walked this distance from an Arab village nearby and had brayed. A scorpion is crawling across the stage.

Ilana and Beatrix shiver in the night air, but yet it is warmer in Ein Hod than in Jerusalem, Tel Aviv, or Haifa. The days are sweltering. Beatrix cannot bear her clothes upon her body. Ilana works naked in the pot shop. The women sweat while the clay dries.

"I am the daughter of collectors," says Ilana. "My parents came from Leningrad with a shipload of furniture and with a large library. My father is a man of culture."

"And your mother?"

"My mother is paralyzed. She gave birth and saw it was a girl and never spoke again. She walks slowly with a cane. She writes her requests shakily. She sleeps separately."

"What did you do in your father's house?"

"I admired the samovars, the art books on the Hermitage. I admired our piano, our phonograph, our sheet music. He is an importer. I fingered the materials he brought from France, the lace from Belgium, the Indian silk. I went to Bezalel Art School to make more objects for his collection."

"Then he is pleased with you, Ilana, that you are a potter?"

"No. He has disinherited me. Cousins inherit the sheet music and piano. An aunt inherits the Belgian lace. The samovar belongs to my mother. The paintings are bequeathed to the Israel Museum. The empty apartment will go to a nephew."

"Why did he disinherit you?"

"Because I would not stay home and be part of the collection."

Bearers of the Dream (4)

Beatrix visits Rut'y. Rut'y has a car and will drive Beatrix to the airport at Lod when her research is complete. She is a social worker in the Ministry of Absorption.

Beatrix and Rut'y have coffee and onion soup at a Jerusalem restaurant.

"Tell me your story, Rut'y," says Beatrix.

"My father was a labor organizer."

"And your mother?"

"She was organized by my father. She was carefully placed in the kitchen where she met the plants that needed watering, the flour and sugar and shortening that needed baking, the neighbors that needed gossiping."

"What was your life like at home?"

"I went with my father to strike meetings. I went with him, as a child, to women's prisons, where he helped to bring reforms. I went with him to the Arab communities, where he brought the Israeli Arabs into the labor movement."

"And then what did you do?"

"I went to Hebrew University to study sociology."

"Then your father is proud, for you are working with the new immigrants."

"No. My father is cross. He has disinherited me."

"Why is this?"

"Because I am not there for him when he returns from the rallies."

"But your mother is."

"Yes, but her head is in the oven, or over the flower pots, or peering in a neighbor's door."

"Your father is disappointed in you?"

"Fathers are always disappointed in us. We bear the dreams they have already shed."

Beatrix marked her tapes, paid her rentals on the apartment in Jerusalem, the hotel in Haifa, the sublet villa in Ein Hod.

Then she searched out her own remnants. She looked for a brown-haired girl in the branches of olive trees, in the towers of minarets, in the citadel of the YMCA, in the bunk beds of youth hostels, the sulphur baths of Tiberias, the shops and bazaars in the markets of the Old City and of Jaffa. She looked for her in the sunset over the Mediterranean and in the sunrise on Mount Carmel. She listened for her call when shepherds passed with their goats on their way to the Judaean Hills. She took a bus into the Sinai and slept in the sand, hoping the girl would be at Eilat or Sharm es Sheikh. She climbed Mount Sinai at 2 A.M., arriving on the summit at six, for sunrise. She thought if Moses received the tablets there, she might receive some word of her remnant, her commandment. But when the sun rose, she fell asleep on the ground in exhaustion. Her guide had to return from the rest of the group that had already descended in order to lead her back down the mountain.

Beatrix looked among Russian-speaking cafés of Tel Aviv, Roman and German cafés, cafés of the young, actors' cafés, cafés of the intelligentsia, the journalists' cafés. She looked in abandoned Arab villages and in development towns.

171

She returned to Rut'y, the woman in the Ministry of Absorption.

"Absorb me, Rut'y," she pleaded.

"I cannot," said Rut'y. "You are already absorbed in something else."

Rut'y took Beatrix to the airport at Lod. No terrorists had landed during this month to machine-gun tourists. No women had boarded planes, during her visit, with hand grenades stuffed into their brassieres. Yet Beatrix was terrorized.

What if all messages from the brown-haired girl went undelivered or undeciphered? What if clues dropped were undetected? What if the brown-haired girl was in the Midwest while Beatrix was traveling in the Mideast?

"Mother, I am pregnant with a baby girl and she has left me."

"Then you must spend the rest of your life looking for her."

Looking for Daughters

Primer: Ten Ways to Lose Daughters

I. Talk Too Much

"Listen to me," says Beatrix.

She wants ears uncovered, eyes attentive, mouth closed. She wants no squirming, no plucking at clothes, no twisting of fingers. Beatrix speaks without pagination, inserting marginalia, notation, documentation. She bolsters her arguments. She stuffs in data. She fills out with fact.

Lena is weeping.

"I have said nothing to offend you," says Beatrix.

"Shut up," says Lena.

II. Compare

When Lena was at puberty, when she started the forty years of walking through her menstrual desert, her skin erupted.

"*I* always had good skin," said Beatrix.

"Shut up," said Lena.

III. Be Helpful

In the Ninth Grade Lena was up all night writing a report. It was dawn. The first class would be in two hours.

"Let me help you," said Beatrix.

"No," said Lena.

"I wrote a book. I can help you write a report."

"Shut up," said Lena.

IV. Have Historical Perspective

The girls in her class are invited to a pajama party. Lena is not. Her friends have made the Honor Roll. Lena has not. They have new holiday clothes. Not Lena. They all have fathers. Lena has none.

"It's only of importance at this stage of your life," says Beatrix in a kindly voice.

"Shut up! Shut up! Shut up!" says Lena.

V. Be Silent

From oration, exhortation, explanation, divination, Beatrix went to an offended silence. She decided not to return accusations with refutations, opposition with a reasonable proposition. Beatrix answered ire, rage, fury, wrath, insolence, meanness, unworthiness, vengefulness, irrationality, anguish, defiance, grief with paragraphs of silence, pages of quiet. Days would go by and the only sounds in the House of Palmer would be in the kitchen or bathroom.

One day Beatrix went into Lena's bathroom. Lena was sitting on the covered toilet, crying into a thick towel.

"Lena," said Beatrix in a kindly voice.

"Shut up," said Lena.

VI. Have Goals for Your Daughter

Lena graduated *cum laude* from Junior High. Beatrix kissed the mouth she had allowed to wear lipstick. She kissed each eyelid she had allowed to wear eye shadow. She kissed the right wrist for which she had bought a watch.

"From high school," said Beatrix, "you'll be *magna, summa, supra, dea*—."

"Shut up," said Lena.

VII. Be Organized

Lena is going on a trip with her class.

"Did you take a face cloth, a hand towel, portable toothbrush with its small tube of toothpaste, Arrid, Noxema, Selsan shampoo, nail clipper, nail file, Cutex Oily Polish Remover Pads, Junior-Size Kotex, clean sanitary belt, address book, notebook, sharpened pencil?"

Lena is going for a four-day weekend.

"Shut up," said Lena.

VIII. Teach Politeness

"Did you shake hands? Did you ask about their kids? Did you write Thank You notes? Did you offer to carry their packages? Did you say, 'I'm sorry'? Did you apologize? Did you excuse yourself? Did you say, 'Pardon me'? Did you say, 'Would you repeat that, please?'?"

"Shut up," said Lena.

IX. Teach Caution

"Did you double-date? Did you carry bus fare? Did you keep your pants on? Did you stay away from the park and dark side streets? Did you let him know what kind of girl you are? Did you make sure he met your mother?"

Lena is silent.

"I'm speaking," said Beatrix.

"Shut up," said Lena.

X. Be Energetic

"Here are your vitamins, this for your cold, here's for night blindness, this for the white spots on your fingernails. Do you have lunch money? Did you get your research from the library? How much time will you have for homework tonight? Are you prepared for the Friday test in Algebra II? Have you worked on Group Project for History? Did you get to the cleaners? Did you take your run-down heels to the shoemaker? Did you practice for Piano? Have you checked out Swimming at the Center?"

Lena is silent.

"Did you hear me?" asked Beatrix.

"Never again," said Lena.

Looking for Daughter—In Purses

She searches in her purse. She searches for the *right* purse. One is a red, drawstring Indian bag. Another is an oilcloth traveling bag. A third is a cheapy bag. Fourth is a classy leather bag. Fifth is an antique bag.

The mirrors are falling out of the red, drawstring Indian bag. She bought it at World Bazaar. The mirrors are falling out and the white beads are loosening from the white thread design. Several rows of mirrors are intact.

Bea sees herself in the horizontal row of tiny mirrors, a bit of an eye, an arch of brow; next row, the nose; two rows down, the mouth. Above, near the missing drawstring of the drawstring bag, Bea sees bits of her black hair reflected. She is faceted like *The Fly*. Vincent Price would recognize her. She sees a broken mirror of world. As the mirrors loosen from their embroidered pockets, Beatrix also sees what's behind the mirror: the red cloth of the purse, red behind eyelid, sun coming up, bloodshot red of eye, gouged-out eye, empty socket of eye where mirror has fallen like a tear.

In this purse she has no clue to daughter. She has a black bobby pin, although she cannot remember when she last used bobby pins. She used to pin her hair up, but the heavy uncontrollable hair would begin to creep out of pins, barrettes, and nets. With her hair up, her cheeks fattened and her eyes narrowed. As the hair avoided its holders, her face would be restored to her. She stopped putting up her hair and tried to curl ringlets above her ears. They stuck out like springs or slipped horns.

In the purse Beatrix has a key to an office. Lena is not using this bobby pin or the key to the office. The purse also once had a binding, that time when she took it to Buffalo—looking for daughter.

She looks into her large, oilcloth traveling bag. It is black-and-white polka-dotted, with double handles. The zipper is ripping from the binding, for she had overloaded the purse when she went to California—looking for daughter. Bea overloads everything, plugs, her arms with laundry that falls on the stairs as she mounts them, books to be returned to the library, books that are lost between car and library return box.

In the black-and-white shiny purse is a health card to a clinic, a phosphorescent green pencil that says GLOW and Cixon 250-2. She has these clues if only she could read them.

The plastic partition of the traveling bag is torn. The bottom of the bag is full of gleaming black beetles of pins. Now she knows where all pins go, to the bottom of purses. She finds a black wide-toothed comb for which she's been searching. It's the only comb that does not tear her hair and that can fit into her five purses. Between its wide teeth lint lodges. She finds a nickel, a dime, two pennies, and an Israeli *lira*. She is surprised to find the two pennies in her purse for she has always saved pennies for Lena and still automatically puts them into a large coffee can in case, when Lena is found, she is penniless.

Beatrix finds a poem on green ditto paper, a poem someone pressed into her hand when she gave a lecture. The poet is anonymous for the poem continues and is signed on page two and she has lost page two. She has marked the green ditto ink in red pen. She sees that she objected to "leaking heavens," "the sneer of the mouth and mind," "snakings of the soul." She has no idea what this poem is about or how it can lead to Lena's whereabouts.

She picks up that cheapy bag, light-green cloth with garish

orange beads. The bag has a white fringe at its base like a lampshade. She bought it on sale and thought to send it to Lena in case Lena wrote. Then she became insecure about her purchase. Lena would object to the color, the excess of beads, the gaudily beaded flower and peacock design, and would have one more excuse not to return home. Beatrix uses the purse and is ashamed of it, yet she finds it more practical than her other bags for it has a simple zipper, closed compartments, and shoulder straps.

From this cheapy bag she takes out her wallet. The plastic of the photograph insert is discolored. It is blackened like a disease across Lena's baby forehead. The eyes are worried in the mother's arms. The bonnet is too small. She has rims of fat showing through the gauzy white pinafore. Bea is holding her and leaning back with the weight. Bea's earring hangs crookedly. Her blouse is unevenly buttoned. Bea is plump after childbirth. The mirror of this wallet is a shiny aluminum paper. It is scarred. Bea sees her scarred face in it.

She has a photograph of Lena wearing a Girl Scout cap. Lena is fourteen and joyously smiling. Behind Lena lurks a shy friend, hidden by Lena's rich brown hair and Girl Scout cap. Between the baby and the Girl Scout is a four-year-old in plaid dress with white collar and cuffs, with a red ribbon on the back of her head and small bits of bow sticking up like terrier's ears. Lena has bangs. She is smiling. But the photographer used a flash and her face is flattened, and the smile is faded. Lena is fifteen and is holding Beatrix's hand against a tree trunk. The tree divides and separates their heads. Their hair is foliage. They are holding hands tightly but not looking at each other.

"LENA!" screams Beatrix.

Her window is slightly open to let in air. It is early Spring and her call sails like a kite. A child outside brakes his bike and looks up at her window.

Beatrix has one classic bag, purchased with her royalties. It is a Judith Leiber Inc. bag. It is to be admired as sculpture, standing on the dresser on its accordion base. It has elegant thin straps. There is gold trimming on the lovely clasp and on the rims of inside compartments. The name of the designer is in golden script. But it is too small to carry supplies.

And then there is a French bag, an antique. It has tiny golden beads, tiny white beads on a golden satin background, with pale pink and darker pink and golden buds with green embroidered leaves edging the purse. Inside, it is rich golden satin. Lena bought it for her, out of Lena's allowance, one summer in London.

Beatrix Palmer had been given an advance by *Commentary* to cover her expenses while she researched: The Jew in London: (a) Immigrant Jewish-British Literature; (b) The Jew in Parliament; (c) The Jew in Society. She wrote half of (a), never completed (b), and did not know how to contact society for (c).

But it was a summer for Bea and Lena like the golden satin lining of her embroidered purse. Sunsets came gradually, from cool yellow to golden. The coverlets on their twin beds were white satin. French windows opened above a garden with rose trellises and English cherubs riding tricycles. Birds sang while Lena nestled on Beatrix's lap. There was no time to write an article.

There was time to locate Lena's lost pocketbook at the Lost and Found on Baker Street. They found no pocketbook there but many Chamberlain umbrellas and bought one. There was time to teach Lena to read chapters, books, series with the Narnia adventures. There was time to cut hair, to buy Lena a matching Scottish skirt and tam, with a dolly also in Black Watch.

There was time for Portobello Road where Lena found Bea's purse. She bought it for her mother out of her allowance, borrowing ahead until the Fall.

Inside of the antique purse is a flowered paper napkin on which is written the telephone number of a French couple whom she met at a party and who invited her and Lena to visit them in Nice. There is nothing else within the purse. But when

Beatrix thinks of her French beaded bag, of the old woman in a French garret, eyes fading, laboriously stringing those hundreds of beads, Bea feels a great sense of responsibility to the bag, to the allowance of Lena, to her child's love for her on the day of Bea's summer birthday in London.

"Mother, I am pregnant with a baby girl and she has left me."
"Search for her."
"Where should I be searching?"
"Look for the father."

Looking for Fathers

Looking for Fathers

If you're a daughter, where do you look for your father?

You used to look in crockery and glassware. In the moustache cup you hunted for his moustache. In the drinking glass next to his bedstead, you found his teeth drinking the water. The jaws are slightly ajar, the teeth smiling.

They toast you. *"L'haim,"* say your father's teeth.

If you are at the beach, you look for your father in his bathing suit. If he has changed in the tall grass, or under a beach towel, to avoid paying for the shower room, you may catch a glimpse of clams without their shell, of unkosher, unscaly seafood, scallops maybe. Or, if it is like meat, more like pork.

You used to be able to find your father at the furnace, carrying out ashes. That was before gas and oil heat. You can still sometimes find your father pulling down the garage door, after he has parked the car there for protection in winter.

If you listen for your father at night, he is sending out a code with staccato snores. If someone in the family has died, your father is crying. If you creep into his bedroom to look, there are no tears on his face.

When your father comes home from work at five, you rush into his arms. When your mother comes home from work at five, you nod at her. It will take her an hour and a half to get dinner on the table.

Looking for Fathers (1): Off to Buffalo

"Mother, I'm pregnant with a baby girl and I want to know what she's learned."
"To shuffle."
"Where?"
"Off to Buffalo."

Beatrix receives an announcement. Annual Buffalo film festival. Her coordinator on *The Pioneers* has sent it to Bea, with a name encircled and an arrow pointing to a face.

That face is obscured by a camera, as are all the faces on the announcement. The filmmakers have probosces, tubular organs of lenses, attached sucking snouts, as they focus on each other or on the reader of the announcement. Jonas Mekas has his thin, pale face and his thin, pale hair obscured by the camera. Stan Brakhage has gray earlocks, puffy cheeks, and binocular eyes, with a lens snout over his full, petulant face. Stan Vanderbeek's beard is cropped by the camera. Bruce Baillie's light eyes do not show nor does Ed Emshwiller's smile.

"If he's there, she's there," said her mother, about Bea's husband and daughter.

"It's a hundred percent sure she's found him," said her father.

Changes occur in one's life, not in the search or in the pain, but in physical accomplishment. Beatrix had learned to dive in

186

elementary school, to bike in Junior High, to type in High, and now, in middle age, to drive.

Beatrix leaves for Buffalo. It is a four-hour trip. It takes Beatrix six and a half.

Her father phoned before she went.

"Give him my regards," said her father. "Tell him I bear no hard feelings."

Being a parent means being once removed from the experience of one's children.

Her program had listed: HAROLD STEINER, the name and face her photographer coauthor had encircled. Showing: Birth, Sunrise, Stillness.

What did he know about birth, running away before the time? Sunrise? He grumbled each morning because he had stayed up half the night. Stillness? He paced like a formerly free-roving creature, now caged. While driving or riding, at his desk, in classroom, on the bed, he moved, tapped his foot, shifted his seat, drummed his hands, jerked his head, climbed over her and under her.

It could not be the same Harold Steiner.

Beatrix stops in Canada for coffee. She nervously takes out her wallet in the dining booth and, into her coat, counts out her money. Has she enough? Did she take too much? Should it have been in Travelers Checks? In larger denominations? Smaller? The pleasant waitress serves her coffee and adds toast without charge. She gives Beatrix change in American silver. Beatrix is drawing and loosening the drawstring of her Indian bag until she breaks the string and has to carry the purse out to her car like a grocery bag, holding it by the bottom. She sets the purse on its haunches in the front seat and it falls over. Photos slip out of the plastic case. The girl in the plaid dress curtsies and her bow wobbles. The baby in Bea's arms struggles to climb down. The Girl Scout flings off her cap. The teen-ager holding hands with her mother against the trunk of the oak, wrenches loose. Lena wobbles on her fat knees, walks proudly with her bow on her head, boyishly without her Girl Scout cap and bangs her mother's arm against the bark of the tree in her hurry to flee. Where did they all run to? Here, there, everywhere.

Here is Buffalo.

Beatrix turns the wrong way off the expressway and goes deeper downtown, along the street of businesses, cleaning plants, diners—Red Barns, White Towers, a delicatessen—churches, churches.

She stops in front of a pawnshop to ask directions. People, waiting on the curb before that grille of closed pawnshop, wave her back in the opposite direction. She makes a U-turn and drives away from the business district to the grassier area of the university.

The conferees register at the same motel. She registered while her suitcase rested like a poodle beside her legs, her purse spilling out the contents of its red stomach.

Beatrix wanted to ask the desk clerk if she could examine the register to look for the signature of Harold Steiner. She would, if she remembered mystery films with James Dunn and Glenda Farrell, palm a five-dollar bill. The skinny, pimply, voice-crackling clerk would, at first, refuse, then he would see that handkerchief corner of green and would say, spinning around the hotel log, "Oh, certainly!" Perhaps with inflation the price had gone up and was now ten dollars to look at someone's signature, or two tens, or maybe not even in American dollars. It wasn't worth it.

Because she had arrived two and a half hours later than she had anticipated, the first event on the schedule was already in session in the auditorium of the U, across the street from the motel. She washed, cleaned her nails, put water up her nostrils, astringent on her skin, Lady Esther on her hands, foot powder inside of her shoes, Murine in her eyes, and went across the street.

Billy the Kid is on. It's not *The Outlaw* with Jane Russell and the late Audie Murphy, late war hero, late alcoholic in a shoot-'em-up. It's not Southwestern deserts and mountains; it's not cowboys and Indians. Somewhere in the Northwest the camera is walking through the woods. The camera bearer is crackling twigs with his feet, is looking into rock pools. The camera bearer makes love. There is a body without a head. The camera bearer squeezes her breasts. She is astride the camera bearer. Her stomach is working and the tape recorder of the camera bearer picks up the sobs of the headless woman, her sighs.

Beatrix is the voyeur. All of the probosces of the filmmakers rape the woman. They poke into her vagina, into her opened yelling mouth, linger on her nipple, up her thigh; the filmed subject climbs in bed with the camera. There is no private moment. There is nowhere a drawer, a closet door, a closed window, drapes, a shaded lamp. All bulbs are nakedly shining: tips of penises, tips of nipples, faucets dripping.

There is a break for dinner. All the conferees join together in the same dining hall. Beatrix has pinned her Festival of Filmmakers badge—green and white—onto her sweater, but she forgot to magic-marker her name on the paper that slipped into the badge. Beatrix, wearing her blank-name badge, is looking around for a table to seat herself and for the table that seats Harold Steiner and Lena Gurnev Palmer-Steiner.

Beatrix sees Jonas Mekas sitting quietly, speaking Hungarian with his brother. She sees handsome women filmmakers sitting together. Their work is not being shown. Only women are being shown, women lovers and mothers, typecast. She hears Stan Brakhage talking. His voice goes into the soup and climbs out, nestles in the mashed potatoes, rolls on the brussels sprouts. His voice eats her dessert.

She had walked from table to table. One table of men ignored her although there was one empty seat at the table. If she sat in it, their conversation would boredly include her or rudely exclude her. She wants to sit with the women. One is tall and has dark hair pulled back in a pony tail. The other is short and has ear-length curly gray hair. They smile and nod to her but continue deep in conversation. Beatrix would never insert herself without knocking, ringing, phoning, apologizing, writing ahead.

She sits at a table with one other person. He is alone, head down, fingering his fork. He is not wearing a badge. He is startled that she has seated herself and he half-rises to touch the back of her chair.

"How do you do?" he says.

He studies his empty plate again. He scratches inside of his wrist. His eyes are hazel. He is bald. He wears a torn sweater and boots.

"Excuse me," he says, "I'm preoccupied."

So is Beatrix, searching the tables. Will Lena be with Dada? Will her hair be long, as in her high school photo? Short, as under her Girl Scout cap? With a ribbon, as when she was four? With a bonnet too small for her fat cheeks and big head?

"What did you say?" said Beatrix. "I'm a bit preoccupied. You'll have to excuse me."

Immediately her table partner falls in love with her, a love that will last unswervingly for the whole weekend conference.

Stan Vanderbeek passes. His golden hair is held back with an elasticized band. He wears a white turtleneck.

"Hello, Barney!" he says.

"Yes," says Barney, Beatrix's table partner.

Ed Emshwiller passes. He has carried a camera to dinner. "Barney!" he calls.

"Right," says Barney.

"Do you know Harold Steiner?" Beatrix asks.

"No," says Barney. "Do you?"

"I don't know," says Beatrix.

Barney cups his hands around his mouth.

"HAROLD STEINER! HAARROOOOLD STEII-NER!"

Everyone is silent. A gentleman rises from one of the white-clothed tables and makes his way to Barney's. He is slender, of middle years. He is not bald like Barney, not blond pony-tailed like Stan Vanderbeek, not gray-bearded and camera-carrying like Ed Emshwiller, not puffy-faced and booming-voiced like Stan Brakhage.

"Hello?" he questions Barney.

"Harold Steiner?"

Beatrix has said nothing. She would like to unpyramid the napkin and put it on her hair and be a white-haired old lady sitting sedately there. She would like to raise the forks and look out between the bars of the tines.

"This is—" Barney looks at her empty name card. "Miss Film Festival."

"How do you do?" says Harold Steiner.

Harold Steiner is the right age, probably the correct weight and accurate height. She cannot see his eyes. They were, in the announcement, peering into a camera. Now they're blinking behind sunglasses.

"Yes," says Beatrix. "Thank you."

Barney is frowning. He had planned to neither comfort nor discomfort his seat partner.

"Just checking, Harold Steiner," says Barney. "Keep that in mind. We've got our eye on you."

"Fuck off!" says Harold Steiner.

Perhaps that is a clue. That angry voice sounds right. Bea cranes to see his table, his companions. A young woman is next to his emptied chair. Half of Harold Steiner's age. Beatrix stands up. Barney's hand covers hers.

"Anybody else we want me hollering for?" he asks.

The young head at Harold's table turns its profile. Does the nose have a slight hump? The eye she sees in that frieze is following Harold Steiner back to his chair.

"No, thank you," says Beatrix. "Would you excuse me a moment?"

"No," says Barney. "I would not."

"Then," says Beatrix, "I will have to cry, pee, wash up at this table."

"Help yourself," says Barney.

He is holding on to both of her hands now. She cannot leave.

"I am Harold Steiner," says Barney.

Beatrix is shaking. Her soup spoon, pea spoon, fruit compote spoon spill: broth, summer green peas, and canned colorless grapes.

The festival resumes. A California filmmaker shows films, and, afterward, is insulted in the question-and-answer period by a New York filmmaker. A New York filmmaker shows electronic films and is insulted by an Oregon filmmaker. A Florida filmmaker shows beach and surf and is attacked by an Arizona filmmaker, who is into deserts. Barney sits alone in the last row of the auditorium, picking at his sleeve. A Boston filmmaker shows experimental, hand-painted films and his *raison* is questioned by a Colorado filmmaker who has just shown his family in films. Barney, in the last row, rises and paces.

Beatrix is sitting on an end seat, closer to the middle of the auditorium. She had wanted to be where she could survey the crowd ahead of her, behind her.

Harold Steiner had changed after dinner. He is without the half-his-age companion. Even at night he is wearing sunglasses. Beatrix leaves the auditorium during one of the Q's & A's. She has diarrhea.

Barney is standing outside of LADIES. He is more than standing; he is standing on his head.

"I needed that," he tells her. "Everything else was on its head tonight."

He takes her hand and leads her away from the conferees, who will be at the motel bar discussing, cussing, consulting, insulting each other.

He takes her to the elevator, up to six, onto his bed, and elevates her further yet, like the torso in the film, breasts grabbed, sobbing, stomach muscles pulling in, releasing. Beatrix has no head. She has no legs. She is a torso and under her the ground is rolling.

"Go home," kisses Barney later. "I like to sleep alone."

Beatrix has left her key at the desk. A message awaits her.

"Is there something I can do for you?" HAROLD STEINER.

It is lettered, not scripted, nondescript, and she does not recognize it.

Beatrix is calm. Perhaps any man can do it for her. Does she need *one* man to do it to her? You meet a man in a taxi. He offers you a stick of gum. You tell him, "Never mind the preliminaries. Do you like to be on top or below?" A bus driver engages you in conversation. You admire the way he turns corners. "Drive to my house," you tell him. "Let the passengers wait."

A waiter serves you gracefully. The plate slides before you. His hands are slender. You rise and take his arm. "I'm not hungry yet," you say.

A student is studying in the library. He is at the table near you. His hair curls on his neck. He looks up and blinks, his eyes tired from the book. "Come rest your eyes," you say, and press his head into your breast.

Beatrix sleeps soundly.

At breakfast Barney is sitting at a table with the two handsome women filmmakers. Beatrix hesitates. He smiles; they smile at her. She has been invited, formally, as to a baby shower, a wedding, an anniversary, a New Year's Eve party. She can now sit with them.

"Harold Steiner," one of the women is saying.

"What?" asks Beatrix.

"His films are on this morning."

BIRTH

The camera bearer's hands are birthing the baby. They pull the baby from the womb. Everyone in the womb room exclaims. Blankets are rushed over. Pan over mother's sweating, exhausted face.

"Are you happy?" asks the voice of the camera bearer, the hands holding the mike up to her.

The woman smiles into the mike. The baby cries into the mike. The guests exclaim around the mike.

(Applause of audience. Next film.)

The sun is coming up slowly. A young woman is seated in a chair. She is naked. Her baby is sleeping. The camera focuses ECU on hardening breasts. The baby stirs. The breasts lactate. One white drop falls over the curve of the breast, rolls down her ribs past her hip to her thigh.

(Muffled applause.)

CU on sleeping baby. Fists closed, fists opened. Head turns slightly. CU on baby's blanket, white like egg whites, puffing with breath of baby. CU on butterfly against window—long-distance lens—on trees outside, walk to windowpane. Kettle boils on stove. Birthing, lactating young mother stares out of window while steam from kettle mists the room. Young mother wipes windowpane. A clear circle. A butterfly whirring within the circle.

Harold Steiner goes on stage for Q & A. He is without sunglasses. He *is* with birthing, lactating young mother, now fully clothed and carrying the child. They all bow.

"Why did you make this domestic scene?" asks one of the women filmmakers. "It's a clichéd topic."

"Are you telling me," says (not asks) Harold Steiner, "that the birth of my child, my nursing wife, are clichés? Clearly, madam—or is it miss—you have had no child-bearing experience, or, if you had, it is in your dim past and you cannot bear its being recalled."

Lena is not here. If this is Harold Steiner, it is not Beatrix's Harold Steiner. The half-his-age woman is neither Beatrix's daughter nor her ex-daughter.

Barney is smiling.

"Anybody else I can call for you?" he asks.

She calls for him at night and he answers the call. He fills her ears with his fingers, his tongue. He fills her eyes with his poking nose. He fills her mouth with everything that probes— all his digits. And, she discovers also, the next day, his films are very good.

They are not of lactating mothers, riding torsos, butterflies pressed against panes, childhood, electronics. They are shots that move slowly, dreamlike, so that one would want to recline while viewing. As one watches carefully—the way he makes love—the leg steps forward, the other; then, a hand swings toward you; the eyes meet yours. It is mesmerizing. That night, when Barney takes her upstairs, she tries to stand on her head. She fails. She hurts the back of her neck. But she *has* tried to stand on her head. He returns to his somnambulist world when the conference concludes and she to her nightmarish one.

Peopleography

In loss, people are titled. I know a woman who is divorced. She is entitled to divorcee. I know a woman who has outlived her husband. She bears the title of widow. I know a woman who has survived the deaths of her parents. She is an orphan. But what am I, a mother without child? To what am I entitled? To grief. I am aggrieved. To sorrow. I am sad.

> *Sad: sated, satisfied, surfeited.* . . . 3a. afflicted with . . . grief . . .
> 4b. a dull somber color or shade—sad brown and black.

I am not satisfied, despite definition. I am not *sated;* I do not find this loss overappetizing. There *has* been a *surfeit* of sighing. My hair, between beauty parlor appointments, is "a sad brown."

I know of a woman who is legally separated from husband and child. Each day she counts her features, takes her pulse, shakes her sleeping foot. She can bear no further losses.

I know of a woman who is legally married to a roaming man. She sleeps with toy chimpanzees, poodles, rabbits, and bears.

She puts her head on their soft bellies, encircles them with her arm. She places them between her legs. Each day she counts her animals. She can bear no further losses.

I know of a slaughterhouse. I would place people into the stocks. I have a list for my cattle truck to pick up.

The Fathers: Lois's, Janice's, Pauline's, Shirley's, and Lena's. The Fathers of Naomi, Rina, Ilana, and Rut'y. Lavan, the father of Lea and Rahel.

Husbands: Lois's medical husband in his Medical Building office, wearing his white lab-and-butcher coat; Pauline's liquor-store owner and nonhusband; Harold Steiner, wherever he is, whoever he is, whose ever he is.

Mothers: Who cannibalize their daughters, contest their sisters, molest their sons.

Them would I send screaming down the shoot. On their heads, between the eyes, would my hammer descend. Against their necks would I, the ritual slaughterer, draw my blade.

Looking for Fathers (2): The Conference

Bea is offered two hundred and fifty dollars to participate in a panel at State U—where Janice had eaten creamed *drek* on toast. The subject is "Literature of the Immigrant." Bea will represent The Oral Tradition.

Bea is sent the list of copanelists. There is the name of Professor Harold Stone: *Stone,* an English professor, an anglicized *Stein.* Harold, if she remembers him from those years ago, could anglicize, even uncircumcise himself to fit into English Departments.

She drives slowly to State, unhappy on interstate highways for speed freezes her and expressways slow her. She perspires when she arrives, perspires in the winter chill. She, a panelist, is given a suite with color TV, besides her two-hundred-and-fifty honorarium.

A cocktail party precedes the conference. This is State U beloved by State Legislature. It has no urban problems, no urban courses. It has no Blacks, no Communists. So it is well provided for in yearly legislative budgets. State U can afford martinis in unlimited supply. Beatrix has one. Beatrix has two. Beatrix has unlimited supply. Beatrix has three and is in somebody's lap. The lapel above the lap bears his name: Professor Harold Stone, Indiana U.

Indiana U to you, Prof. Stone.

She can see well enough to realize it is not her Harold Steiner. It is an old man, this Prof. Harold Stone, as old as Dr. Long of *Sane Sex Life and Sex Living*, as old as Pauline's late grocery store father or Lois's late Romanian pharmacist father.

"Well, this is very pleasant," says a deep, rich, not old voice. It has timbre. He must have sung in church.

He hugs her to him. He rocks her in his arms. She decides to stay in that cradle.

She sits next to him on the panel. His topic is Henry Roth, and Roth's sleeper, *Call It Sleep*. Bea does not listen to the criticism. Rather she and the audience are taken with his anecdotal, nonscholarly speech. He knows Henry Roth. He knows everybody. He knows Meyer Levin, who tried to get a second edition published of *Call It Sleep*, after the book failed during the Depression. He isn't even Jewish and he knows all those immigrants.

Beatrix is less oral about the oral history of the immigrants. She speaks softly, forgetting the mike, until the back rows of the conference shout: "Louder!" Prof. Stone readjusts her throat mike and holds her shaking hands under the table while Bea's voice and thoughts firm.

They have dinner together with the other panelists. Prof. Stone regales them with tales of his family and with reminiscences from his book, *Love and Other Affairs*.

Bea studies his face. His nose is arched; his cheekbones are high. His eyes are not faded blue. His hair is not wispy white.

His hands are not age-spotted, arthritic, or shaking. He is the handsomest man in the room.

"Will you excuse me, my dear?" he asks her.

Bea is disappointed. He must circulate to greet his colleagues and former colleagues; his former students and lifelong friends, his admirers, his publishers. It is a cotillion and he is gracefully weaving in and out.

She goes to the bar. A man with turquoise belt buckle, turquoise ring, black straight hair pulled back with a leather thong, is popping shots of whiskey into his mouth like oysters.

"What is your specialty?" she asks him.

His eyes are turquoise. His smile is greenish.

"Want me to show you?" he asks.

She, the member of the panel, becomes haughty.

"I'm an American Indian from Wounded Knee," he says. "I'm here to buy guns and to fuck women."

She wanders away and is introduced to a Black Lit specialist who is angry that his specialty was not included in immigrant literature. His suit is elegant, more formal than any panelist's. His shirt is silky, his tie an amazement of colors. He talks about his wife in law school, his daughters taking ballet.

"Why are you here?" Bea asks him.

"I'm here to make contacts for my people," he says, "and to fuck me some women."

She is introduced to an Egyptian novelist. He speaks English beautifully, as well as French and Russian, besides his native Arabic.

"Why are you here?" Bea asks him.

"I demand equal time with the immigrant Jews," he says. "There are many Arab-Americans writing also, and they are not represented."

"Then that's why you're here!"

"That, and to fuck some women."

She is introduced to a magazine publisher. He is an angry young Jew. His magazine is angry, young, and Jewish.

"Why have you come?" asks Bea.

"Because I represent the Jew as Eternal Immigrant," says the publisher, "and because I want to fuck some women."

She searches for Professor Harold Stone. He is searching for her. He gives her his arm and escorts her away from the Indian, the Black, the Arab, the Jew.

"Why have you come to this conference?" Bea asks her aged, charming friend.

"To reacquaint myself with old friends," he says, "and to fuck some women."

Beatrix has her monthly, her cycle, her bad time, her period, her exclamation and question marks, her curse, her ovulation, her menstruation.

Professor Stone is horrified. He releases her arm.

"There are certain taboos that are signposts to mankind," he says. "Incest is one. Menstruation is the other."

He gags. His lips become white and his firm hands shaky. His blue eyes milk over.

"Blood," he says bloodlessly.

She is at the back of the cave. She is Rahel sitting on the totem of her father Lavan, and he will not enter his daughter's tent because of her filth. She is every chicken cut open, every entrail, liver, and heart lifted, leaving dark blood spots. She is the Blood Woman, Blood Worm, Blood Blister, Vampire. She sucks blood from the neck of sleeping boys; she sucks her own napkins when she is finished with them.

She is moony and loony. She is a trap and the penis could be snapped off inside. She has bear teeth in her womb, claws in the vagina, tusks in her Fallopians.

She is an accident, a murder. She is the body thrown from the car, or under the wheels of a train. She is assault, rape, wound. She is Homer's Strife, striding through battlefields. She is the Norse Hel, at the mouth of the underworld.

Her womb snaps, cracks, barks, whispers, whines, gasps, gags, snores, curses. Her womb says secret words that no one can define. Her womb is the Rosetta Stone. Its writing is cuneiform. Its walls are papyrus.

The tool he uses is the stylus. Prof. Stone takes his tool in his hand, upstairs. Color returns to his lips, firmness to his hands, a light to his eyes.

In the same building at State U as the one housing The Conference on Immigrant Literature is a Conference on Abortion and a Counterconference on Friends of the Unborn.

Women who anticipate the unborn are picketing the abortionists, psychologists, penologists, environmentalists of the Conference on Abortion. They push their bloated stomachs at Beatrix. They try to hand her pamphlets. The cover of the throwaway is lurid, a fetus expelled. "They Have Souls. They Have Hearts. You Have A Heart, Too." Beatrix shakes her head. She has no heart. The picketers spit upon her.

Looking for Fathers (3): Hillel House

Her publishers are sending Beatrix out to the West Coast for Jewish Book Fair. She will speak on the paperback of *The Pioneers* and on the new hardback, *The Remnants*.

Her artwork for *Remnants* was a problem. Her photographs with Instamatic were instant but trivial. She wrote to her interviewees asking for other photos. They went to studies that posed them: women with the fingers of one hand touching a cheek, the other hand covering up a tattooed wrist. Men standing, one hand on the back of a chair, to show how much taller they are than the chair.

The women were Israeli beauty-parlored, hennaed, back-combed, and sprayed. Their lips looked as if they had been pressed onto a handkerchief and removed from the reality of face. In the lighting of the photograph the lips were the same shade as the hair, flattening the effect of nose, cheeks, brow. Their eyes were penciled, also their brows. Some wore false lashes and falsies. She recognized no one from their photos. Each received a Thank You note and a small check for the photo from the publishing house.

A cartoonist was then hired to do Steinberg-ish line drawings. But the Holocaust cannot be caricatured. Then Chaim Kupferman, from an Israeli kibbutz, was asked for permission to use his concentration camp series. Rico Lebrun was approached. It became a search for barbed-wire art. The book became more abstract and the voice sepulchral, prophetic, beyond the one face, that set of gestures.

Beatrix will be preparing her audience for *Remnants* by playing them tapes of the interviews.

Unafraid Women is postponed but the publishers have taken an option on Beatrix's proposed anthology, *Mothers and Daughters*. Beatrix has submitted a list of stories, excerpts from novels, and synopses from films dealing with that relationship. Now Beatrix is looking for one of those characters of that special relationship, from San Diego up to San Francisco, looking for Lena Gurnev Palmer-Steiner.

Beatrix is worn, her hair and skin dry from too much sun too quickly absorbed. She has spoken at the San Diego Conservative Synagogue, at the Brandeis Summer Camp, the Emma Goldman Jewish Landschaft Hall, the Los Angeles YM & YWHA, the reform temple in San Francisco.

The elevator of her hotel is filled with Retired Principals. They are definite, corseted women who crowd Beatrix at the Information Desk, the newsstand, and into the cafeteria. When she wants to sit alone, they seat themselves in her booth and then ignore her. The cafeteria has taken on a special character, like a Teachers' Lunchroom. Beatrix, over chicken salad, is back at McAfee Intermediate or is posing for Yearbook in High. She is ignored and begins to worry about promotion and self-promotion. She worries about grades, report cards, honor points among the critics. It makes her nervous to rise and leave her dishes on the table. The women glance at her plate to see if she's cleaned everything off. Beatrix wonders if she should carry soiled silverware and plates away on an aluminum tray.

She lies down on the textured spread of her hotel-room bed, which proceeds to spread its mottled pattern over her arms and neck. Beatrix reads the literary gossip column of the *San Francisco Chronicle*. Despite thirteen speeches in two weeks, Bea is not gossiped about. She has failed to be promoted. Who is gossiped about is HAROLD STONE: ex-restaurateur, ex-educator, ex-promoter of prize fights, rock concerts, and poetry readings. He is into something new, porno-promo, working out of his own film company, Hillel House. They are shooting in Mill Valley. Beatrix goes on location to locate her ex-husband.

She ferries across the Bay in a boat that is hours off schedule. A woman stands next to her on the pier waiting, wearing a long skirt and carrying a basket of eggs. She never moves, never tires. On the boat ride the woman stands at the prow, the wind billowing her skirt, scrambling her hair, her basket steady under her arm.

Bea has been wearing a pantsuit and carrying an overnight case. She has been restless during the wait, sitting on the dock, asking the time every fifteen minutes. During the boat ride, Bea goes into the rest room to change pantsuit for folksy smart, reappearing in a Pakistani purple skirt, Yemenite silver coin earrings. She stands next to the solid figure of the woman with the eggs. Bea picks up and puts down her overnight case. She stands at the prow, walks to the stern, and passes Alcatraz and other rocks without thinking about them.

The boat docks near an amusement hall full of nickelodeons, pianolas, animated wooden figures engaged in running trains or in training animals. Ticket booths of mechanical fortune-tellers move their eyes, heads, arms but deliver vague fortunes to Beatrix.

It is near the amusement palace that she finds Harold Stone and the Hillel House crew. They are surrounded by signs: "HEALTH HAZARD."

"THIS IS AN EXPERIMENT CONDUCTED BY THE DEPARTMENT OF HEALTH, EDUCATION AND WELFARE."

His cast is standing or sitting in a series of booths.

"Harold!" calls Beatrix.

"Shh!" someone tells her.

"HAAROOOOLD!" says Beatrix.

Harold turns.

"No thanks," he says. "You're too old."

Beatrix advances on him. There is no possible way for them to recognize each other from over twenty years ago. How could Harold recognize her when he knew that Eugene V. Debber in slacks, size 44 men's shirts, no makeup, uncontrolled hair, puffy brows, someone given to shrieking at her mother or tearing into him? The woman confronting him is no crybaby. She must be somebody's Old Lady, wearing careful hair and Pakistani purple. She's wearing dude shoes, rings on each finger, bells and coins on her ears.

"Get her off the set," says Harold.

"What's happened to you, Harold?" Beatrix asks in astonishment.

Nothing, except age, disease, baldness, and corpulence. His head is a doorknob. His features are squeezed together. His chin reverberates after each phrase. He is wearing a vest over no shirt. His stomach is lifted by his pants belt until it is riding high on his chest. Harold is wearing leather cowboy boots.

"Where is Lena?" she asks.

"Will somebody do something about this personage," says Harold.

"LENA GURNEV PALMER-STEINER," says Beatrix. "Where is she?"

"What's she doing? Calling for her Pomeranian?"

"LEENA!" shouts Beatrix. "Where are you?"

She is becoming frantic. She is sure that in the cast of young men and women she has seen Lena. She runs around to the other side of the set where the booths are open. They are outhouses. It is a row of toilets. The name of the film is posted: WC ON THE WC.

In each booth someone is active. In one, a camera is filming a young boy urinating, a boy about twelve. In the next, a man is defecating and grunting. He holds a mike against his mouth. In the third, a spread-legged girl is busy with urination, defecation, and constipation. In the fourth, a man is urinating between a girl's legs. In the fifth, a man is urinating into a girl's mouth. In the sixth—.

Beatrix backs away, aghast. In this pose Harold recognizes her.

"Beatrix," he says. "Baby. . . . My wife," he tells everyone. "My child bride, from whom I had a child. I never saw the child, didn't, in fact, see much of that child bride." His cast has gathered around him.

Beatrix, however, was right. She did see someone else whom she knew. Someone in orange wig, someone lined up to use the "facilities." Lena slips away.

"Let's go to the chow wagon, honey," Harold tells Beatrix.

They go, instead, to an ice cream parlor in this quaint town, an ice cream parlor with homemade ice cream, homemade rough wooden booths.

Harold is chatty. His voice becomes an English major's:

"It's a new subject. Water Closet on the West Coast. Hasn't been dealt with visually. Got the idea from Documenta 4 at Kassel, Germany, when they showed German artists into these trips, cutting pieces off their penises, slashing themselves—the body is the canvas. They defecated into each other's mouths. The body is the receptacle. I hated it, Beatrix. I loved it. Very Swiftian, scatological. I am trying to bring the satirical methodology of the eighteenth century to this hypocritical age. . . ."

Beatrix, giver of thirteen recent speeches, is speechless.

"Know how I got into it?" asked Harold. "From instinct. From honoring my past. What did I love the most from the past?"

Beatrix is looking at her coffee. There is no cream in this quaint place. There is that ersatz vegetable milk that oils on the surface of the coffee. She is drinking chicken-soup coffee.

Clearly, she was not what he loved best from the past.

"My job as a movie usher," said Harold. "In High I ushered at the Linwood LaSalle. I wore a uniform the color of your skirt and carried a flashlight. I poked into balconies with it, at the sides of the theater, the back rows, up girls' legs, into people's eyes. That was power. To cast a little light into the Midwest darkness."

He is consciously overstating. His eyes are also shifting. He wants to go back to his set, and she has unsettled him.

"Where is Lena?" asks Beatrix.

"I don't know any Lena," says Harold. "Honest, Bea. I never knew a Lena."

"Maybe she changed her name," says Beatrix forlornly.

"For God's sake," says Harold. He waves for the restaurant check.

"My daughter," says Beatrix. "She left home a while ago, a year—maybe three."

"Why would I know where your daughter is?"

"She's *your* daughter!"

"No," says Harold. "What you don't have isn't yours. She isn't your daughter, either."

He holds her by the elbow, releases the elbow to pay the overpriced bill.

"It's a Brechtian concept," says Harold, "as exemplified in *The Caucasian Chalk Circle*. There's a rather crude translation by Bentley:

> what there is shall go to those who are good for it,
> . . . the children to the motherly . . .
> The carts to good drivers . . .

Were you motherly, Beatrix? Or a good driver?"

While Harold is holding forth, off the set goes Lena, wearing her orange wig, her spangled Liza Minnelli glasses. She is cheap *Cabaret*. As mother tracks, she backs off. As mother searches, she disperses.

Where Do Daughters Go When They Go Out?

Into the receiving blanket of the world.

> Lena Gurnev Palmer-Steiner
> Went to the East, went to the West
> Looked for the very ones
> That she loved best.

She found: a talking live oak. The tree spirit inside of the knot called her into the forest. Its gnarled mouth spoke. Toothless gums opened. Woodpeckered freckles flashed at her. The Spanish moss made it hoary and the old face of the tree said,

"Lena Gurnev Palmer-Steiner, go out of the woods to the sea."

She goes to the sea, ankle-deep, she the embryo reentering the brine. Her legs goose-pimple. Her knees freeze. Her thighs sigh. Her cunt grunts.

Arms of waves beckon, further out. Fingers of waves clutch at her. Her nipples shrivel. It's high tide. She's thrown back on shore.

She goes into the sky. She floats wispily across the moon. She indulges in clouds, sparkles through stars.

Lena Gurnev Palmer-Steiner, descend! She is a balloonist, an ascensionist.

On land her mother pulls the umbilical cord. The balloon of Lena Gurnev Palmer-Steiner floats to earth.

Looking for Fathers (4)

Can one follow father? Into the front seat of the auto, putting your head on his shoulder. Onto the dance floor, arm on his. At a restaurant, eating by candlelight across from him.

You and father retire, carrying lanterns to light the stairway. You pause on the landing to kiss good night.

206

"Good night, my father."

"Good night, beloved daughter."

You enter your separate rooms, turn down the covers, plump the pillows, remove lounging garments, and recline. You cannot sleep. You rise from your bed and tiptoe on thick carpeting to his room. He is awaiting you.

Looking for Fathers (5)

She looks for fathers: behind doors, inside of offices, through revolving, department-store entrances.

She looks for fathers up escalators, down elevators.

She looks for fathers from the dental chair, for they will drill into her.

She looks for fathers breaking up cement, drilling next to her.

She looks for fathers in uniform, whistling and directing the traffic of her.

She looks for fathers with reflecting shields, operating on her.

She looks for fathers behind desks, remonstrating her.

She looks for fathers filling out forms, informing her.

She looks for grandmothers.

She folds her writing into their laps and they envelop her.

She opens her beak in their kitchenette and they cut her meat into bite-sized pieces, blow into her soup spoon to cool the broth, mash the carrots with butter to slide it down her gullet.

She puts her mouth against their ear. They hear all she has never uttered.

She puts her mouth against their breasts. The milk of the grandmothers flows again.

She puts her ear against their mouths and they fill her hungry ear with the words of lovers.

Lena Gurnev Palmer-Steiner, come home.

Beatrix at Home

Beatrix at Home

"Mother, I am pregnant with a baby girl and she criticizes me."

"What does she criticize?"

"She criticizes me for dyeing my hair, shaving under my arms and on my legs, for trimming my pubic hair, for putting on Mitchum super-dry deodorant, for clipping my cuticles, reshaping my hairline, piercing my earlobes, pedicuring my feet, polishing my nails, exercising my ankles by stepping on and off thick books."

"She criticizes you because she will be doing that, too."

Beatrix has returned home. She is reading the local press.

WOMAN'S BODY BELONGS TO MAN, SAYS MINISTER.

"The abortion reform bill is wrong," the Rev. Charles Williams, president of the . . . Baptist Ministers Conference said Monday, "because it sanctions killing and because it leaves the decision to

211

doctors, most of whom don't believe in God, and to women whose bodies don't really belong to themselves.

"No woman's body belongs to her," he told a press conference sponsored by antiabortionists. "I don't know who told them a dream like that. My wife belongs to me. She belonged to her daddy until she belonged to me."

Buttressing his statements from the baby-blue-bound, gilt-edged Bible . . . Williams read, "In sorrow thou shalt bring forth children."

Some of that is true.

Weighty Bea

Bea has gained weight. She will soon develop thick ankles, high blood pressure, lethargic habits. She will have to buy her clothing at the Big Girls Shoppe.

She goes on a diet with Pound Watchers.

For Breakfast: 1 egg or hard cheese and 1 slice bread

For Lunch: fish or lean meat and 1 slice bread

For Dinner: lean meat, broiled fish, and fresh vegetable salad.

Bea must not despair. Pound Watchers will not leave her cupboards bare. It is all compensation. For no husband, husbanding ways. For no children, childish habits. For no lover, self-love.

Pound Watchers carefully arranged for her snack.

Snack Bowl at Night: slices of green pepper, cucumber, celery, shredded red cabbage.

"Nosh to your heart's delight!"

Bea Gives Thanks

Beatrix makes a Thanksgiving turkey. She tapes the menu onto her refrigerator so she won't forget any of the side dishes.

She is serving:
    Turkey
    Chestnut stuffing
    Cranberries and orange slivers
    Candied kumquats
    Onions and white sauce
    Sweet potatoes in glazed apples
    Eggplant salad
    Carrot torte
    Pumpkin and pecan pies
Her parents are invited to eat at an aunt's.
Beatrix eats alone.

Muscley Bea

If she cannot do it for herself, Exercise Ed will do it for her.

There he is on the cover of her exercise book, crouching as if doing the *kazatzki*. If she does her knee bends, she, too, will be a cossack.

"Hi girls!" says Exercise Ed. "Let's exercise!"

If she lies on her back, lifts her knee, and touches it over the other leg to the floor, if she reverses this process with the other leg, at least fifteen times a day, says Exercise Ed, "Watch those hips shape up!"

There is a double knee over.

"The waistline will benefit a good deal from this one, too," promises Ed.

"Ed, do you promise?"

"Bea, I solemnly promise."

She can do the "Sitting Bounces," which Ed calls "a fun exercise." Bea can do the Scissors Legs and "snip the hips away." Bea can do arm exercises, tummies aweigh, and bust exercises, but, warns Exercise Ed, "They work best when you're SMILING!"

Bea will exercise and exercise but she will never look muscular like Exercise Ed.

The Faces of Bea

Bea readily admits that she is ignorant about her facial muscles. She never knew, as Fanny Face-Saving tells her, that "every muscle of the face is there to do its job." Bea never knew that "every muscle of the face has a beginning and an ending."

Bea is ready. Bea is set. Bea will go:

First her forehead and scalp muscles have a beginning and an ending, then her eyelids, upper lip and mouth, cheeks, nose, chin, and throat. All, all working for Bea.

Each scalp raise will lower her age. Time will freeze with every eye squeeze. She will firm the skin of the chin. She will smooth every facial groove.

Bea does this one-half hour every day. She becomes flushed, easily tired, and bad-tempered.

Tinting Bea

Bea does not want to be her age. Bea does not want to be her color. Bea does not want to be her shape.

Bea's hair wants to be gray every two weeks but Bea must combat colorlessness with various hues, Natural Auburn, Natural Brown, Natural Black.

Bea readies the operation:

    rubber gloves
    plastic shoulder cape and towel
    scissors
    newspaper covering sink
    cold cream to wipe off streaking on the face
    a clock
    a book to read during the 25 minutes or the additional 20
        minutes to make sure the stubborn gray is pene-
        trated.

The directions begin with a warning: "to do so may cause blindness."

You are promised that your new hair color will leave your hair extra shiny, extra manageable.

It has taken Bea the whole morning. She will have to do it again soon.

Bea and TV

One Sunday, August 26, Bea reads the listing of TV movies for the day.

At noon on Sunday she can see *Student Prince* (1954) with Ann Blythe and Edmond Purdom (voice by Mario Lanza) or *Ride Beyond Vengeance* (1966) or *Stopover Tokyo* (1956) with Robert Wagner and Joan Collins.

At 1:00 P.M. she can see *My Six Loves* (1962) with Debbie Reynolds and Cliff Robertson.

At 2:00 P.M. she has vast choice: *Jennifer* (1935) with Howard Duff and Ida Lupino; *Kenya, Country of Treasure; Heart of the Golden West* (1942) with Roy Rogers and Gabby Hayes; *They Won't Believe Me* (1947) with Robert Young and Susan Hayward.

At 4:00 P.M., Bea can watch *Three Brave Men* (1957) with Ray Milland and Nina Foch.

At 6:00 P.M., *We Joined the Navy* (1962) is playing.

At 7:30 P.M. is *Twist of Fate* (1954) with Ginger Rogers and Jacques Bergerac.

At 8:00 P.M. is *That Certain Woman* (1956) with Bette Davis and Henry Fonda.

At 11:45 P.M. is *Three Bites of an Apple* (1967) with Tammy Grimes.

At midnight: *Danger Has Two Faces* (1966) or *The Last Adventure*.

Beatrix need not watch a movie. She has other choices open to her.

She can see "The Partridge Family" on Channel 5. She can see "Eleven Year Itch" at 8 P.M. where "Danny learns the vagaries of the female heart."

If Bea wishes to rise early or if she cannot sleep the night through, she can see "Agriculture USA" at 6:22 A.M. on Channel 5. Eight minutes later, at 6:30, on the same channel, she can see "Agriculture Today."

At 7 A.M. is "Fantasy Funhouse" or "Gilligan's Island," or "Pebbles and Bam Bam." "Lassie" is still around at that hour.

At 11 there is "Wrestling" on Channel 56. At 12:30 there is again wrestling. At 1 there is "Golf for Swingers" or "I Love Lucy." There is more wrestling on Channel 12.

At 1:30 is "Roller Derby." At 3 there is wrestling or, if she wishes, "I Love Lucy" repeats yet once more at 6 P.M.

Bea can go through the whole day without a movie. But if she wants to see a film that night on TV, she can see *Dark Victory* (1939) with Bette Davis and George Brent. Bette Davis has an unnamable disease, and before she passes on (we should also not name our ending) she selects a worthy wife to service George Brent.

Tomorrow night Beatrix can watch another film with Bette Davis, Mr. George Brent, and Mary Astor. Both women service handsome, moustached George. He is reported missing in an airplane crash in the jungles of the Amazon.

"Give me something to live for! His child!" cries Bette to pregnant Mary.

It is *The Great Lie*.

Or Beatrix can watch other films in which Joan Leslie services James Craig (1948), Gloria Grahame services Rory Calhoun (1957), Claire Trevor services Robert Ryan (1951), and, in that same good year, June Allyson services Van Johnson in *Too Young to Kiss*.

Diet, darling Beatrix. Have your recreation. Everything in moderation. But don't deprive yourself.

216

From Embryo to Out You Go

Embryein (gr.), to swell inside. Compare to *sauerkraut; qairu* (Goth.), thorn; *veru*, spit; *bryein*, to swell.

That sauerkraut is swelling inside. Each leaf is added, each thick, veined sheet; the sauerkraut of the brain is growing. The cabbage of the head and belly are layering. The *thorn* of the body is pricking. The *spit* is gathering in the sewer.

Fetus—see *feminine*. Feminine is *female* (ME variant influenced by male, diminutive). *Dhei*, to suck reduced form *dhe-mna*, in Latin *femina*. Suffix reduced form *dhe-to* in Latin *fetus* . . . *dhe-kundo* in Latin *fecundus*, fruitful . . . fertile, lucky, happy (*felicity*). *Delu* (OE), nipple; *tila* (OHG), feminine breast. Also see *fellatio*.

If an "unhatched young vertebrate," an "embryo," soaks in that female brine, is to be nourished by the *delu* and the *tila*, and all of life is pickled and floating and will be suckled by that originator, that fruitful, happy, lucky originator, no wonder then that men, not feminine, must hate us. We are the inception, the water jar, the nourishment, the expelling from the Garden of Eden.

How could they not hate us? There is little for them to do if we are conception, reproduction, resurrection. They must hate our breast. Why else do they grab it? They must hate our brine. Why else do they jab it?

They grow too big to slip back in through the slits of nipple, the eye of the navel, the mouth of the womb.

So they punish us at birth and give us pain and punish us in life and give us pain.

Periodical Bea

For no good reason on this earth, Bea still fertilizes.

Being an imprecise person, Bea cannot possibly follow exact tampon directions. She cannot make decisions between:

217

a. placing one foot on the toilet or chair, or
b. sitting on the toilet seat with knees apart, or
c. squatting slightly with legs apart
whichever seems most natural and comfortable for you.

None did, none was. Poking with that cardboard Tootsie Roll between bladder, rectum, vagina, hoping, as in some dime-store game, to fit rolling object into right hole, she invariably ended up leaving in the cardboard and pulling out the cotton. Or she would end up with bloody fingers and the tampon floating inaccurately in a sea of blood.

Those careful explanations of what to do with grasping thumb and forefinger, aiming directly at the small of the back, removing the forefinger to free the withdrawal cord, all of that required an engineering student, a mechanical genius, or someone less shy about poking into cavities like a dental assistant.

Bea sidles up to the drugstore counter, trying to avoid the gray-haired man behind the cash register, trying not to stand near the male customers in line. She has selected her napkin, her dinner napkin, her breakfast napkin, her man-sized napkin, not folded next to her plate, not folded under her chin, not folded in her lap, her neat napkin folded between her legs.

She can have Stayfree and run, like the black-haired beauty in gossamer dress, through green fields. In gossamer dress? Nowhere under that transparent material can Bea make out belts, pins, metal tips, wads of cotton batting.

Bea, all of her life, has failed the menstrual ads. They were so discreet, they whispered. She would never, if she heeded them, be inconvenienced by bleeding, backaches, nausea, bad circulation in feet and hands, twitching of leg muscles, chills, or cracked lips. The girls in the Land of Magazine Menstruation, the girls with periods in the periodicals leap immediately into the water, wearing tight swimsuits or, in short, crisp, white, swinging tennis skirts, there they were out on the court!

Bea was taking mincing steps from bed to bathroom, bed to

218

teakettle. Not those girls who won blue ribbons at horse meets, who attended balls gowned in Modess.

At the store she bought boxes, daintily marked like handkerchief or stationery boxes. Soon all sanitary products would be sold in stationery stores. On each napkin would be the wearer's initials. Have them monogrammed for your best friend!

She carries these boxes home proudly, not in the old brown paper bag. Her Stayfree goddess trips through a blur of green. On each box, flora, fleurs-de-lis, green mint leaves, Kotex-blue roses. The boxes vie for euphemism and fantasy. Tear along the perforated edge for a visual experience of napkins backed in green or pink. Smell them. They are perfumed. Wear them as edgings on cashmere sweaters. Wear them as earmuffs in cold weather.

Bea wonders if she is normal, if she has ever really menstruated in her life. Perhaps it is all psychology and if she were less neurotic, she, too, could roll in dewy flowers, jump hurdles with her stallion, or dive from the highest board.

The Orphan

Beatrix has bursitis. Beatrix has dandruffitis. Beatrix has colitis.

Factory smokestacks have entered her lungs. She is developing emphysema. Soot has settled on her skin. She has burnings and itchings. She never leaves the house in winter. Her ankles swell.

Nevertheless, Beatrix Palmer is regal. She is receiving royalties from *The Pioneers, Remnants, Mothers and Daughters*. She is given her third advance for *Unafraid Women*.

Her parents have passed away into the unmentionable place where Bette Davis goes when she goes out.

Beatrix is tired. When parents go, you are not only orphaned, you are stepped up a generation. She wants to retire.

Good-bye, French teacher, *ma chère*, who has suffered from an unmentionable disease. Good-bye, Bald Chemistry, now bald all over. Jewish Math is hanging on, working out problems.

Romanian Lois has jumped out of the window of the Medical Building. Her two daughters are sent to boarding school. Her husband marries the daughter of the doctor in the next suite.

Janice has reunited with her husband. He is fading. He is becoming a white man.

Shirley descends from the attic and takes over the kitchen. She flushes out her old aunt, hitting her with a crutch. The old aunt falls down the steps of the porch, which she had so well guarded, and bruises her knees on the cement.

Pauline's liquor-store-owner friend dies and leaves her his savings. Her mother dies and leaves her alone. Pauline enrolls at the Yale School of Architecture.

The high school Yearbook for fifteen years had a black cover and Black graduates. This year it has an Arabic cover and Lebanese graduates. City University no longer enrolls whites. One has a choice of majors: Black Literature, Black Music, Black Arts, Black History, Urban Law as Related to the Third World, Third World Psychology, Third World Medicine, The Third World and Women, Third World Dance, Teaching Skills for the Third World.

Beatrix's past has fallen from the embankment.

She is thinking seriously of commencing Old Age.

Looking for Shells

The Sheller

This is a story.

It is feeding time. A man in tan shorts, whose hem has become unpressed, throws bread to the gulls. The gulls are noisier than the passing motorboats. Sandpipers, walking daintily into the surf, peck momentary holes in the sand. Pelicans, upside-down diving for fish, are long, long under water.

She walks the beach, Beatrix Palmer. From heel to toe shells are crunched, her soles scratched by gastropods. The Florida Cerith, a miniature Siamese tower, drills into her heel. The slipper shells collect between her toes. She picks up a red-veined slipper, turns it over, sees the pearly half-ledge, discards it, thinking someone else's heavy tread broke the other half of the ledge. It is not Beatrix Palmer's first mistake.

No letters arrive along with the *Key News*. No phone calls vibrate. At her window Australian pines drop their cones. An albino cat mews to be let in, then becomes frantic to go out again. From her window a blue heron perches on the wooden pilings.

She forgot to put the sand dollars into the sun. They are on the coffee table, like uncut cookie dough, with their five petals and five slashes cut into the off-white uneven circle. They are molding. Green almost obliterates the daisy-shape and speckles, like poppy seed, the slight hump of the animal. It is offensive to her to see that spreading mold. She turns it over. The shapes are inclusive on the flat back, like claws, fronds, like clusters of leaves. They remain upside down on her coffee table.

All is upside down—the diving birds, the sand dollars, and her day. For the sun is too hot to sun in, she discovered, lying on the sand, the sugary-white sand, that first day of arrival and burning her eyelids so that she had to wear sunglasses for a week. She looked puffy-lidded and Oriental, but then, when the puffiness deflated, the lids shriveled and she became older, like the leathery retirees around her.

So she covers herself tightly in the sun with a green overpriced cotton hat from the shopping center near Sarasota.

If she shells she stoops, rising suddenly. Far down on the public beach she thinks she sees green, green moving slowly toward her, expanding brightly, her own light-green hat, walking on a stick, on branches of legs. There are no eyes under the hat. The mouth is smiling; no, sneering.

There is another green hat tickling, like a blade of grass at the back of her neck. Years ago. A green paper crown cut out of bunting. Under it straggles a green-dyed mop, the strands separating over the shoulder, curling on a nylon curtain, dyed light green, over a green dress, whose cap sleeve is visible, as is the pinkish arm through the gossamer curtain. The hands are folded on the lap. The pink lips—is it the color film, too brownish?—are slightly separated and the light sparkles on a bit of a tooth. What has come into her head with the shimmering green queen? Is it Halloween? A St. Patrick's Day affair?

224

She stumbles over spiny shells, spiky shells, abalone fish scales, shells stuck inside of other shells until she is at her own efficiency apartment with its indoor-outdoor green carpeting (for grass in winter climates, for grass in sandy ones). She pulls the drapery cord against the sun and the aquamarine Gulf, purple further out where the sandy bottom is not visible.

She glues scallop shells to driftwood.

"Elmer's Glue," said the crackly voices at the Art Club. "That makes it really stick."

They glue their shells and sell each other their own arrangements.

Beatrix Palmer glues a white scallop shell with its finlike projections next to a red-ribbed scallop shell. The coloring is fading from the red shell as the shell dries, so Beatrix sprinkles water on the shell and bluish gray appears under the red. She fancies selling the shells with a circulating spray, a pump that will wet them so they can retain their sea color. The two shells, white and damp bluish gray under red, are turned sideways, facing the center. There, slightly elevated, is the most beautiful scallop of the beach—a sherbety peach with white edges and projections like whiskers.

The room darkens, a squall storm coming up. Rain—and more of her shells drying outside!

A storm is at another cottage. She reads, in a lettered rather than scripted hand:

You always hear seagulls and boats' horns and a little repair work on the docks in the morning. Right now the foghorn is booming every few seconds:

> B-o-o-o-o-o-o-om.
> B-o-o-o-o-o-om.
> B-o-o-o-o-om.
> B-o-o-o-om.

Pardon me, but due to an unquiet rest last night, the author of these reminiscences has just fallen asleep. Therefore, in the author's stead, I bring this odyssey to a close. Fin.

It was Lena, after a summer in London, during a summer in Maine.

The same cabin, some years before "the author" could write, could only print, could only print capital letters, Beatrix had a record of The Weeping Willow, The Seagulls, The Pretty Clouds, The Dark Room.

The Weeping Willow rested on tall grass, crayoned red green yellow blue green. The trunk was shaped like an ice cream cone and was colored blackish brown. The willow leaves were each a separate color, red, yellow, black, green, alternating.

The Seagulls were plants of gulls with wings like leaves, with head and beak of flowers. The Pretty Clouds were more conventional, with purple-aquamarine-green-yellow-black-crayoned clouds. In the same order of color, flowers sprouted below.

The Dark Room had red dark walls, dark blue drapes, purple rug, dark green lamp, brown lamp cord, huge brown electrical outlet. Although Beatrix has now opened her drapes, in the light of the squall it is still The Dark Room.

To the tune of "Swanee River" ("The home of Stephen Foster," said the billboards on her way down through Ohio, Kentucky, and on to Florida), the oldies had sung: "Now we are gathered for Barney Greenstone, who's sixty-three."

He was also the baby of the group, a bouncy, overweight baby boy. They cuddled him, treasured him, would have glued him on driftwood to set their own memories of ten, twenty years before. He was also, until Beatrix arrived, the only Jew on Dolphin Key. He had widely spaced teeth, a moustache, and an aggressive stomach, and he aggressed toward Beatrix with his hairy mouth and aerated teeth.

He invites her into the pool of his condominium. But he is so busy greeting people at both the shallow and deep ends of this small pool and introducing her that she has no chance to swim. Mr. Greenstone is very social.

He calls to take her to Marina Jacks. They will view the sunset from that ideal spot, but he has been busy greeting people before he picks her up and they miss the sunset, park too far from the restaurant and have a several block walk. They do have a table overlooking the water but with no streaked sky or dramatic sun. It is better when twin lights go on above and then below, shimmering in the water. It is better when the green turtle soup arrives. It is *not* better when Barney talks about his *netsukes*. It is *not* better when he drives her back to his condominium to show them to her, Japanese toggles, behind an ornate glass case. Each is dwarfed, humped, a gargoyle; each is a scowling big-headed miniature; each is a peasant carrying fruit or a miniature baby. It is *not* better when Barney reads her their papers, the history of each toggle and of their carver.

He goes to get her a glass of wine. Beatrix is fast asleep on his couch, not leaning or stretching out but sitting stiffly, head erect and snoring.

The jingle shells around her jingle, common in these warm waters. She holds them in her palm, a monochromatic study ranging from pearly white, mottled bluish gray to a dark gray, about or less than an inch, none regular, none flat or in smooth circles.

She has collected ten eared-ark shells, heavy, clumsy, thickish things, strongly ribbed, irregularly marked. The rich black around the edge looks as if it were dipped in tar. The eared ark is less clumsy upside down with its regular fluted, toothed hinge line.

These smooth ears of shells.

The sun through Baby Lena's ear, a red sun, for Baby Lena has a port-wine stain.

"Nothing serious, just a cosmetic difficulty," Beatrix is told by her pediatrician.

When Baby Lena grows up and can see herself in the mirror, she never again allows her hair to be cut or her ears to show.

The squall storm is over. Light mottles the front yard of Australian pines. The pines clean their own grounds with fir needles. The sun mottles in her eyes.

There is Baby Lena by flecked light, ears projecting, eyes squinting, green gingham dress faded in the snapshot, green rattle faded in her mouth. The background, seen above the ledge of the yellow-lined carriage, is in splotches of greens and yellows and is not recognizable.

Before that. The baby stretching its arms on the couch.

"How big?"

"So big!"

The baby, not yet strong enough to sit up alone, leans over the balancing weight of her Buddha stomach and thickly diapered bottom. She has fallen backward in the yellow-lined carriage. Her mouth is spread. Her ears are spread. Her hands hug each other. The belly button winks, and holes of cheek, elbow, and knee dimple.

That's when Beatrix had gained too much weight. She is in red jeans and red-checkered shirt. Her thick hair is fastened back. Her legs fill the jean pants. Her hips fill the pockets. Her breasts, milk-filled, stuff the red gingham shirt. She, although a young woman, has fatty pouches under her cheeks.

Black and white snap. She has her red shawl over one shoulder, her nursing shawl. It is dark gray in the photograph. Her hair is very black, pinned in place as befits a nursing mother. There is the soft black of new baby's hair against her hand. There is the receiving blanket, photographed white. There is the black cord of the watchband against her wrist, the white sparkling face of watch, the lipstick 1950s red, a beauty mark on her left cheek. There is her plaid pull-out couch losing a button. There is the infant's fist lost on the hill of the breast. There is the nipple a circle around the mouth. No one is reading the time on the watch. Harold Steiner has since disliked both faces, the watch's and her own.

She has a two-burner efficiency kitchen behind the blinds and reaches over her head to the shelves for a plate. She bought cheese and fruit at the supermarket, but the cheese is sweating and the fruit is molding.

There is a scramble on her hand, a leap, a scream. Who screamed? It could not have been that big South American cockroach that screamed. She chases it with a wet beach towel, slams it, kills it, and kills it again. She cannot let it go, not the tiniest quiver of the legs, of the antennae, the wings. It is curled and small when she flushes it down the toilet.

Barney's car drives up and he laughs at her breathless account of the hunt and the bagged game. He will take her to the Ringling Museum. It is still hot out. She puts on her green sun hat, a towel dress in greens and blues that she has worn every summer for ten years. She needs no bra for her breasts have not been milk-filled in many years.

"I can't identify everything," she tells Barney.

He can for, along with his condominium, he purchased *Golden Nature Guide, 475 Marine Subjects in Full Color*.

She can identify people along the beach.

They are, besides the oldies, a few bikinied grandchildren, golden rather than leathered. Surprisingly, there are the Amish, bonneted, bearded, suspendered, sitting near the hot dog stand and picnic tables, in the hot sun.

Do the Amish, through their beards and bonnet crowns, look at the smooth flesh of the bathers? Do those old men, with white shirts and black pants, see a colorful world beyond them, under the palms, away from the garish red of hot dogs, the falsely colored orange drink? Do they see that world of blue, green, brown of eye, pink of lips, curve of hips?

Beatrix Palmer's cheek.

Beatrix Palmer's cheek is to be scratched. On the day of the visit. It is to be a thin red vein of a scratch, as on the slipper shells. It is to be a thin rib of blood along her shell of cheek. The nail will catch her cheek, Lena's bitten, jagged nail, so that the mark on the cheek will not be a straight line but a dot-dashed one where the nail is or is bitten away.

Beatrix Palmer's face will have the scowl of Barney's *netsukes*. In a broken whirl, in sun that seems to glare from bits of mirror, Beatrix Palmer will strike back at the attacker and will catch the corner of an eye with her own sharp, mist-pink nail polish, and will pull Lena's eye Oriental.

Barney takes her into the hot sun of the Ringling Museum courtyard. They walk through a transplanted Roman villa, gauche, not grand, into the art gallery. Circuslike paintings, crowd-catching biblical scenes are playing. A particularly repeated theme is Judith with the Head of Holofernes.

There are large paintings of Rubens' bulging bodies from his body factory. There are those three circus rings of biblical scenes, everything visible from the top of the bleachers. There is Barney, stomach bouncing, hairs of moustache blowing as he explains, as he explains. Beatrix becomes thirsty and irritable.

"I can't write, I can't speak," said the loose-leaf sheet which Beatrix found after one of the disappearances and revisits. "I no longer think. Feeling and pictures have taken over. Now Mrs. Kennedy is pregnant with an eleventh child and there are the constant assassinations, assassinations as common as births. I cry & mother weeps, tears falling on my head in her lap. I don't understand and therefore no words, no logical, comprehending words come to calm me. I am 16 & it is unfair that people at 16 must think about the country's fate, must experience the pain.

"Come, Hades, give me a taste of your medicine. Cure me of the life force. Last week at Jim's I tried your medicine, powerful Hades. And mother found me and laughed and screamed, 'You are sick. If I had the money I'd put you in an institution,' and I, in my pain, hear her laughing scream, and she slaps me to show me how much she loves me, and the doctor on the radio tells of slapping Kennedy to hear a heartbeat and the pulse, and he hands the stethoscope to Ethel Kennedy to listen."

Barney goes into the carpentry shop to buy Mrs. Palmer a Coke. There is a box for dimes on top of the refrigerator. He helps himself, puts in his dimes and carries out the bottles. The guard stops him, so they drink the Cokes in the carpentry shop.

They drive back, Barney one hand on the wheel, the other holding Mrs. Palmer's. The waves are high and there are the high-pitched cries of the sandpipers. Barney parks the car at her rented efficiency and walks with her along the beach. Waves implode, a dull thud as of distant thunder. Later the waves slam against the groins that jut out from each beach home. The pilings have been built recently to stop the loss of the beach.

"That's forty thousand dollars worth of pilings," says Barney. "I don't know if the Gulf takes away more than it gives."

Shells are piled against each wooden beach barrier. There are the most delicate fingernail pink of shells, spirals of shells, jellyfish shimmering on the sand. When the sea recedes the shells are left behind like buttons on a mattress. Black-headed gulls stand on the water's edge.

Barney and Beatrix find tar on their sandals. The odor is brackish. Beatrix will not let Barney come into the apartment for he has tar between his toes. They stretch out on the steps and wiggle their toes at each other. In the greening evening their toes are like seaweed.

Beatrix remarks on the Spanish moss draped on a neighbor's trees.

"Like lace shawls," says Beatrix.

"Like cannibals," says Barney. "They eat up the trees."

Moon shells are drying on the stoop, each a carnivore that engulfed and smothered other shellfish. Barney studies them with his porpoise eyes. There is the Shark Eye staring back at him.

Beatrix is proudest of her Florida Fighting Conches with their pagoda tops, the orange, golden, purple pearly interiors. She has found a West Indian Fighting Conch also.

Barney wants her to return with him to the condominium.

"Not *netsukes*," he promises. "I have the largest conches in the Crafts Club, twelve-inch Queen Conches, fourteen-inch Emperor Helmets. I have Giant Tuns. I have Fig Shells."

As she sits there, she again becomes sleepy and yawns. He is hurt and puts on his sandals. She is yawning too hard to apologize, but does wave as he drives away.

"NO THING UNITES US," said the outside of the airmail envelope, still capitals, all caps, no matter where the voyage overseas. But why write to say that? The yawning brought tears to Beatrix. The daughter had written to say more: a visit was pending, impending, rending.

Beatrix kept several ugly yet fascinating shells. One huge thing had barnacles all over it. Another was a thick, corroded, white oyster shell. Sand cemented small shells together. Beatrix kept a piece of sponge. And she kept letters, those corrosive letters.

"Was in Hawaii. Pretty uptight."

From some country whose postmark was obliterated:

"There's a cat on my lap listening. The light is dim afternoon before the rain. One auburn cow in all this green. Supersonic crickets. Everything that's still appears to be moving."

Months later, another card:

"One day a person entered a room feeling confused. I am nowhere. What can I do? A person answered saying when one is nowhere there is no thing to say and nothing to confuse. One is nowhere."

And where was Beatrix Palmer, who was considering investment in Old Age, in a condominium with her royalties, who was consulting a stock broker and a Dolphin Key bookmaker?

No child crossed her path. The oldies on the Key fled when a youngster approached. Their leases, Barney informed her, banned children under fifteen years of age. The few longhairs the Key people saw were hitchhikers on their way to Fort Lauderdale or Georgia kids down from Atlanta for a bit of warmth. The old drivers would grip the wheels of their cars tightly not to swerve suddenly upon them.

There was traffic through Dolphin Key, those schools of dolphins that leapt by in the early morning, the blue heron, cormorants, pelicans, and gulls. The oldies put these symbols on the doors of their houses, metal arching gulls, wrought-iron ships, tarpons, and dolphins.

The next morning Barney is by.

"Breakfast?" he grins.

"I have strawberries," says Beatrix, "cantaloupe, eggs."

She has not been spending her mornings writing. Afternoons she naps. Evenings there are social affairs.

"No," says Barney, "waffles, bacon, sausages."

It is a joyous thought for him, eating forbidden foods, bacon and pork sausages, the clams and lobsters from the other evening at Marina Jacks. He obeyed not Leviticus and set himself down in a condominium in this land of Gentiles.

In Beatrix Palmer's car were boxes of books. She took her research for *Unafraid Women*, her business contracts, her photo albums, her correspondence.

Last night Beatrix had opened her photo album. The album is of imitation leather with imitation golden tooling. She is kneeling in an early shot. Her arms are spread. She wears a black velveteen, sleeveless blouse. Her hair looks like black velveteen. Everything is darkened and lightened. Her skin is light Northern. Her flared skirt is very white with large black polka dots. On one knee is her daughter's head, her daughter's arms hugging that knee, the little girl's black hair a little bluer than the sleeveless black velveteen blouse that is its backdrop, the mouth closed but upturned, the eyes soft, the ears protruding, the port wine stain almost as red as the red knee socks. Mother and daughter are kneeling in the grass.

When had the sad pictures begun? The portents? The one with the red knitted hat that fastened under the chin, the red knitted sweater with large white pearl buttons, where she is seated on a furry pony and the pony's face, under its harness, is worried, not knowing who is on the saddle, on its velveteen red blanket with silver stars. The little girl is clutching her own hands rather than the reins. Her face is almost serious enough to be grim.

There is a picture in front of that screened-in cabin by the lake, long ago. The wind is blowing. The mother's hair is piled on top of her head in curls. The daughter's hair has loosened from the ponytail. She is holding something. A tube? Beatrix Palmer thinks it might be a frozen ice cream drumstick. The mouth is twisted. Worry? The sun in her eyes? Or just because she's been eating the drumstick?

Younger still. Lena on a park bench. Someone took the photo, not Beatrix Palmer for there is Beatrix Palmer in the background. A tiny part of Beatrix's rounded cheek, slender nose, a bit of her red-lipsticked smiling mouth, three or four upper teeth visible. Obscuring the rest of Beatrix's face is her daughter's, one eye large and round with worry or fear or resentment of the photographer. Lena's brows are knitted. The mouth is definitely in pain, the hair in need of combing. The dress is neatly ironed, the press marks showing on the cap sleeves.

Another photo, Lena at six with six of her upper baby teeth missing. Is that smile gay, impish, or malicious? Beatrix Palmer never knew, would never know.

At the Howard Johnson: waffles, sausages, toast, pats of butter, encapsulated marmalade, and old people.

In the next booth are a round-bellied, jeweled man with bulldog face and his prune-faced wife. With the wife everything had tightened to a scrunch; with the husband everything was loosened.

Another old man nearby was tight-faced, a stretched

skinned man with cheekbones cutting through the skin. Out of the window Beatrix Palmer saw a barrel of an old man with tiny feet skimming along the sidewalk.

They heard two couples talking in the lobby, while they awaited their tables.

"You can't trust California for the earthquakes," said one old man.

"You can't trust Florida for the sudden freeze," said the other.

"Trust Arizona," said one of the old ladies, holding her purse handles. "It cools down at night in Arizona and you can sleep."

"Looking all over," said the couples, "for a place to sleep."

Barney had listened, amused.

"Nobody dies in Florida," he tells Beatrix.

Beatrix Palmer will look down into the water. It will be clear. She will see depressions under her eyes. She will see the skin around her eye, left eye, is becoming cracked like mud. Too much sun? She will see several chins, or is it a slight hanging of the skin under the one chin? And a slight, light growth of colorless hair on the chin that she will not be able to see in the dark efficiency apartment, and therefore, cannot pluck. Her forehead will be drying and lining. Her bathing cap will be pulled off by her opponent and hurled away. Her hair will be pulled down toward the water by her opponent. Her mouth will be open above the water, stretched so wide the loose skin of the chin is taut. Soon her upper teeth will be covered by her upper lip as she will sink toward the water.

Barney has a surprise for her. A pen shell, a gross, ugly thing that he unwraps for her at the Howard Johnson table. It is almost a foot long, rough-shelled but inside it shines as if it were oil in sunlight, with glowing golds, bluish greens, purplish blues, and silver.

"I have another," Barney says. "Even larger. You're not depriving me of anything. Take it."

But does she want it?

"Do you want to watercolor with me on one of the other Keys?"

"I don't have paint or paper."

"You know me, old Barney from CIT."

"I know MIT. What's CIT?"

"Cleveland Institute of Technology."

"How well do I know you?"

"Well enough so that it will come as no surprise, after I pay the bill, leave the fifteen percent, that I came prepared with paper and watercolor paints."

They paint at the beach. She paints the froth of waves left against the groins of pilings, frothlike meringue, chiffon-jello. She paints the shells spilled to one side, the twinkling froth, sinking into the shell pile. She paints chips of shells, holes in bells. She paints brown seaweed, light green sea lettuce clinging like thin rubber.

He paints a little boy with a fishing pole, a little Black boy with a pail of worms, leaning over the bridge connecting the Keys. He paints the boats moored there. He paints an Amish man sitting on a rocking chair on the bridge.

There is a sudden bark. She drops her brush into the sand.

"Did my dog scare you?" asks the passing man. "She's exuberant this morning."

Beatrix's leg is bitten in a few minutes, the mean bite of a red ant.

He takes her to a cocktail party given at the Crafts Club. She is a new neighbor, maybe a permanent one. *The Saratoga Times* has listed her under Distinguished Visitors to the Keys and the Tampa paper has her in its column, Visitors Receiving Keys to the Kingdom.

The drinks are too strong. The men all look and sound like W. C. Fields. The women are sand-keeping machines, sweeping their men, flattening the white hair, tying their ties, dampening their faces, keeping their men in working order.

The men, freed of work, become the lives their women have always had to lead, frivolous, useless, full of crafts but not crafty, filling the time. Their bodies become their own floating rubber tubes in the condominium pools. They change clothes several times a day for changing social events.

No one hears the news or talks of it. No one reads the paper or talks of it, except for the listing of plays at the Ringling Museum, of movies in Tampa or Sarasota, of religious services, and those lists of visiting dignitaries to their Keys.

They discuss shelling with Beatrix. Only one man in the group works and he has to pay for it by missing the boating excursions, the craft classes, and the cocktail parties, or the swims in the heated pool.

They are proud that Beatrix has gathered a fairly rare gastropod, an olive shell with unusual markings, for the shell had cracked and had repaired itself. The shell is passed about.

Beatrix's hand will press down on the hair that is floating like seaweed and that, through the greenish water, is brown. Under water the strands separate like the strands of that St. Patrick's Day mop hair. Beatrix will press down more. Bubbles will appear and Beatrix will move her legs away from the scratching hands, the kicking legs. Beatrix will punch at the opened brown eyes, the gasping mouth, the stalk of neck. Beatrix's hand and face will become tired. The lines along her cheek will groove more deeply; the mouth will turn downward in strain.

One of the red-, swollen-nosed gentlemen of the Crafts Club is speaking to her.

"Your name's been bandied about, yes indeed, bandiieeed about."

The chairperson of the Crafts Club has clipped the items on Mrs. Palmer, encircling with magic marker the paragraph in which she's mentioned and obliterating the other names with the thick stroke.

In this world, Mrs. Palmer is decades younger than Barney, the baby.

"Come here, youngster," says Barney.

She is his exhibit, his seashell on driftwood, his enameled copper earrings and cuff links that he exhibits in the Crafts Members Gift Shop.

Beatrix will shell, walking as she always does, head down, early mornings or early evenings. She is becoming acquisitive and annoyed at another sheller's turkey wing or lovely pinkish tellin.

As she will walk head turned downward, there will be an obstinate shadow before her that will not move. She will step to one side. So will the shadow. She will look up into the eyes of a shadowed green sun hat, a bikini, a sneering smile, a daughter.

"I wondered where . . . I wondered when . . . ," says the mother.

"No where," says the daughter.

"Have you eaten?" asks Beatrix.

"Same mother," says Lena.

"Same daughter," says Beatrix.

They go into the efficiency. The daughter is a vegetarian so never mind the tuna or lamb chops. Now Beatrix has somebody to share the fruit, the too-soft avocado, the wilting greens. She wishes Lena would wash up, comb her hair. She wishes her daughter would take off the mother's green sun hat.

Beatrix rinses her hands, standing on the indoor-outdoor carpeting that extends from the wall kitchen into the bathroom.

Once there was a pink plastic birthday comb with a pink-framed mirror and a pink bow in Lena's hair. The pink comb combed the brown bangs. The eyes were looking at the mirror. The collar was frilled and fading into the neck. What color was that collar, was that dress? The mouth is open in concentration, almost in a smile at the mirror.

The mother can hear the Gulf, regular, splashing against the piles. They eat the salad, the fruit. The daughter finishes and laughs.

"I'm into meat again," she says.

"I can't please you," says the mother.

"That's right," says the daughter.

The night is full of: "Which of us is the kid?"

                         "Your cowardice or is it disinterest?"

                         "Answer me!"

                         "Are you afraid?"

                         "Who's your boyfriend this time?"

Who is talking? Beatrix cannot always tell.

"I still love you," Beatrix Palmer says to her daughter.

All the pain in the dressers of her bedrooms, all the pain that groaned with the opened drawer, the pain of notebooks, filled with drawings of drawn women. Later, from other lands, the drawings are crying, the eyes have tears but the tears have become hearts, pearls, seashells. The drawings are in a lovely, hand-bound book (bound by her nowhere-bound daughter) from India. They are on soft paper and the ink of the Indian fantasies has spread slightly.

There will be a bite under water, the mouth will turn on the mother's arm and bite it until the hand lets go of the hair. The daughter will slowly ascend to the surface, floating upward, while the mother will rub the teeth marks in her arm. Slowly, slowly the daughter will walk the water back to shore, back to the efficiency that housed a night of accusation. The daughter will pick up her mother's sun hat and put it on her wet hair.

The mother will be left, bereft. They had drowned each other first in tears and then had almost drowned each other. The daughter will leave, wearing the mother's favorite towel dress and the mother's overpriced light green sun hat. The daughter's thumbs will work the road. The oldies will pass her by until a Fort Lauderdale (probably) bound, long-haired blond boy will stop. The mother will watch from behind the Australian pines, from behind the neighbor's trees being consumed by Spanish moss.

"Where to?" the boy will ask.

"Wherever," the daughter will say.

Last shot. Window down, daughter staring straight ahead to the bridge connecting Dolphin Key to the other Keys. The daughter's mouth will be widely smiling.

Beatrix is now a retiree. She is now an oldie.

"What *do* these young people want? What *do* they want?"

There is a shadow on Beatrix's upper lip. The hairs there are darkening. Will her stomach thicken? Should she attach herself to Barney? Would two retirees be less tired?

Would the sun be enough to make up for growing old? Will she spend her time gardening, trying to grow rosebushes in this sandy, salty soil, leaving the bushes in planters and bringing them in every night? Would she mother those thorny bushes as she could never adequately protect from sand and wind her daughter?

Was intent to murder equal in the eye of God to the commission of murder.

The insults, the vile insults, the slaps, the slaps returned, the punch, punch revisited, the flailing, kicking, scratching, uprooting of hair, ripping at cheeks, the attempts to destroy the photographs of face in the water.

Beatrix Palmer is still at the road, staring past departure. Had she wheeled the yellow-lined carriage into the Gulf? Was she strangling that baby with her red scarf when she nurtured her? Was she pressing that face into her chest to keep the nose from breathing?

All of that happened in the moment of immersion. At that pushing down of Lena's head through the water, albums were spilled and snapshots cracked. Ink ran from letters, stamps loosened, envelopes opened.

Beatrix destroyed the present, but, much worse, the past.

Did the sea surface with her to crack her against these pilings, shuck her, leave her with other empty shells of people?

She will lock firmly the luggage of her life, her typewriter, suitcase, cosmetic bag, and record nothing, accomplish no distance, alter no tired appearance.

A car comes down the road. Beatrix's vision is blurred. It honks. Noisy Barney?

Her green hat comes out of the car. Her green-and-blue towel dress comes walking toward her.

"No more assassinations," says Lena.

Birth me, Mothers. Carry me in the brine of your belly and your tears.

Let us sit on each others' laps, daughters and mothers.

We have hired our own hall. We hold hands. Our engagement rings do not scratch. Our wedding bands do not disband us. The musicians are women. The one ascending the podium is a woman.

"Mother, I'm pregnant with a baby girl."
"What is she doing?"
"She is singing."
"Why is she singing?"
"Because she's unafraid."

Acknowledgments: To more of my mothers, the following young girls and women who loved and sustained me

MOTHERS UNDER TEN

Jenny Freedman, Haifa, Israel
Sarah Cole, Cambridge, Massachusetts
Effie Galnoor, Jerusalem, Israel

MOTHERS UNDER TWENTY

Nahama Broner, Detroit, Michigan
Tamar Weinstein, Englewood, New Jersey
Claudia Weinstein, Englewood, New Jersey
Susan Broner, West Hempstead, New York
Maya Sonenberg, New York, New York
Jill Brose, Highland Park, Michigan
Erica Bogin, New Rochelle, New York

Mothers in Their Twenties

Sari Broner, Detroit, Michigan
Finvola Drury, Jr., New York, New York
Aliza Masserman, Ann Arbor, Michigan
Lois Clamage, Detroit, Michigan
Doron Galnoor, Jerusalem, Israel
Cathy Bogin, New Rochelle, New York
Ilana Kanska, Jerusalem, Israel

Mothers in Their Thirties

Virginia Kelley, New York, New York
Davida Cohen, Hof HaCarmel, Israel
Julie Jensen, Detroit, Michigan
Marcia Freedman, Haifa, Israel
Arella Bar Lev, Tel Aviv, Israel
Sue Brose, Highland Park, Michigan
Karen Klein, Royal Oak, Michigan
Prof. Linda Jaron, Providence, Rhode Island
Marylou Zieve, Bloomfield Hills, Michigan
Prof. Elizabeth Meese, New Brunswick, New Jersey
Prof. Jane Eberwein, Rochester, Michigan
Marian Wood, New York, New York
Sally Lund, New York, New York
Nomi Nimrod, Haifa, Israel

Mothers in Their Forties

Joan Weinstein, Englewood, New Jersey
Evelyn Orbach, Detroit, Michigan
Dina Saxer Margolis, Toronto, Canada
Margaret Lowinger, San Francisco, California
Rina Kimche, Hof HaCarmel, Israel
Phoebe Hellman Sonenberg, New York, New York
Lucille Field, Providence, Rhode Island
Joyce Weckstein, Southfield, Michigan
June Snow, Detroit, Michigan

Dr. Elizabeth Kubler-Ross, Flossmoor, Illinois
Barbara Fussiner, New Haven, Connecticut
Ruth Kroll, Detroit, Michigan
Prof. Alice Shalvi, Jerusalem, Israel

Mothers in Their Fifties

Dr. Sylvia Fried, Tenafly, New Jersey
Malverne Reisman, Southfield, Michigan
Judith Lieber, New York, New York
Annette Freedman, Southfield, Michigan
Eleanor Torrey West, Bloomfield Hills, Michigan
Sylvia Gingold, Teaneck, New Jersey
Harriet Berg, Detroit, Michigan
Nancy Bogin, New Rochelle, New York
Miriam Ben Arie, Jerusalem, Israel
Elizabeth Weiss, Oak Park, Michigan

Mothers in Their Sixties

Ilse Schrag, New York, New York
Hannah Pokempner, Detroit, Michigan
Dr. Hansi Mark, Oak Park, Michigan
Phyllis Bowman, New York, New York
Priscilla Merritt, Deer Isle, Maine
Florence Crowther, White Plains, New York
Evelyn Scheyer, Detroit, Michigan

Mothers in Their Seventies

Beatrice Masserman, Oak Park, Michigan
Pearl Sternlight, New York, New York
Antoinette Opperman, South Bend, Indiana
Agnes Bruenton, Detroit, Michigan